BUNTER BY APPOINTMENT

BUNTER BY APPOINTMENT

DANIEL GREEN

Hodder & Stoughton
LONDON SYDNEY AUCKLAND TORONTO

British Library Cataloguing in Publication Data
Green, Daniel
  Bunter by appointment.
  I. Title
  823'.914[F]   PR6057.R33/

ISBN 0 340 38790 4

Hodder and Stoughton Editorial Office: 47 Bedford Square, London WC1B 3DP.

CONTENTS

Now, a comic romance . . . differs from the serious romance in its fable and action in this; that as in the one these are grave and solemn, so in the other they are light and ridiculous; it differs in its characters, by introducing persons of inferior rank, and consequently of inferior manners; whereas the grave romance sets the highest before us; lastly, in its sentiments and diction by preserving the ludicrous instead of the sublime.

HENRY FIELDING: Introduction to
The Adventures of Joseph Andrews

PROLOGUE – *Calculating My Chances*

It stood to reason that the Begum of Sumroo* would resent it
when we scarpered, if only because I was, at the time, the sole
inhabitant of her male seraglio. It also stood to reason that, if
the *sowars* she sent after us could overtake and recognise us at
any stage of our long, long journey to Kurachee, they would
drag us back in chains. And then, like as not, it would be boiling
alive in oil for all four of us.

Kurachee is a pilgrimage port on one of the mouths of the
river Indus in the state of Scinde. And because we had to travel
disguised and Scinde is inhabited by devout Muslims who'd as
soon cut an Unbeliever's throat as look at him, we decided to
disguise ourselves as pilgrims bound for Mecca. Gurmakh
Singh, my aged Sikh retainer, would become Hadji Habiboolah Khan, a Patan horse coper making his second pilgrimage for the spiritual benefit of his three new young wives. Fyzoo
and Ghulabi, his late sister's daughters-in-law, would travel as
two of those wives. I, William Frederick Augustus Bunter,
would be the third. That would allow us to remain concealed by
veil, chadoor and purdah from the gaze of men, as pious
Muslim women should. In short, we could huddle under the tilt
of the *hackerry* whilst bullocks pulled us across the plains of the
Punjaub, and then we could do the same in the curtained-off
zenana area of the *bhottiah* that would carry us down the Indus.

But *hackerries* and *bhottiahs* and months of travel ain't to be
had for nothing, and that didn't take into account what we
would have to pay for our passages to England if we ever got to
Kurachee. Our first problem, therefore, was how to pay for our

* A description of the Begum and of some of the other characters
mentioned will be found in an earlier instalment of these Memoirs
published under the title of *Bunter Sahib*.

scarper. Gurmakh Singh, looking to the future, was prepared to invest all that he had saved and stolen during his long career in service. The daughters-in-law were willing, if necessary, to sell every scrap of the jewellery in which their capital was invested. But all I had that could be turned into cash was my locket. So I took this from around my neck and gave it to Gurmakh Singh to sell. He examined it with an expert eye for, like most Indians, he knew a bit about jewellery.

'It's a costly enough sort of trinket,' he said, 'and the gold weighs well. But the brilliants on the front have little value and will add nothing to the price.'

'There is a portrait inside,' I said, 'which can mean nothing to the Indian you sell it to, so throw the painting away and sell only the case.'

He opened the locket, looked first at the portrait and then at me:

'Surely,' he said, 'he who is pictured here is of the House of Bunter.'

'Why do you say that?'

'He looks exactly as you will look, Bunter Sahib, in twenty years' time. And what except family piety could have persuaded you to carry the picture of one so ugly? Yet he has an air of wealth and authority to him. Is he some great *Angrezi* Nabob?'

I answered sharply, for I disagreed about the ugliness: 'Far greater, O ignorant one, than any *Angrezi* you have ever looked upon.'

Gurmakh Singh had in his youth served John Company as a sepoy in the 17th Bengal Native Infantry and prided himself on his connections with, and understanding of, the English: 'When I served the Company in Calcutta I often saw *Angrezi* Colonel Sahibs and Collector Sahibs. Once I even saw the great Governor General Sahib himself.'

'You compare sparrows with eagles. Know that he whose picture you now look at is brother to King Georgey and Sirdar of all King Georgey's armies.'

Gurmakh Singh was determined to demonstrate how much more he knew about military matters, whether Indian or

British, than a mere civilian such as myself, and he now changed from Urdu to his personal version of English to emphasise the point.

'Commander-in-Chief British Army,' said he, 'is ruddy well being bloody old Duke of Yuck.'

'That's right,' said I.

His eyes wandered once more from the locket to myself.

'Ever since my eyes were first gladdened by the sight of Your Excellency I have always thought that one as fat, as ugly, and as wonderfully well-hung as yourself has to be of the blood of kings. This painting proves it.'

'Nevertheless you will throw it away to make the case more attractive to whatever moneylender you sell it to.'

'Money speaks loudly, Bunter Sahib. But even if I got many lakhs for the case, the rupees would not speak one-tenth as loudly as that portrait does so long as it remains around your neck. For does it not proclaim King Georgey's kinship to you? And what Feringhi sea captain would refuse Bunter Sahib and his followers passage to Bilatee once he has been shown that the great king of Bilatee is himself a Bunter?'

So I kept the locket and Gurmakh Singh became noticeably more deferential. And if I often caught him looking at me with the satisfied air of a man whose investment was turning out better than he ever dared hope, I realised it was because he had such an exaggerated idea of the opulence of Britain and of the richness of the pickings to be made there. For him it had become a sort of gingerbread land where even the least enterprising Sikh must prosper, and where one who had had the foresight to be of service to so great a man as Bunter Sahib would certainly find favour, fame and fortune.

PART ONE

HIND

1 Kurachee Doldrums

There was hardly a moment of that journey across India and down the Indus when I wasn't in a state of more or less absolute funk. The daughters-in-law, however, hadn't enough imagination to be scared. They were simple women who had never before travelled even ten miles from their village, so the world, or what they could see of it from behind purdah, seemed to them an enchanted place. And when the enchantment palled, they giggled and chattered together, principally about me.

Gurmakh Singh, I'm sorry to say, had whetted their appetites with highly coloured accounts of what I had done to the Begum. Not that their appetites needed very much whetting, they being two lusty young women who'd been too long a-widowed. Which was why they soon progressed from giggling over my equipment to making practical tests of it. I dared not struggle or scream for fear of attracting attention to myself. So once again, and over and over and over again, I became the victim of masterful women. What they contrived to do to me in those confined spaces would have made one of Astley's acrobatic riders envious. By the time we got to Kurachee they were both of them several months into their pregnancies.

Kurachee, because it makes so much of its living out of pilgrims, has to be a more conspicuously devout place than anywhere else in Scinde. So we took an upstairs room in a serai much favoured by pilgrims which was situated close to the waterfront and in the heart of the brothel area. And there, for day after day and eventually week after week, the daughters-in-law and I lay low, for we dared not risk the streets even in chadoors and veils. But Gurmakh Singh wearing his green Hadji's turban was a quite different kettle of fish. And so I set him about the business of finding a ship whose captain would be willing to give all four of us passage to England.

It wasn't such a simple business as we had assumed when we were planning our escape months earlier in Sumroo. For one thing all that was now left of the cash and jewellery we had set out with were a few gold mohurs, sixty-five sicca rupees, and the gold studs in Ghulabi's and Fyzoo's noses. These, as Gurmakh Singh pointed out, didn't add up to anything likely to tempt a sea captain, always supposing he could find one.

And this, for several weeks, he failed to do. The rulers of Scinde have always refused to allow John Company to trade into their territory which, seeing what has happened to some of the other Indian rulers, was probably quite wise of them. John Company, for its part, sees to it that no other European ships trade where their own East Indiamen can't. So, although there were a good many dhows, xebecs, feluccas and suchlike in port, and a few larger vessels lying out in the Roads, they were all native-built and manned and never went farther afield than the Red Sea pilgrimage ports or the slave and spice ports of East Africa and Zanzibar. Besides which the captains of such were unlikely to accept as passengers out of Kurachee three Sikhs posing as Muslim pilgrims and one Englishman posing as a woman posing as a Muslim pilgrim.

So we stayed, as you might say, in the Doldrums until the day a large three-masted topsail schooner flying the Stars and Stripes dropped anchor in the Roads. American ships, it seemed, didn't rank as European any more than Americans ranked as Unbelievers. Just as soon as Gurmakh Singh reported her arrival I sent him out to her to bespeak four passages.

'For,' said I, 'if we can't get passage to England, damned if we don't take it to America. Anything to secure our passage from India.'

It was a dejected Gurmakh Singh who returned nursing a black eye to tell me that he'd met the American sea captain, and that he was, in Gurmakh Singh's opinion, an ignorant, bad-tempered religious crank who didn't properly understand English.

'For,' said he, 'all the American could talk about was greens.'
'Greens?'

'Greens. He must belong to one of those sects whose followers are forbidden to touch meat. Never have I met a man so deeply interested in vegetables.'

Gurmakh Singh, apparently, had been walking down the Street of the Pastry Cooks when, outside one of the lower-class eating-houses in that thoroughfare, he had come across an angry Kurachee eating-house keeper and an even angrier and extremely bosky Feringhi who were swearing and shouting at one another. As the one was doing this in Urdu and the other in something very close to English Gurmakh Singh offered his services as an interpreter.

'Tell the infidel pig, O Hadji,' said the eating-house keeper, eyeing Gurmakh Singh's green turban with respect, 'that he has to pay me for the kebabs.'

'He is,' Gurmakh Singh said to the Feringhi in his very best English, 'requesting the Sahib to be paying him for the pieces of meatses on skewerses.'

The Feringhi, who was very tall and very thin and wore tight white strapped pantaloons, a light blue swallow-tailed coat with a double row of brass buttons, a flowered satin waistcoat and a tall white stovepipe hat, took the hat off, threw it on the floor and jumped on it.

'Yo' kin tell him,' said he, 'ter be sticking them skewers straight up his ass. Ah ain't in the market fur smelly little scraps o' mutton. Ah'm in the market fur mah greens. An' it were greens I asked him fur.'

'You are wanting only greens?'

'What else would any red-blooded Amurrican be wantin' after three months at sea with only seamen fur company?'

Even though Gurmakh Singh couldn't properly follow what the fellow was saying, his calling himself an American suggested that here was someone who had to be humoured in the hope of its leading, eventually, to a meeting with the captain of the American schooner. So he said to the eating-house keeper:

'The unbelieving, uncircumcised dog is one of those who eat

only vegetables. It is something to do with their unholy religion.'

But to the American he said: 'This is being a low, O a very low eating-house. If you are kindly allowing me I shall be showing you very much better place for greens.'

'Did you say eating-house? Ah sure as Hell thought it wuz a cat-house. Ain't any wonder Ah set Sambo there a-hollering. Here, boy . . .' and with that he tossed a silver dollar to the eating-house keeper who broke into a series of smiles and benedictions.

'If your Excellency,' said Gurmakh Singh, 'will please to be following me.'

The American followed.

There was, in the Great Maidan, the most famous and the most expensive of all the eating-houses in Kurachee. There they served all manner of curries, pilaus, tandooris, vindaloos and suchlike dishes. And to complement these they also served a great variety of vegetable and salad dishes. Gurmakh Singh realised that to treat the American to a meal in such a place would, in our present financial state, be an act of folly unless it produced a very definite return in the shape of our passage to America. So he stopped in the middle of the Maidan and asked:

'You are, Sahib, off the ship with the starry and stripey flag?'

'That flag, mah coloured friend, is known as Old Glory. The ship it flies over is the *Gay Georgian*, owner an' master Captain Gaylord Griffiths, who now has the honour of remindin' you that he's fair itching fur his greens.'

'You will find here,' said Gurmakh Singh, leading him straight into the Kurachee Garden of Gourmets, 'the very best greens in the whole of Scinde.'

The layout of the Garden of Gourmets clearly puzzled the American. A series of cooks, assistant cooks and scullions squatted over charcoal braziers in a central courtyard whilst waiters bustled backwards and forwards carrying great trays of food from the braziers to the alcoves where the more prosperous of Kurachee's citizens were guttling and guzzling. Those waiters looked suspiciously at the American in his stovepipe hat but when Gurmakh Singh clapped his hands and called loudly for a table his green turban won them an alcove to themselves.

If their waiter was surprised when Gurmakh Singh ordered two large dishes of spinach, two of cabbage, two of green beans and a large bowl of salad the American was even more surprised by what he saw going on around him.

'Are you sartin-sure,' said he, 'that we've brung up at the right house?'

'Sahib asked for greens. If Sahib will have small pieces of patience, he will soon have them.'

'Hain't ever knowed a cat-house where a man has ter tuck into his vittles afore he kin tuck into his piece o' tail.'

Gurmakh Singh, who was sure by now that the Americans ought not to be described as English-speaking, said, 'Please?' and looked even more puzzled than Gaylord Griffiths. The latter drummed his fingers impatiently and kept muttering something about wanting to look at the merchandise before actually purchasing it. And then, with a triumphant swoop, the waiter placed a steaming dish of spinach in front of each of them. Griffiths looked at his dish in amazement:

'What in the name of the Great Whore of Babylon is this?'

'Is your greens, Sahib,' said Gurmakh Singh. Then, seeing the American's face flush with anger, he added:

'If Sahib is not liking this sort of greens is no worry. Plenty, plenty of other sorts coming. All the bleeding greens Sahib can be wanting. Is green beans. Is green cabbage. Is green lettuces. Is . . .'

Griffiths stood up and said: 'Where Ah come from we never allow coloured men ter make fun of us.'

'Is not fun,' said Gurmakh Singh. 'Is food.'

It was then that the American hit him on the right eye, turned sharply left, and marched out of *The Garden of Gourmets*.

Long before Gurmakh Singh had finished it was clear to me that an opportunity had been missed, solely because of

problems of idiom. It was difficult to explain this to Gurmakh
Singh who was convinced that he was master of every idiom in
the English language, and proceeded to tell me so in English,
which he swore he spoke far better than any American.

'Just remember,' said I, 'that when a sailor talks about
wanting his greens, he ain't necessarily referring to vegetables.'

'Then what else can he be referring to?'

'Women.'

'Never,' said Gurmakh Singh, 'am I completely understanding bloody English language. When I was in Bengal Native
Infantry and one of my English squaddy friends is wanting
woman, he says he is wanting his bleeding oats. But now you
are telling me that if he is not squaddy, but English or
American matelot, he is not wanting his oats. He is wanting his
bleeding greens.'

'It is,' I agreed, 'all a little confusing.'

We were spared further discussion by the sounds of a violent
argument that came floating up from the street below. Normally
I would have ignored it, for we were in a brothel area and *The
Paradise of Pleasing Houris* was just the other side of the street.
But as at least half of the argument was being conducted in
what sounded vaguely like English, I looked out of the window.
One of the disputants was a fat, toadlike woman whom I
recognised as Amina Bibi, the bawd mistress of the establishment opposite. The other was a tall, thin, better-than-half-
drunk fellow wearing tight white strapped pantaloons and a tall
white stovepipe hat.

The two were completely at cross purposes. Amina Bibi was
urging him in Urdu to enter her establishment and taste of its
joys, while he, taking her for someone who was trying to sell
him souvenirs, was demanding his greens in Anglo-American
and telling her to let go of his sleeve and get the Hell out of it as
he wasn't interested in little ebony elephants.

'Gurmakh Singh,' said I, 'is that the American sea captain?'

'It is,' said he.

'Then hasten down to him, get him away from Amina Bibi,
and bring him up here.'

'But how to do that, Bunter Sahib? Have I not already told you that he is a very savage, very uncivilised man who has already blackened one of my eyes?'

I thought for a while and then said:

'You must tell him that you hadn't understood that he really meant oats when he talked about greens. And after that you can say that the finest oats in the whole of Kurachee are to be found upstairs here in this room.'

The daughters-in-law and I presented three fairly amorphous bundles of clothing when the American arrived, for we were hidden behind our veils and huddled into our chadoors. But he immediately decided that we must be females and so swept off his hat, staggered, clutched at Gurmakh Singh, recovered himself, and said:

'Gaylord Griffiths, dear ladies. Cap'n of the *Gay Georgian* an' yores ter command.'

The daughters-in-law, who hadn't understood a word, didn't even giggle, and I said nothing, for I was wondering whether he was too drunk for the business I had to propose. Our silence must have struck him as much too frigid a start to an evening of pleasure for, with a wild 'Yaroo', he hurled his stovepipe hat into a corner and broke into an extraordinarily energetic song-and-dance display that would have done credit to a courting peacock.

Of the dance I shall say nothing. But the song, so far as I could follow it, ran roughly as follows:

> Ah'm a roarin', rockin', shockin', Georgia lad,
>   Yow Siree!
> An' the dames they drive me mad,
>   Yow Siree!
> But since A'm full o' beans
> Ah'll jus' rock, rock roun' mah greens,
>   Yow Siree! Yow Siree! Yow Siree!

Gurmakh Singh, who had watched and listened with a nodding head and a tapping toe, chuckled coarsely and said:

'Even so, Bunter Sahib, did I once sing and dance to the girls of my village when I was a *khub jewan*, a randy young buck. We call such carollings and caperings *rukhs* in the Punjaub, and I would I had a gold mohur for every maidenhead I took with my *rukhings*. I do not boast when I say that in those days I could leap higher and sing louder than any other man in Sumroo.'

Griffiths couldn't have understood a word of this. Nevertheless his *rocking* must, like Gurmakh Singh's *rukhing*, have been some sort of mating rite. For when he had *rocked* himself to a stop and recovered his breath he pointed straight at me and said to Gurmakh Singh:

'Ah think Ah'll jus' start with the fat one, Sambo. Ah don' suppose she unnerstands any English, so kindly inform her that Cap'n Griffiths is about to come aboard.'

2   *A Georgian Gentleman and the Great Game*

Gurmakh Singh, who had never before been addressed as Sambo, didn't know what to say. I did. The time had clearly come to get away from *rockings* and *rukhings* and talking of greens, and to start discussing the question of our passage from India. So I said, in my clearest tones, for he was clearly fuddled:

'Captain Griffiths, how would you like to earn ten gold mohurs, sixty-five sicca rupees and two gold nose-studs?'

He was, at that stage, too fuddled to be surprised.

'That's a wholly elegant sort of English you speak, Ma'am, 'most as elegant as what our ladies speak in Savannah. Never expected an Indian whore, Ma'am, ter be so accomplished. But Ah have ter tell you as you've gotten Gaylord Griffiths wrong. Ah don' know about Indians, but Ah was born an' raised a Georgian gennleman, an' all gennlemen in the South are brung up ter have the mos' proper respect fur the fair sex. So you don' pay me, Ma'am. Ah pays you.'

Whilst Griffiths thought I had got him wrong I knew he had got me wrong. So I pulled down my veil and flung open my chadoor, thus revealing that I hadn't shaved for some time and was wearing a grubby, floral-patterned smock over purple baggy drawers. This time he was surprised, and he fairly goggled as I said:

'Your sentiments do you credit, Sir. But the payment I offered was for a passage . . .'

Fuddled or not, he now found his tongue.

'Bugger me,' said he, 'it's a transvestite.'

'My appearance, I assure you . . .'

Anger began to replace surprise as he cut across me again. 'A transvestite! A bloody Limey transvestite! Well, Fatty, it don' work with me, no matter how many gold nose-studs you're offering. Griffiths won't play, an' that's that.'

'I don't want you to play. I want a passage. . . .'

'No Siree! Ain't ever bin mah line o' country. Ah may be a seafarin' gennleman what's bin too long from his greens, but Ah'm also an' always a Georgian one. An' so Ah leaves buggery an' all such capers ter Yankees, Abolitionists, an' other pore white trash, an' ter the officers an' men of yore Royal Navy.'

The Bunter part of me don't offend very easily. The Guelph part – if that's what it is – does. Which was why the blusterings of this drunken, de-colonised descendant of rude colonials helped me to understand what George III, my possible grandfather, must have felt about the Americans when they rebelled in 1776. So it was a Guelph rather than a Bunter who drew himself up and said:

'You may, Sir, come from Georgia. There may even be some Georgians one could describe as gentlemen. But you, Sir, ain't one of 'em. You're a low, ill-bred fellow, Sir, and unless you stop blustering and start listening I'll have nothing to do with you.'

That made him so angry he stuck his face into mine and yelled: 'Ah've a good mind, Mister, if that's what you are, ter cut yore tripes out here an' now. Fellow, is it? Low, is it? Ill-bred, is it? Ah'll have you know Gaylord Griffiths don' jus' come from a long line o' Georgian gennlemen. He's also a direct descendant o' Llewelyn ap Gruffyd hisself.'

My nose is really too snub for sneering down. Nevertheless I did what I could. 'Llewelyn-ap-Who? Never heard of him. What was he? One of your Georgian gentlemen or a Welsh horse thief?'

I thought, for one ugly moment, that he was about to strike me. Instead he drew several deep breaths before he said:

'He wuz, God rest his martyred soul, the last Prince o' Wales. And you bloody English murdered him.'

'What nonsense you do talk. The last Prince of Wales wasn't murdered by the bloody English or by anyone else. He may have become monstrously fat and dropsical, but he's still alive and kicking, and these days he's called King George IV.'

'And what is being more,' said Gurmakh Singh, determined to help things along, 'Lord Bunter here is being same King Georgey's own bloody nephew, other side of bleeding blanket.'

'You,' Griffiths told him, 'are just about the lyingest coon Ah ever did come across.'

Gurmakh Singh, fortunately, did not know what coon meant. So he did no more than ask Griffiths, quite mildly, why he called him a liar.

'Didn't you,' said Griffiths, 'swear that this wuz where Ah'd find the best greens in town? An' what have Ah found so fur? A fat Limey transvestite, that's all Ah've found. An' now, damn my eyes, you're a-tryin' ter make me believe that same transvestite is some sort o' kin to the King of England hisself. Ah tell you what, boy. If'n you wuz mine Ah'd have you whupped 'till they'd whupped some truth into yore hide.'

Gurmakh Singh was so intent on proving his point that he didn't resent being treated like an American, and a black one at that. 'If he isn't being what I am telling you,' he said triumphantly, 'perhaps you will be telling me why he is having Duke of Yuck picture inside bloody locket.'

'Locket? What locket?'

Gurmakh Singh pointed to that very sizeable trinket which, now that I'd flung open my chadoor, could be seen nestling in the valley formed by the artificial titties I still had to wear. Griffiths gave it one look and said, scornfully:

'That bit o' brass? There's a Jew has a stall in Baltimore Market will sell you two a good bit bigger for half a dollar.'

'Complete, I suppose, with a cipher and coronet picked out in diamonds,' I said, 'not to mention a famously well-painted miniature on the inside?'

'Diamonds? Who says they're diamonds?'

'I do. And so does anyone with intelligence enough to tell a diamond from a lump of coal.'

That shook him a little, so he shifted his ground. 'Well, what's all this about a coronet then?'

'As you've abolished them in your country its significance will escape you.'

'Lookee here, Fatty. America may be a republic, but that don't mean that some of us Americans can't appreciate the significance of coronets jus' as well as we appreciate the significance of dollars an' cents, or the significance of pork an' beans.'

His anger at that moment was so immoderate that I started to revise my estimate of Captain Griffiths. So I took the locket from around my neck, gave it to him and said:

'In that case, Sir, you will certainly recognise the distinctive features of the coronet on the front of this locket.'

'Ah wull?'

'Come Sir! Everyone knows that only the brother or younger son of a King of England can have fleur-de-lys *and* crosses pattées *and* strawberry leaves on his ducal coronet. This one, may I point out, has 'em all.'

'Sure it has,' said he, 'but what is the significance of this other stuff?'

'This other stuff is the cipher of His Royal Highness Frederick Augustus, Duke of York, after whom I am named, and who himself placed this locket in my infant hand at my christening. You will find his portrait inside.'

He fumbled so with the fastening that Gurmakh Singh had to open it for him. Griffiths then spent so much time looking from the portrait to me and then back again that it was plain he was trying to picture me cleaned and curled and barbered and dressed in a Field Marshal's uniform with the broad ribbon of the Garter across my chest and the Round Tower at Windsor in the background. And he was succeeding.

'You swear he's the Dook of York?'

'I do'

'An' you'll take your Bible-oath he's yore Pa?'

'Come, Captain Griffiths, you know as well as I do that no wise man will swear to his father. But I would have you remember what that fellow Hamlet said to his Ma in the play.'

'An' what may that be?' Ain't never bin a man for playgoin'.'

'He said, "Look here upon this picture and on this." '

And with that I pointed in a series of restrained but dignified gestures to the Duke's lofty, not to say balding forehead, his bulging light-blue eyes, his receding chins and straining waistband, and then to my own.

At that point he gave a bob of the head and a scrape of the foot in my direction and I knew that I had him. I'd have had him a deal earlier if only I'd realised more promptly that he was far more interested in Kings and Dukes and royal by-blows than he would ever be in sicca rupees and gold nose-studs. For, to put it at its plainest, Gaylord Griffiths thought of himself as a patrician.

For myself, I've never really known what a patrician is. As the grandson, on the one side, of a King of England, and on the other of that William Bunter who was the greatest artist the British pie-making world has ever known, I've never needed, – other than in the way of business – to look up to, or for that matter to look down upon, anyone. But that don't mean I can't recognise a snob and a tuft-hunter when I meet one. Griffiths, if he'd been a true-born Briton, would have been one of the more ludicrous examples of both: as an American, however, he was more to be pitied than laughed at. One should never laugh at the socially deprived.

Griffiths's deprivations all followed from the sad fact that any American who thinks of himself as a patrician will always be a stranger and a misfit in the land of his birth. And that entirely because it is a land which has denied itself the benefits of an hereditary monarchy and aristocracy and has, instead, officially dedicated itself to the very doubtful proposition that all men are born equal unless, of course, they are born black.

It was quite natural for Griffiths, therefore, to start getting excited at this, his first contact with royalty, even though it was in the unlikely person of Bunter and the even more unlikely setting of the Kurachee brothel area. What I had to do was encourage that excitement and persuade him that helping me escape from India would, more than likely, win him his entrée to the Court of St James.

It wasn't, I'll always maintain, a half-bad job of persuading I embarked on, quite impromptu. Griffiths, I said, would certainly remember how at Tilsit in '07 Boney and the Tsar Alexander had divided the world between them. Russia was to be given a free hand in India whilst the French would be given an even freer hand almost everywhere else. The French had been obliged to abate their ambitions since then but the Russians were still determined to secure their part of the bargain, just as we were determined they should not. India, as a result, was full of Russian and British agents struggling for control. And that struggle was known on our side as the Great Game.

'If I now call myself plain Mr Bunter,' said I, 'it is because the Great Game requires me to travel incognito.'

'Incog . . . ? But of course, Your Royal Lordship.'

I frowned, tapped my foot and said: 'Incognito *means* incognito, Captain Griffiths.'

'Ah mos' humbly beg yore pardon, Sah, but . . .'

'But what, man?' and my foot tapped again.

'But why do you have to be incog-whatever-it-is in Kurachee?'

'There are, Sir, certain high matters of state concerning relations between one reigning house and another that must never be talked about.'

'Does that mean,' said Griffiths, looking as eager now as a schoolboy in a sweet-shop, 'that there's more'n one set of you Royal Highnesses involved?'

'My lips, Mr Griffiths, are sealed.'

'Quite so, Yore Honour . . . Sah . . . Mr Bunter. Ah understands puffickly. But . . .'

'But again, Griffiths?'

'If Ah might, humbly an' with all due respeck, ask why, even though you have ter be incog . . . in disguise . . . you have to be disguised as an Indian . . . an Indian . . .'

'An Indian what?'

'Well Sah, as an Indian whore.'

If he was puzzled to find an explanation for this, so also was I. To gain time I drew him towards the window, and by the time we got there I was able to mutter into his ear:

'It's because they're after me, Griffiths.'

'Who are they?'

'The Russians.'

'Oh, ah, the Roosians,' said Griffiths, looking more puzzled than ever. 'Are you sartin it's the Roosians? Ah ain't seen hide nor hair of one.'

'You wouldn't. Like myself, they have to travel in disguise. But they know about my mission and are determined to stop me completing it, and that's why they're in Kurachee with orders to cut my throat. If they trace me here, I'll be dead before morning. And that, Griffiths, is why I had to be an Indian whore.'

'Ah don't quite follow.'

'Why man, I had to get you here, and I could only do so by appealing to your natural instincts as a mariner. I am sorry to have misled you in the matter of your greens, but I had no alternative.'

'Nothing wrong,' said Griffiths, 'with a mariner's natural instincts.'

'Nothing at all. And very healthy too. But now you are here I have to appeal to your higher instincts as a Georgian and a gentleman. You're the only man who can get me safely out of

Kurachee. And so I place my life, my mission, and the future, perhaps, of the British in India, in your hands.'

Griffiths did a little jig of excitement which ended in another bob and a scrape.

'Flattered,' said he, 'flattered *and* gratified to be called to yore royal assistance.'

'You will understand,' said I, 'that I was forced to abandon my treasure chest in the course of my flight from those Russian fiends. So all I can offer you in the way of immediate reward are the sicca rupees and gold nose-studs already mentioned. But get me safely to England and you'll not find the government ungrateful. And then there will be the family. When you and I, Captain Griffiths, drive up to Windsor together, you will have earnt the gratitude of every single member of it, from the King downwards.'

Griffiths couldn't decide whether to be indignant at being offered money or delighted at being promised a monarch's gratitude.

'As between one gennleman what's in distress, which is you, an' another what's in a position to assist, which is me, all talk of gold nose-studs mus' be insulting.'

'Of course it is, and I apologise for mentioning 'em.'

'The thanks of yore Royal Uncle an' yore Royal Pa will be reward enough an' more for Gaylord Griffiths.'

'Surely,' said I in a murmur that suggested I was communing with myself quite as much as I was talking to him, 'surely you will have deserved more of His Majesty than mere thanks. A peerage, perhaps? And not one of your functionless Irish affairs but a regular, slap-up House of Lords job.'

'But Ah'm an American.'

'No matter. Your also being the descendant of that Prince of Wales fellow you were talking about not only makes you Welsh, which is a damn sight closer to being English than you could say of several of our present peers; it also makes you more or less one of the family, so I wouldn't be surprised if it weren't the Garter rather than the Bath.'

'The Garter!' said Griffiths ecstatically, looking down at a long and skinny limb covered in white duck and obviously wondering how it would look in knee breeches, silk stockings and a Garter.

Just then a series of menacing screams came floating up from the street to remind us all of where we were. I looked out of the window. It was Amina Bibi who had suddenly decided to give tongue, and from what I could make out she'd been waiting under our window for Griffiths ever since Gurmakh Singh had snatched that potentially rewarding customer away from her. But now, as Griffiths hadn't re-emerged, she'd decided she'd lost him to Gurmakh Singh and his three so-called wives. This naturally made her angry. No honest and long-established tradesman likes losing custom to a Johnny-come-lately whose very identity and respectability are still in doubt. And so Amina Bibi was now announcing her displeasure to the world.

'Listen, O ye men of Kurachee,' she screamed. 'What sort of Hadji is this Habiboolah who comes to our pious city of Kurachee in order to sell the favours of his three so-called wives to an Unbeliever? Is he not taking bread out of the mouth of a devout and honest woman who has served you well, and your fathers before you? Is not my son the Chief of Police in this city? And is it not his duty to preserve this city's reputation and the good name of all true Hadjis lest the pilgrim trade by which we live fall into disrepute? I swear to you all that just as soon as the cock and the muezzin herald in tomorrow's dawn, I will have brought the Chief of Police and his Vice Squad to investigate this Hadji Habiboolah, and the doings of those he calls his wives.'

Gurmakh Singh turned pale. The daughters-in-law stopped giggling and chattering between themselves. I cursed my luck. And Griffiths said:

'Ah don't know what it is she's a-screaming. But she's the woman who tried to sell me some little ebony elephants a while back. P'raps Ah should buy one now ter shut her up.'

'That woman,' I said, the idea coming to me in a flash, 'is no more an Indian woman than I am. And she deals in far more deadly things than little ebony elephants.'

'Is that so? Who is she then?'

'That, Captain Griffiths, is the Countess Anna Gorbachovna, the oldest, ugliest, and most evil of all the Russian agents in India. And what she's a-screaming is that she's found me at last and that her savage gang of Cossacks and Kalmucks will have slit the throats of each one of us by breakfast time tomorrow.'

'You don't say!'

'I'm afraid I do. So if you can't get us aboard tonight and clear of Kurachee by dawn it will be too late to do anything.'

'Yore pardon, but did you jus' say "us"?'

'I did. My companions must, of course, travel with me.'

'But they're coloureds.'

'They ain't, if you look at them, all that much darker than your average Sicilian or Algerine.'

'They're still darkies, an' the only darkies ever carried on the *Gay Georgian* have ter travel spoon fashion.'

'Spoon fashion?'

'That's the only way to pack 'em in when we're on the Middle Passage. Each darkie's head in the lap of the one behind an' all of 'em chained to their benches on the slave deck.'

I should have anticipated this, seeing that I was dealing with a Southern gentleman. But I wasn't going to give in to him. Bunter ain't the sort of chap to leave friends in the lurch, leastways not whilst there's still a chance of smooth-talking 'em out of it, and especially not when two of 'em are carrying demi-Bunters as cargo. So I said, still feeling my way into it:

'I regret that I can't reveal the true identities of my companions. To do so would be to reveal State secrets.'

'Darkies is still darkies,' said Griffiths in an obstinate sort of voice.

'And yet,' I went on, beginning to see my way forward , 'and yet, Captain Griffiths, the moment I clapped eyes on you I said to myself,"There's a man I could trust with even the most secret secret."'

He flushed with pleasure and said: 'Mum, an' more'n mum, has always been the word with Griffiths.'

'In that case, know this. My secret mission was to Britain's most important ally in India, Runjeet Singh.'

'Ter who?'

'To the Maharajah of the Sikhs, the King of Lahore, Peshawur and Kashmir, the Lion of the Punjaub and Lord of the Land of the Five Rivers, the lands which guard the north-west frontiers of India and the man whose armies hold those passes against the Russian hordes.'

As I rolled out, one after the other, each successive title borne by that one-eyed, sodomitical little monster Runjeet Singh, Griffiths's eyes grew wider and wider. And when I had rolled them all I turned and waved to Gurmakh Singh and the daughters-in-law and said:

'And now, Captain Griffiths, I shall introduce you to my companions. That venerable gentleman is, in real life, the Sirdar Gurmakh Singh, cousin and Grand Vizier to the Maharajah Runjeet Singh. And those two ladies in the corner are the Maharajah's only offspring, the Princess Fyzoo and the Princess Ghulabi.'

Griffiths's eyes were, by now, popping out of his head. 'Do you mean,' he gasped, 'that there ain't jus' one o' you royals in this room, but four?'

'You could even count us as six, for you will have noticed that both the Princesses are pregnant. All Runjeet Singh's hopes of perpetuating his royal line rest on what they carry in their wombs. If the Russians can get at us before I can get them to safety, the Punjaub will, sooner or later, be without a ruler, the passes will no longer be held, and the Russian hordes will have the whole of India at their mercy. So you see, my dear Captain Griffiths, that the fortunes of more than one royal house, not to mention the future of one of His Majesty's greatest dominions, now depend on you and the *Gay Georgian*.'

The prospect of being of service to such a multiplicity of royals, whether *in esse* or still only *in posse*, clearly delighted him beyond measure. He crossed to the corner where he'd tossed his stovepipe hat, picked it up, flourished it, bowed first to Fyzoo, then to Ghulabi, and finally to me, and said:

'Yore Royal an' Maharajal Highnesses, Gaylord Griffiths an' the *Gay Georgian* stand ready this very moment to carry you-all to London, England, or to anywhere else as you fancies.'

3   *Adieu Kurachee*

It was all very well for Griffiths to offer us instant escape as confidently as though it would take no more than a hop, skip, and a jump to put us aboard the *Gay Georgian* and away. He was still in a state of high elation brought on by drink and proximity to royalty. But I was in my habitual state of funk, brought on this time by Amina Bibi. I knew that getting to the *Gay Georgian* would be no easy matter. She lay at anchor out in the Roads, and to get to her we had first to reach her jolly-boat which was tied up at a wharf a full mile away where her crew were waiting patiently for Griffiths to satisfy his craving for greens.

I also knew that, so long as Amina Bibi hadn't shut up shop at the Paradise of Pleasing Houris, we couldn't put even our noses out of the door of the serai. She let no one pass unobserved and was quite capable, in her present mood, of rousing the neighbourhood if she caught us trying to scarper. Unfortunately, she didn't normally shut up shop much before dawn, and dawn, if her threats were to be believed, would bring not only her son, the Chief of Police, but the whole of the Vice Squad down on us. To make things more difficult, dawn in India ain't one of your slow-breaking affairs with rosy-tipped Aurora dawdling over the horizon. Your Indian dawn goes off like a rocket, which was why we'd have to make our dash for it just as soon as the last of Amina's customers had departed and before Aurora's touchpaper had been lit.

It was all, therefore, a matter of fine judgment. The trouble was, I was the only person fit to do any fine judging. Gurmakh Singh, who was in even more of a funk than myself, had hidden himself under the charpoy, from which he would, eventually, have to be dragged. The daughters-in-law were too simple to keep abreast of what was happening, and were certain, in any case, to do nothing more constructive than giggle. Griffiths, when he was not offering his services, as the descendant of one Prince of Wales, to Bunter, the descendant of another, kept sadly remembering that he'd not yet had his greens. And every now and again, when the grog fumes got to him, he would dance a few steps and sing a bar or two of his *rocking* song, although there was now little *joie de vivre* in the rendering.

Few, when they first meet me, would recognise in me a leader of men. But I had had leadership forced on me. So, when I dared wait no longer, I led my little band of funks, drunks and gigglers out into the silent and still moon-dappled streets of Kurachee. And a damned rum-looking crew we were.

There were four of us in chadoors, for we had given Griffiths our spare one. One – myself – was constitutionally bulky. Two – the daughters-in-law – were bulky because of the buns in their ovens. And the fourth – Griffiths – was so tall that he was no more than demi-chadoored. When, in correct style, he pulled the garment over his head, the whole of his bottom half, which was covered in white duck, was left fully exposed. And as he insisted on clapping his crumpled white stovepipe hat on his head over the chadoor, he looked taller and more bizarre than anything seen in the streets of Kurachee since the days of the *djinns* and the *afrits*. Lastly, creeping along timidly in the rear, came Gurmakh Singh still wearing the showy Patan dress and green turban of the Hadji Habiboolah Khan.

We didn't so much dash to the wharf as get there by fits and starts. Every time I heard a noise behind me, when one of my followers kicked a stone or stumbled in the gutter, I felt sure the

Chief of Police and the Vice Squad were already on our trail. Thereupon I would dart for cover into the nearest doorway where Gurmakh Singh always attempted to join me. But as Kurachee doorways are narrow and neither of us was wasp-waisted, this was like pouring a quart into a pint bottle and we spilled out into the road again. At which the daughters-in-law would giggle and Griffiths dance a little dance.

I have always counted it a singular piece of good fortune that we eventually got to the wharf without being noticed or followed by anyone. We were even more fortunate in that the jolly-boat's crew hadn't dispersed to the grog-shops and so were sober enough to row us out to the *Gay Georgian* without making too much noise or ramming anything. No one aboard, however, was prepared for the swift and silent departure the situation demanded. As the first mate explained when he was rousted out, the crew had expected to spend at least another week in port taking on cargo and enjoying, as their captain had done, shore leave plus greens.

But the moment Griffiths trod the deck of his ship he became a different and much soberer man, so it didn't take him long to rid the first mate and crew of their illusions. He soon had all hands on deck preparing to sail without any of the yelling, cursing, shantying and blowing of bosun's whistles customary on such occasions. The crew grumbled, of course, but when one of them grumbled too loudly Griffiths showed him what he meant by silence by laying him out with a belaying pin.

It was still quite dark as the anchor came home, but then, as jib and headsails started to fill and we slowly got under way, dawn broke and suddenly it was light. Gurmakh Singh and I, taking what we hoped was our last look at Kurachee from the quarterdeck, were able to see that the *Gay Georgian* was not, after all, being allowed to slip away unchallenged. A ten-oared barge was pulling so vigorously after us that it seemed certain to overtake us.

Already it was close enough to make out the features of two figures standing in the bows and gesticulating to us to return. One was Amina Bibi. The other was a corpulent fellow wearing a choga so heavily encrusted with gold that the sun, although still low on the horizon, was setting him a-sparkle. It flashed off the daggers and silver-mounted pistols stuck into his kummerbund and off the tulwar he had drawn and was shaking menacingly at us. Behind him half a dozen sinister-looking men in black were beating the oarsmen with their staffs to make them row even harder. Amina Bibi was screaming at us, but the breeze carried her words away, and all we could make out was a protracted wail of 'Habiboooolah . . .'

Gurmakh Singh groaned. 'Amina Bibi, may she burn in Hell, has kept her word. Heavens help us if her misbegotten son, the Chief of Police, and the Vice Squad catch up with us.'

But at that moment the offshore breeze started to fill the maincourse and spanker, which had just been set, and the barge, instead of gaining on us, began to drop behind.

The Vice Squad used their staffs even more vigorously. Amina Bibi screamed even louder. But the Chief of Police was waving his tulwar so vigorously that he lost his balance and fell overboard. The last we saw, the rowers were resting thankfully on their oars whilst the men in black were diving to recover their Chief, weighed down as he was with his embroidery and armoury. Amina Bibi was massaging her throat.

Only then did Gurmakh Singh relax. He spat triumphantly into the sea and said: 'Rejoice! Rejoice! Bunter Sahib. We have beaten the bastards. And I have done what I promised to do so many months ago in Sumroo. I have put us safely on our way to Bilatee.'

And then, in a dignified manner befitting an aged Sikh got up as a Patan horse coper, he did a little dance on the quarterdeck which may or may not have been a statelier version of one of the *rukhs* of his youth.

I didn't dance. I leant, instead, against the taffrail watching our wake and thought of the hitherto unappreciated advantages that attached to my locket and to the present importance of being Bunter. As I'm an optimist, I didn't spend much time wondering whether these advantages would survive our arrival in England. But I did give a passing thought to Captain

Griffiths's possible reactions. When he discovered that the King and the Duke of York were not waiting for us, tippy-toe, at Windsor Castle, that the ovens held no fatted calf and the wine coolers no champagne, would he, I wondered, return to the subject of cutting my tripes clean out?

PART TWO

BILATEE

4 *Who, then, is King Georgey's Nephew?*

It was as we rounded the Cape of Good Hope that the daughters-in-law finally gave birth. This they did within a very few hours of one another, and each to a lusty and quite remarkably plump male child that took greedily to the breast. Griffiths was so excited by these additions to his cargo of royals that he gave orders for the mainbrace to be spliced and for the crew to dance and skylark in honour of the event. The crew, however, were all Georgian by birth and, coming for the most part from the labouring classes, were democratical rather than aristocratical by conviction. So even though they enjoyed the extra rum, they skylarked only reluctantly, for they weren't inclined to celebrate the arrival of what the ship's black cook described as 'jus' another coupla piccaninnies'.

I'd already discovered – in the case of Bishop Heber's wife, for instance – that mine is such a dominant strain that there is never any mistaking anything that is of Bunter's begetting. So I wasn't a bit surprised that the babes should look so Bunterish in spite of being wholly Singhs in their colouring. Griffiths, however, commented on the resemblance so often and so pointedly that I thought it wise to provide each infant with a high reason of state for looking the way he did.

'You see in these two bouncing boys,' I at last said to Griffiths, 'my response to the British imperative.'

'To the what, my Lord?'

'To the demands of our British Empire.'

'With all due respec', Ah'm damned if Ah kin see how yore Empire comes into it.'

'That's because the United States never has had, and never will have, an empire. It's also because I never gave you the true reason for my mission to Runjeet Singh.'

41

'No more you did, Sah.'

'So long as Runjeet Singh stays alive, British rather than Russian influence will prevail in the Punjaub. But the Maharajah must soon snuff it of debauchery and old age, leaving the Princesses as his only heirs. The Sikhs will not for long consent to be ruled by women. So how would you, Captain Griffiths, set about ensuring the continuance of British influence in the Punjaub?'

'Ah'd send in the troops jus' as soon as the old fellow turned up his toes.'

'And what, pray, would that achieve?'

'Why, Sah, you British would then be in a position ter win over the hearts an' minds of the natives, an' ter knock Hell out o' those of 'em as didn't want their hearts an' minds won over.'

'That, Captain Griffiths, is exactly why you Americans can never be an imperial people. Send in the troops, indeed! Hearts and minds, indeed! You need something a deal more subtle when you're dealing with a country as large as the Punjaub and a people as warlike as the Sikhs.'

'Such as what, Sah?'

'Such as the difficult task I will only complete the day you land all of us, but especially these babes, safely in England. For you see, Captain Griffiths, it was to ensure male grandchildren for Runjeet Singh and male heirs for his throne that he sent for me.'

'Ah don't know as Ah understand you.'

'The Duke of York, as Commander-in-Chief, is responsible for the perpetuation of our influence in India. So try to look at it from his point of view. Unless Runjeet Singh's daughters can be put in the way of producing male heirs the whole of the Punjaub will, sooner or later, fall into anarchy and the Russians will come in. But if, through my exertions and self-sacrifice, the Princesses are made to produce demi-Bunters, they will also have produced demi-Britons. And who, when their time comes to rule over the Punjaub, could possibly do more to sustain our influence there than a couple of demi-Britons?'

'But, Sah, you ain't married to either, or both, or any of the Princesses.'

'Of course I'm not. Each of 'em was very properly married at the age of six to another six-year-old Sikh. But husbands who start as young as that ain't much good at the heir-producing business even when they've grown up. What Runjeet Singh needed was a copper-bottomed, one-hundred-per-cent heir-producer guaranteed at Lloyd's – That's why he asked the Duke for me. And as you can see, he was right to do so.'

'Then why, if Ah might ask, did you all have to leave India in such a hurry?'

'The Sikhs hate miscegenation. So it was important to get the Princesses well away from India before they gave birth. And, of course, it was equally important to the Russians to prevent it. But we have evaded them, Captain Griffiths, and in a few years' time the Princesses will be able to return to Lahore with their sons because the Sikhs will have forgotten what Bunter looked like.'

'Ah'm jus' beginnin' ter understand, Sah,' said Griffiths, trying to look respectful and knowing at one and the same time, 'all that can be involved in what you people call the Great Game.'

'We may call it a game, but those of us who are its players think of it as a sacred duty. One for which no sacrifice can ever be too great.'

'With all due respec', Sah, Ah wouldn't exactly describe yore Indian mission as a sacrifice. Not if the Princesses wuz as willin' ter suffer fur King an' country as you wuz. They're pleasant-enough lookin' wummin. British imperatives or not, Ah'd never mind making that sort o' sacrifice twice a night. Damned if Ah would.'

He looked for a moment as though he was about to nudge me in the ribs but, seeing that I was frowning, he quickly reverted to his rude-deferential.

'But o' course, fur one in yore position, Sah, it mus' be a sacrifice when you think o' t'other high-born, home-grown greens you could have bin enjoying. Ah honours you fur it, Sah.

It's deeds like yores, Mr Bunter, as made an' saved yore Empire.'

I was happy enough to leave it there. The arrival of the babes had given me much to think about and I had neither the time nor the patience for long arguments with Griffiths. The fact was that I could, if I'd not been an optimist, have fallen victim to an increasing melancholia as we got closer to England and I got closer to having to prepare for what lay in front of me. It was not only that, with two extra Singhs to look after, I was in serious danger of acquiring more responsibilities than I could hope to discharge. It was also that my own future, once we'd landed, seemed quite as uncertain as the Singhs'.

Griffiths may have been counting on the Duke to be waiting for us with outstretched arms, but I didn't even know whether the Duke was alive or dead. When I had to cut and run from Calcutta in '27 the rumour was that the brandy was getting to him and he hadn't much longer to live. But in truth alive or dead made no difference. If he were alive, he couldn't be expected to remember who Bunter was; if he were dead, Bunter couldn't be expected to mourn him. In either case the amount of welcoming and succouring would be exactly the same.

My alternative sire, the Hon. George FitzThistlethwaite, had been rotting in his Lisbon grave these twenty years past. And as for my mother, I'd only seen her once since her little affair with Lord Byron had sent her into exile in Europe with a wee Byron in her oven. Which left, parentally speaking, only Mr Wilberforce. He had promised my mother, just before she scarpered, to stand *in loco parentis* to her child. But, try as he might, he could no more understand than he could approve of me. He was so clearly delighted when he was able to ship me off to India – that bourne from which so few Britons return, and then only when they are of pensionable age – that I couldn't expect him to do much in the way of welcoming if I suddenly arrived on his doorstep after a mere six years' absence and with a whole parcel of Singhs at my back.

But was he still alive and, being alive, feeling charitable? Mr Cobbett had unkindly pointed out that Mr Wilberforce poured out so much of his saintliness on negro slaves that Devil a bit of it was left for English children slaving away in the mills, or out-of-work English farm labourers slowly starving to death on parish relief. He could have added there wouldn't be too much of it left, either, for Bunter and his family of Singhs.

It was by this process of elimination that I generally arrived in the end at the Jewkeses. And my spirits would then rise even though I couldn't be sure all of them or any of them were alive and still living at Number 19 Great Coram Street. They were no relations of mine whether from under or over the blanket but something considerably better, namely friends. It had been in my first year at Christ's Hospital that I had met John Jewkes Junior – known to everyone as J.J. – and he, although in the Upper School, had constituted himself my guide and protector. It was he who had introduced me into the bosom of his family. As a quasi-orphan, I had nowhere to go on leave days, so he had taken me to his home to meet that most sporting of Cockney grocers and wholesale tea-merchants, John Jewkes Senior and Mrs John Jewkes, whose heart was as large as her bosom, which is to say beyond measuring.

They had all made me welcome, but the two senior Jewkes had been getting on in years and had always done themselves rather too well, so it was reasonable to assume that they were now lying side by side in the churchyard. If so, J.J. would probably have taken their place in Great Coram Street, in the grocery business and in the hunting field, and he, I felt sure, would welcome me and take me in whether I had Singhs at my back or not.

But most of all I wondered whether Maria, his sister, relict of the late Lieutenant-Colonel D'Arcy Huggins, had managed to get back from where I had last seen her in Lahore.

Maria I had known and liked ever since she was a remarkably stout and plain small girl, not least because, like myself, she had always taken an intelligent and informed interest in grub. Had she, I wondered, made good her escape from Runjeet Singh's Vizier after Runjeet Singh had had D'Arcy Huggins torn limb from limb by wild elephants for a quite trifling offence? And – which was even more important – had she managed to return to Great Coram Street with any of the loot I had entrusted to her that momentous evening when I fled to Sumroo to escape the sodomitical lusts of Runjeet Singh and she had to flee to Lucknow to escape the more orthodox lusts of his Vizier?

I acted out of character that day by trying to play the hero, something Bunter ain't physically or spiritually equipped for.

'We shall,' I said, 'meet again in Great Coram Street. How we shall laugh then at our present predicament. And how joyfully will we share, as true partners should, whatever is left of this Indian loot.'

Stolid and undemonstrative though she is, that reference to partnership moved her deeply. She gave me a quick bear hug, sniffed, wiped her eyes on the hem of her sari (she was wearing her ayah's clothes at the time), said, rather gruffly, 'See you in Great Coram Street, *partner*,' and went shuffling off down the road which would take her eventually to Lucknow.

Whenever I thought back to that moment I found myself hoping that she'd managed to get back to England, preferably with most of the loot. Even if she'd had to get rid of every scrap of it I still hoped she'd got back. Indeed, there were moments when I found myself wishing the voyage were already over so that I might discover whether she was now snugly tucked in and tucking in at Great Coram Street.

But as soon as I began to think about arriving I also began to worry over how I would then deal with Captain Griffiths, at which stage I would get close to wishing that we might start sailing backwards in order to delay the dreadful moment when the truth about Bunter had to be revealed. Meanwhile his weakness for royalty and his unquestioning belief in Bunter as a card-carrying member of the House of Brunswick kept him dancing attendance on me. And one of the first things he did when I told him that a shift and a chadoor weren't the best togs for a long ocean voyage was to make the whole of his wardrobe over to me.

'That's all very well, Griffiths,' I'd said in my royal yet

affable way. 'But you're built, dammee, like an understuffed scarecrow on stilts whilst I, as you can see, am built otherwise.'

'In that case, Sah, I shall send my sailmaker to wait on you.'

For a moment I wondered whether he proposed to have me stitched into his second-best storm jib to protect me from the sharper sea breezes. But Griffiths was an-all-or-nothing man, and where Raleigh had sacrificed no more than a cloak, he wanted to sacrifice his entire wardrobe, which was a large one. Anyone who turns up in the Kurachee brothel area wearing a flowered waistcoat and a white stovepipe hat has to be a dandy.

So the sailmaker did all Griffiths's togs over until they fitted me to a T. The only time he came near defeat was with Griffiths's best shore-going winter rig. This had been made of such a heavy and expensive material that the tailor, thinking to save a few shillings, had skimped on the seams. The sailmaker, as a consequence, had little to let out and the suit, even after he'd done his best with it, sat on me uncomfortably tight.

Luckily neither Gurmakh Singh nor the daughters-in-law needed to be kitted out. This was because they none of them came on deck from the time we left Kurachee to the time we dropped anchor in the Thames. Gurmakh Singh was too sea-sick to leave his cabin. The daughters-in-law were at first too heavy and later too busy to be going up and down companionways. The infants, however, stood in need of swaddling clothes and these the sailmaker, a most ingenious man, cobbled together from some old bits of bunting he had to hand. The result was that, although one of the babes seemed to be forever signalling for a pilot and the other was always in quarantine, the two of them were kept decently warm.

We made a fast voyage all the way from the Arabian Sea to the Western Approaches, nor did we meet any headwinds until after we rounded the North Foreland. But from then on they blew against us until we were finally forced to heave to and anchor in midstream, not far from the Pool of London, which we could not hope to enter until the winds turned favourable.

Lying at anchor brought Gurmakh Singh on deck for the first time. There was little enough for him to see since all was shrouded in one of those greasy yellow fogs known as London Particulars. It was also trying to snow, for we were no more than ten days away from Christmas. What with the cold and having lived for so long on dry toast and weak tea, it was a mere shadow of the Gurmakh Singh of our Sumroo days who came staggering towards me on the quarterdeck. And yet he looked remarkably determined as he drew me to the stern rail, looked around to ensure we weren't overheard, and even then addressed me in Urdu.

'Praise God the accursed *Kala Panee* is at last still and Bilatee is close at hand. How often in the past months have I had to wonder whether the next vomit would be the last vomit of Gurmakh Singh.'

'I also praise God you have survived.'

'Yet I must tell Your Excellency that when I was not wondering about my next vomit I was wondering about other things.'

'Such as what?'

'Such as the difference between fact and fancy, truth and untruth, appearance and reality.'

'These are deeply philosophical thoughts for in-between vomits. What led you to them?'

'May I answer with a conundrum?'

'Why a conundrum?'

'Your servant fears to give offence.'

'No offence will be taken. Proceed, O Father of Riddles.'

'It runs thus. When village girls become princesses and aged serving men are turned into sirdars, who then is King Georgey's nephew?'

This was indeed a forerunner of the problems I would soon be facing. Gurmakh Singh had always accepted the locket as proof positive of my royal ancestry. I had neither encouraged nor discouraged him in this for I was by no means certain about it myself. Yet now, just because I had told Griffiths a few lies about the daughters-in-law and himself, he had started to have doubts. I've always had doubts, which is why I have never actually lied about the locket. It's difficult to lie about anything when you can't be sure that you may not be telling the truth. But all of this was too difficult to explain, so I tried to pass it off lightly.

'A most ingenious conundrum, and one which I shall answer with two. What, O Gurmakh Singh, must you call a father who does not remember whether he begat a son or not?'

'I would call him forgetful, Sahib.'

'And what would you call the woman who bore that son?'

'Aiee, Huzoor! Would you have me slander your mother?'

'Who talks of mothers?'

'If it is another's mother, I would call her careless.'

'I am glad, Gurmakh Singh,' said I, 'that we understand one another.'

'That your servant should understand is a matter of no importance. But that Griffiths Sahib will soon be trying to understand is a matter of such extreme concern that I fear there could be a great cutting of tripes unless . . .'

'Unless what?'

'Unless we can escape before understanding dawns.'

'It must dawn very soon, but anchored as we are, far from the shore, escape is not possible. And yet like you, I long for it.'

Gurmakh Singh pointed to a bumboat which was dimly visible through the fog, coming towards us. It had got rid of whatever it had to sell to other ships lying nearby and was now returning empty to the Middlesex shore. Its homeward course seemed likely to bring it close under the *Gay Georgian*'s stern.

'In Kurachee,' said he, 'I studied the ways of both sea-going and shore-going sailors. I found that such bumboats are invariably manned by rogues who would sell their mothers for a trifling sum and cut their grandmothers' throats for even less. I have no reason to believe that Angrezi bumboat men are any different in this respect from Kurachee ones. Why then should not Your Honour arrange with the rogue in yonder boat to return late tonight to carry all of us quietly and secretly ashore and away from Griffiths Sahib?'

'How do I attract his attention without shouting and thus attracting more attention than we want?'

Gurmakh Singh fished around in his kummerbund, took out a lean-looking purse, extracted a single gold mohur and gave it to me.

'Here,' said he, 'is the language you must use. If you also have to use words, let them be whispered ones.'

The bumboat was now so close under our stern that I was able to lean over the taffrail and drop the coin at the sculler's feet. He was so muffled up in tarpaulin jackets, shawls and oilskins that I doubted he would be able to bend to pick up the mohur. This he did, however, and as he looked up I motioned to him to lay hold of the anchor cable and pull himself along it until he was within whispershot.

'There will,' I hissed, 'be five more . . .' Gurmakh Singh nudged me in the ribs and whispered fiercely in my ear so I changed feet, as it were, and went on, 'three more of these if you are willing to return here, in absolute silence, at midnight, and carry six of us quietly to the shore.'

He examined the mohur, bit it, shook his head and muttered: 'It will have to be five.'

'Three,' I whispered, Gurmakh Singh's elbow still in my ribs.

'Five.'

'Three and a gold nose-stud.'

At that moment someone emerged from the companionway and started to move towards us, clattering a bucket.

'Settle the price later,' said the bumboat man who, it was beginning to dawn on me, was actually a bumboat woman. 'Until then,' she added, 'mum's the word, midnight's the time, an' Buttercup's the name.'

And with that she sculled quietly away into the fog.

5 *Buttercup, Cabbages, and Commanders-in-Chief*

It's all very well for Walter Scott's and Mrs Radcliffe's heroes and heroines, but escapes in real life ain't often such simple one-leap-to-freedom affairs as they are in novels. We couldn't, for example, sneak away from the *Gay Georgian* half as silently as I would have liked. Indeed, although the night, the fog, and the fact that no anchor watch was kept all worked in our favour, we would never have got away at all if Griffiths and his crew had slept even one snore less soundly.

All of this was due to Gurmakh Singh, and yet he had meant well. If he had spent the hour or two before the arrival of the bumboat filling the daughters-in-law and their brats full of rum, it was because he hoped it would give Dutch courage to the mothers and reduce their squalling infants to a drunken silence. His hopes were over- rather than under-fulfilled. The daughters-in-law were giggling much louder than usual even before we lowered them into the bumboat. By the time they took their seats on the middle thwart they were chanting Punjaubi *rukhs*. The rum had persuaded them that they were on their way to a party, and in the village where they had been brought up, there had always been *rukhs* to sing and dance to at parties. As for their brats, the rum had certainly laid them out, but it had also given them an attack of wind. And so they belched and hiccuped so explosively in their stupors that they might just as well have been firing off musket volleys.

These varied and terrifying noises continued even after Gurmakh Singh had joined them and was hissing. 'Chut! Chut!' as savagely as it ever can be hissed. By the time I had lowered myself into the stern of the boat and the bumboat woman had started to pull away it seemed to me that all that was needed to turn our departure into a public and ceremonial occasion was a full bosun's party piping us ashore.

It was impossible in the dark to tell what size of a woman the bumboat woman was, she having chosen to row her boat from the bow thwart. But it soon became obvious that she wasn't up to my weight. For the moment I seated myself in the stern the bows went up to such an extent that, good waterwoman though she may have been, she took almost as many air shots as rowing strokes. Every time her oars missed the water she fell over backwards and cursed so profusely and inventively that even Gurmakh Singh, that connoisseur of barrackroom profanity, grunted in admiration.

Our departure, taking it all in all, was noisy and spasmodic rather than swift and silent yet the noise failed to alarm anyone aboard the *Gay Georgian* and the air shots failed to prevent us slowly making progress. And, of course, the more progress we made the less the noise mattered. In addition to which the half-gale, which was bringing snowflakes drifting down without doing much in the way of lifting the fog, soon chilled the infants into deeper and more silent stupors and the daughters-in-law into a comparative sobriety.

Nevertheless, what with one thing and another, it was a good quarter of an hour before we saw the Middlesex shore looming up out of the fog and another quarter of an hour before we could see the small, rickety-looking wharf we were heading for. We weren't many yards away from it when the bumboat woman suddenly took the way off the boat and, holding her out in the stream, said:

'Not caring, I didn't ask, an' not asking I don't know who an' what it might be as you're scarpering from. But what I does know is that there's the small matter of payment that 'as to be dealt with afore you does any further scarpering. Now as I recollec', we'd agreed that it would be five more o' them gold pieces with what you called a nose-stud thrown in to round off the bargain like.'

I didn't know whether Gurmakh Singh had five mohurs and a nose-stud left in the treasury or not. But if he had, I was very willing for him to hand them over. Sitting in a smelly bumboat on a snowy, foggy night, with twenty yards of swirling, muddy Thames separating me from terra firma ain't exactly the conditions that encourage Bunter to argue. Not so Gurmakh Singh however. A few hours' respite from sea-sickness had worked wonders with him, and he was rapidly reverting to his former swaggering, bumptious self. He saw himself once more as Bunter Sahib's *khansamah*, and, if there was any rooking of Bunter to be done, it was, in the first instance, to be done by Gurmakh Singh.

This, he clearly told himself, was just the usual bazaar situation in which the bumboat woman was making the opening moves in what would certainly develop into a prolonged and thoroughly enjoyable haggle. The conventions demanded as much when a price had to be established. It was impossible to see in the darkness whether he actually wagged a finger at her, but what he said in his opening remark was certainly said in a finger-wagging sort of voice.

'You are being very bloody greedy, Missus. Five more mohurs was never bleeding well being agreed as you are jolly well knowing. It was three mohurs, and you are being very extremely lucky to be getting that. And never, absolutely never was I agreeing to throwing in bloody nose-stud.'

The next move was the bumboat woman's. She should, by all bazaar conventions, have blubbed a bit, have referred to her poverty, her children, and her reputation as an honest woman, have denied that three mohurs had ever been mentioned, and have pointed out that such a paltry sum would never have induced her to take to the water on such a night as this. But either she had never heard of the conventions or else had no respect for them, for devil a bit of blubbing, denying or protesting did she produce. Instead she said, in a very matter-of-fact voice:

'I ain't a-arguing with you. I'm a-telling you. An' them as won't be told will 'ave to be taught.'

Gurmakh Singh stuck to the conventions even though the bumboat woman did not. 'You are being,' he said, 'a bloody great liar. But because Bunter Sahib is a great man and I am being very very kindly towards you, three mohurs and three rupees . . .'

He got no further. The bumboat woman, having groped under her thwart, had produced a short-handled boathook with which she knocked Gurmakh Singh into the bilges where he lay groaning. If he had not still been wearing his green Hadji's turban, he would have had a split scalp to nurse.

I ain't the sort of man to intervene in a private haggle, and so, when she proceeded to turn the boat's bows upstream and to pull away from the wharf on a course roughly parallel with the shore, I said and did nothing. Nor did I protest when she suddenly swung the boat into a narrow little inlet and tied up to what appeared to be some sort of hulk sitting on the mud at its landward end. As soon as she had made fast she swarmed up a rope ladder hanging over the side, disappeared down what must have been a companionway, and reappeared moments later carrying a lantern which she shone on the rope ladder.

'You can't,' she said, 'see what I'm a-holding in me other hand on account of it being dark. It's a bloody great hoss-pistol what me late third husband used to call 'is Poor Parlay, that bein' becos 'e'd used it to parlay a good many Parlay-Voos to their Maker when he was with the 'Eavy Brigade in Spain. I've seen that same pistol blow a bloody great 'ole through two Frogs at once. What it'd do to a bunch o' civilians don't bear talking about. So you'd best all get up that there ladder just as quick an' as quiet as you can.'

It would clearly be a difficult job to get the daughters-in-law up the ladder complete with infants. Gurmakh Singh was no longer in a position to point this out. So, however reluctantly, Bunter had to.

'Ma'm . . .' I began.

The lantern beam was switched into the boat where, for the first time, the bumboat woman could begin to identify some of the passengers she'd been ferrying. The light lingered on the daughters-in-law huddling into their chadoors, on their babes swathed in their respective buntings, and on Gurmakh Singh sitting on the floorboards and holding his turbanned head.

'Bugger me,' said the bumboat woman, 'if I ain't been a-carrying a cargo of blackamoors.'

'Ma'am . . .' I bleated once more.

The light swung on to me.

' 'Ceptin' for the stout party,' she went on. The light stayed on me, swinging up and down.

'Stand up,' she said. Gurmakh Singh staggered to his feet.

'Not you,' said the bumboat woman. 'The stout party.'

I stood up.

The light kept playing on me, lingering on this part of me and that until I began to wonder what it was about me that could be of such interest to the bumboat woman. In the end I decided it must be my get-up, which had been chosen for a night trip on the Thames the week before Christmas. In short, I had chosen to wear the thickest and warmest clothes in what had once been Griffiths's wardrobe.

This meant that I wore under what had been his heaviest boat cloak what had once been his winter shore-going outfit. This was the one in light blue broadcloth which the sailmaker had been able to tailor only partially to my figure. In short it was hellishly tight and devilish uncomfortable under the arms, around the waist, and in the crotch. But since I had decided, like St Paul, that it was better to be uncomfortable than to freeze, and, since I have always been susceptible to head colds, I wore one of Griffiths's stovepipe hats kept firmly in place by one of his scarlet mufflers which went over the crown and was tied under my chin.

The light lingered so long on all of this that I began to blink through my spectacles and feel self-conscious. Finally the voice of the bumboat woman broke the silence.

'Take that tile off, Fatty,' it said, 'so as to give me a shufti at your mug.'

I did what she ordered but all she said was:

'You ain't much to look at, Fatty, are you? An' why do you keep squirming so an' why are you forever clutching at your crotch?'

It wasn't the sort of question a chap is eager to answer, so she answered it for me.

'If you ask me,' she said, flashing the lantern in that direction, 'you're clutching at your best part – that is if them tight trowsis o' yours ain't lyin'. In fac' I don't believe I've seen anything so worth clutchin' since me second died, an' 'e were the best-'ung man in the 'ole of the 52nd. Black Bob Crauford what commanded the Light Brigade until 'e got isself killed at Ciudad Rodrigo once told me 'e didn't think there was a rifleman in the 'ole of the brigade as 'ung 'alf as 'eavy as my Sam. "'ow do you know?" I said to 'im. "Hobservation," 'e said to me. "Well you hobserved correc'," I said to 'im. "If I ain't any good at hobserving," 'e said, "we shall never lick Boney," an' then 'e gave me a guinea over an' above what 'e owed me for doin' 'is laundry.'

The situation was an intolerable one. There was I, standing up in the stern of the bumboat shivering with cold and funk and with the snowflakes coming down and turning me into a tolerable imitation of Lot's wife; and there was this unpredictable, dangerous, loquacious hag, lantern in one hand, pistol in t'other, expecting me to listen to endless reminiscences about her husbands and Black Bob Crauford.

'Ma'am . . .' I ventured once more.

'You ain't a sheep, Fatty, so stop bleatin' at me and come aboard afore I does something drastic with Poor Parlay.'

It was only after she had hustled us all down the companionway and into what she called her cuddy that I was able to get my first real look at the bumboat woman and her home. Neither was what I expected. The home, I discovered later, had been one of the larger Thames barges, those which, when on the coastal trade, will sail as far afield as the Crouch, or even the Tyne. But if she had been a vessel of war, she would have been described in her present state as being *en flute*. That is to say she'd been immobilised, her masts, yards and rigging had all been dropped, and a large section of her deck, forard of the crew's quarters, appeared to have been roofed over.

The cuddy, which was lit by a number of oil lamps, was

surprisingly large. A pot-bellied iron stove, which still had at least a bushel of sea coals glowing away in its belly, kept it splendidly warm. What I would call its walls, though there is probably a more nautical term for them, were almost hidden by one of the most extraordinary displays of military memorabilia you could hope to see outside a regimental depot.

There was a shot-torn regimental flag keeping company with the similarly battered eagle of a French demi-brigade. A pair of crossed sabres of the straight English type was balanced by a curved slashing pair of the French type, and under each pair were hung counterparts of Poor Parlay. There was a French lance with the guidon of Poniatowski's Polish Lancers still hanging from it and a Lifeguard's helmet and breastplate. There were bayonets, a sergeant's halberd, muskets, bugles, bandoliers, powder horns, cutlasses and a French kettle drum. There was a whole gallery of prints of the better-known of the modern military and naval commanders, starting with Nelson and St Vincent on either side of the companionway and ending up with the Grand Old Duke of York in full fig as Commander-in-Chief on one side of the stove and the Iron Duke, in more sober rig, on the other. Built into the frame that enclosed Wellington was a curious little glass-fronted case or reliquary which contained, sitting up on a little red velvet cushion, something that looked very like a half-set of human teeth.

These were all things I took note of later, for when I first came into the cuddy all my attention was fixed on the bumboat woman. She, without ever getting rid of her Poor Parlay, had managed to get rid of her oilskins, tarpaulin jacket and sea boots before taking up her stand facing us and with her back to the stove. Then, with the pistol still in one hand, she hoisted her skirts with the other and exposed her bum, which was encased in red flannel drawers, to the stove's genial heat.

'It's the sciatiky,' she said. 'Ollers takes me in the arse if I get it chilled.'

And she grinned at me with as much friendliness and good humour as if I'd just invited her to stand up with me for a country dance. She was, I now realised, a comfortably built,

round-faced, apple-cheeked sort of woman with a pair of eyes
that were as small, round and black as a couple of boot buttons,
but had a good deal more sparkle. Indeed her appearance was
very much more pleasing and amiable than her conduct had
led me to expect. And although she was now well on into
her middle age, she still had that confident, open, slightly
masterful manner that a woman who knows she has been
attractive to men never loses. She seemed so willing to be
friendly in spite of her Poor Parlay and the strangeness of the
situation that I embarked on yet another attempt to reason
with her.

'It would distress me, Ma'am,' said I, 'if, by coming to the
aid of those in distress you have exposed yourself to an attack
of sciatica. I have been told, Ma'am, that a good rub with
neat's-foot oil followed by the application of a hot brick
wrapped in flannel to the seat of the trouble will work wonders.
Now you won't want us here, Ma'am, whilst you attend to such
matters. So just as soon as we have settled what we owe you, we
will be on our way.'

'I said five, an' I meant five,' said she. 'But . . .'

Gurmakh Singh, taking care to keep me between himself and
the bumboat woman, made protesting noises which she
ignored.

'But,' she continued, 'now as I've 'ad a look at you I can see
you ain't likely to be flush. I 'ad thought, seein' as 'ow you was
on the run, that you might be on the run with a good bit of swag.
But if you're on the run from anything, it will only be a circus,
an' there ain't much swag in circuses. Now where was it you
was thinkin' of scarperin' to?'

'London,' said I.

'God bless the man, you're almost there. But it's a big place,
London is. Where in London was you thinkin' of?'

'Great Coram Street, Ma'am.'

'That ain't far from Covent Garden, is it?'

'I don't believe it is.'

'Then I'll tell you what. It's well past midnight an' snowin'.
If I turn you out now you're as like to drown in the river or get

lost in the marshes as to get to where you want. But I've a cart
going to Covent Garden with produce tomorrow, an' I don't see
why it shouldn't carry you lot as well and go to Covent Garden
by way of Great Coram Street. You can spend the rest of the
night here, I'll give you breakfast, an' all I'll charge you for
river an' road transport, board an' lodging, will be them three
coins you offered. If you want to throw that nose-ring in, that's
up to you.'

'You are,' said Gurmakh Singh, coming out from behind me,
'very sensible woman. Is pleasure to be doing business with
you. I shall be happy to be giving you three mohurs. But
nose-stud, as you are now seeing, is in woman's nose where it is
belonging, and we are needing special tools before it is being
able to be removed.'

'In that case,' said the bumboat woman, 'we'll forget the
nose-stud.'

'Heavens,' said Gurmakh Singh with the air of one who
knew, 'will certainly be slipping one Hell of a lot of blessings in
your direction.'

'Well,' said she, 'we might as well get what sleep we can.
Now there's only this place an' me own sleeping quarters. If
you keep the stove going an' stretch out on the lockers, you'll be
as snug here as in your beds. But you, Fatty . . .' and here she
turned her gaze and Pour Parlay in my direction '. . . you will
just have to tuck up with Buttercup, on account of my needin'
someone to help me with the neat's-foot oil.'

And then she gave me the most brazenly lewd wink I have
ever seen the human eye perform. Past experience at the hands
of masterful women should have prepared me for this, but it
was such a quick and brutal move, with none of the usual
preliminaries and pourparlers, that I felt enraged.

'Think you,' I said to Gurmakh Singh in Urdu, 'that we two
can rush and disarm her?'

He looked horrified. 'The pistol, Huzoor, which blew the
holes through the Frenchmen, still points at us. Would you
have me commit suicide?'

'Would you,' I replied angrily, 'have me prostitute myself?'

'You must not think of it in that way. It could not, after all, be worse than it was with the Begum. It may even be better for she is of your race and so will expect no more than that you should couple in that simple missionary style which is all you Angrezis ever practise.'

'Yet it is a shame to both of us that I should be forced at pistol-point whilst you, my *khansamah*, snore in the cuddy.'

'Relax, Sahib, and think of all we get in return.'

'Think also of us,' said Fyzoo.

'And of our children, who are also yours,' said Ghulabi.

'You are our protector and our shield,' said Gurmakh Singh.

It was late the next morning when I reappeared in the cuddy where Buttercup insisted that I should eat a breakfast that was restorative in character. That is to say after a dish of fried smelts with an oyster sauce and another of broiled beefsteaks, I had to drink a cream, egg and brandy posset before I was allowed my coffee and muffins.

Whether it was because I was slightly languid or whether it was because of the way Buttercup fussed over me I cannot say. But the daughters-in-law tittered and drew away from me and Gurmakh Singh started to snigger the moment I tottered into the room. I could not help feeling chagrined by this, especially when I remembered how they had appealed to me only a few hours earlier as their protector and shield. There is, sad to say, something of Judas Iscariot in every one of us.

No one, however, could have been more amiable than Buttercup, who, once I had breakfasted, took me in a most friendly fashion by the arm and showed me round her domain. This began in the cuddy with an inspection of her trophies and portraits, each of which earned a lecture. When I remarked on their specifically military nature she said that she had never been a bloody civilian but had followed the drum for more than twenty years.

'Why,' said she, 'I've 'ad no fewer than three 'usbands shot from under me as you might say, for I were never farther away from any of 'em than the baggage train when they was fighting.

I were sixteen when I followed me first to 'Olland in '93 and nigh on forty when I were with me third at Toulouse in '14. Tottin' 'em all up, that makes twelve set battles, three sieges, four retreats, an' Gawd alone knows 'ow many lesser bits o' business when we was on detachment.'

'And that was when you acquired this splendid collection?'

'Of course. What else do you think sodgers fight for?'

'Honour? Patriotism? King and Country?'

'King an' kiss-me-arse. You're talkin' like a miserable politician. Sodgers fight, in the first place, to save their skins. Then they looks around for loot an', if they can get away with it, a spot o' rape. But in the long run what they want most is soovenirs.'

'Souvenirs? What sort of souvenirs?'

'Properly speakin' they ought to be battlefield soovenirs. Things like prints an' tattoos is only garrison soovenirs, but I don't scorn 'em. You must 'ave noticed the 'eart pierced with an arrow I 'ad tattooed 'atween my titties in Gibraltar, though I dare say you missed the snake what runs down me back that were done in Portsmouth. But on the 'ole, soovenirs ain't tattoos but objecks like these 'ere.' She waved an arm around the cuddy from Nelson to Wellington, which allowed me to enquire about the half-set of teeth let into Wellington's frame.

'Ah,' said she, 'you might just as well ask me why I'm known as Buttercup when me real name is Dolly.'

'Then why,' said I, feeling too docile to ignore such an instruction, 'are you known as Buttercup?'

'On account of 'im,' said she, jerking a thumb at the Duke's portrait. 'It were the only joke 'e ever made in all the years I've known 'im, 'an I did 'is laundry all the way from Torres Vedras to Bayonne. You can 'ardly find a better way of gettin' to know a man than by attending to 'is dirty linen.'

'But what was the joke?'

'It were just after Salamanca. Nightshirts an' drawers it were as I was delivering. An' just to pass the time o' day, as I always did with me customers, I remarked as 'ow I'd been at every battle 'e'd fought since the first one at Vimiero. 'E looked at me for a bit an' then said: "Well, Dolly, we'll jus' 'ave to call you Buttercup from now on." "Whatever for?" said I. "On account of your bein' found on every field," said 'e. An' then 'e laughed fit to split 'is britches, which is what no one 'ad ever seen 'im do afore. It were the talk o' the 'ole Army, which is why I've been Buttercup from that day to this.'

'And where do the teeth come into it?'

'They're my personal soovenir of the Dook, they being the bottom 'alf of 'is spare set. Solid ivory – carved for 'im out of an elephant's tusk when 'e was in India.'

'He gave them to you?'

'Not 'xactly. I came across 'em in a bundle o' table napkins what I were washing. 'E thought 'e'd lost 'em during the advance over the Pyrenees, an' 'e raised 'ell about 'em. It weren't just the value. With a nose an' chin like 'is 'e 'ad to be sure of always 'avin' something in 'is mouth what would keep the two apart. So 'e always 'ad 'is ivories in, even when 'e were in bed an' on top. Leastways that's what I found.'

I must have looked surprised, because she bridled:

'You don't think, do you, that all I ever did for 'im was 'is laundry. When he was in the field an' there was no 'igh-born Spanish bits around 'e'd generally send for me. Never could sleep properly, could Arthur, 'less there was four legs in 'is bed. An' 'e were as good in bed as in the field, let me tell you, which is more than anyone every said about Boney.'

These revelations about the two greatest soldiers of our time startled me and it must have shown, which made her grin.

'Lor' bless you,' she said, 'I thought everyone knew Boney's pecker were something a twelve-year-old would 'ave been ashamed of. It din't stop 'im rogering, but it stopped 'im doing it well. Some 'igh-born tart what'ad done the rounds once said that, if you'd been in bed with Boney, all you knew was that you'd been in bed with the conqueror of 'alf the world.'

We had come, by this time, to the picture of the Duke of York, at which she looked less kindly than she had at Wellington's.

''E were my first Commander-in-Chief. Washed 'is linen an'

warmed 'is bed when we was in 'Olland in '93. Never 'ad anything to do with 'im after that on account of 'e went to the 'Orse Guards.'

I thought it might be a good thing to show her that I, too, had a portrait of her first Commander-in-Chief. So I gave her the locket and a heavy hint of what it stood for in my pedigree. Her reaction surprised me. She looked at the locket, smacked her thigh and said:

'Bugger me if that ain't better'n tattooing.'

'Tattooing?'

'For me soovenirs.'

'I don't follow you.'

'P'raps not; but you follow them,' and here she pointed triumphantly at Wellington and York.

'I still don't understand.'

'Why, Mr Bunter, it now turns out that I've not only 'ad me legs around a Commander-in-Chief what's dead an' a Commander-in-Chief what isn't, but I've also 'ad them self-same legs round a Commander-in-Chief's bastard. There ain't many women as can count that amongst their soovenirs.'

'So the Duke of York is dead?'

'Didn't you know? Died almost a year ago. I'd 'ave thought...' and here her brow darkened and she began to look suspicious. '. . . I'd 'ave thought as a son would know about 'is Pa's death.'

'You don't need to worry about your souvenirs,' said I. 'I've been travelling in wild and savage parts of the world these past eighteen months.'

That reassured her and we completed the inspection of her domain which would, under different circumstances, have interested me as an interesting example of a cottage – or rather barge – industry. All that part of the deck which had been given a roof reed thatch had been divided off into pens, some of which held pigs, some of which held goats, and others of which held poultry, pigeons, turkeys and suchlike. There was a stable which held an enormous donkey and a small and very hairy dun pony. The last pen of all was home to Joe Girdlestone, who was a little, bent, wizened, dirty old fellow who looked after the livestock and the smallholding ashore, whose several plots of cultivated land held the reed beds at bay. Some of them, at this time of the year, lay fallow, but others still carried crops of swedes and winter cabbage.

These stock pens and garden plots supplied the produce Buttercup carried out to the ships lying in the river, and whatever they produced by way of surplus to that trade, Joe Girdlestone took to Covent Garden. But Buttercup herself, when not busy in the bumboat, was hard at work in what had once been the hulk's hold. Here she had set up a series of manufactories to deal with the liquors she smuggled in from the ships she traded with. The processes they were subjected to in the hold ensured that, for every bottle of brandy or wine that came in, two fuller-bodied bottles went out to be carried by Joe Girdlestone to the vintner in London who was Buttercup's agent.

There was an economy of materials in every one of these processes that struck me as admirable for, apart from the sugar which was also smuggled, nothing was used that had not been grown in the plots or gathered from the hedgerows. Thus there were burnt sugar and Thames water for the brandies, elderberry wine for the clarets and burgundies, gooseberry wine for the champagnes and a fine beetroot cordial for the ports. And as Buttercup's agent had his shop in St James's and a reputation for selling the choicest wines and spirits in London, it would have been difficult to deny that, besides being a source of profit to Buttercup, these cottage manufactories were of benefit to every drinker in London possessed of a palate.

After this tour of inspection we all sat down to a light meal of spatchcocked eels followed by boiled ham, greens and potatoes, followed by custards and syllabubs, followed by a Stilton cheese and a dish of pippins. After years of tandooris and curries and months of ship's fare, such honest English food persuaded me that the wanderer was, at last, come home to his birthright.

And then the time came for us to set out for London. We did so in the care of Joe Girdlestone, who had a load of cabbages to take to Covent Garden. That load so filled the light cart, which was all that the dun pony could pull, that there was room on top of the cabbages for only the daughters-in-law and the Bunterkins. So they put a pack-saddle on the donkey and me on the pack-saddle though I had to sit sideways as though I were a woman riding side-saddle. Gurmakh Singh walked with Joe Girdlestone at the dun pony's head, still wearing his Patan costume and green turban.

Before I mounted my donkey, however, I had to take my leave of Buttercup. It must not be thought of as vanity on my part if I state that, despite the briefness of our relationship, a good part of which had been adversarial, Buttercup had grown most devilish fond of me. She gave me a great hug and a series of smacking kisses and said:

'You don't make the most o' yourself, Mr Bunter, that you don't. You've got parts as a duchess would be interested in, yet you seem loath to give 'em employment. But you've given me a deal of enjoyment, even though I 'ad to squeeze it out o' you at pistol-point. So I'm grateful to you, Mr Bunter, Sir, an' when Buttercup's grateful she's grateful for life.'

'Come, Ma'am,' said I, 'there's no need to make so much of it.'

'I'll make as much or as little of it as I wants,' she said sharply, 'an' what I mean is this. I know what them Royals is like. Lot o' stuck-up Germans without a decent English sentiment in 'em. I suppose, from what you told me, that you expect to be received as one o' the family.'

'I expect nothing of the sort, Ma'am, especially now that the Duke is dead and my Mama in Corfu.'

'That's just as well. But if ever you do stand in need of a spot o' help, just you remember that Buttercup's got a bit put away, an' that it's an English and not a German 'eart as beats under that tattoo.'

'I will indeed, Ma'am.'

'An' if ever you run into the Commander-in-Chief, just you

tell 'im as Buttercup sends 'er love an' that if ever 'e stands in need of 'em, there's a spare bottom set of 'is to be found 'ere in me cuddy.'

6   *Great Coram Street Matrimonials*

The dun pony, being a trifle small for the job, made heavy work of pulling a cart that held daughters-in-law as well as cabbages. My own animal was large enough even for Bunter, but she was also, I discovered, a female and in season. Her reluctant gait, together with the manner in which she plaintively brayed at every quadruped we passed, were clear evidence of what she was thinking. If she had to be mounted at all, she would prefer it to be by something with four legs rather than two.

Darkness, therefore, was closing around us as we turned into Great Coram Street, for which I was truly thankful. We had, in our passage through the City, attracted a good deal of attention, together with a most undesirable following of street-urchins, one gang of whom would pass us on to their fellows in the next parish whenever they got tired. Nor could I escape them by hanging back and pretending to have nothing to do with the cabbage cart, for that only won us two sets of urchins instead of one. I could understand why Gurmakh Singh and the daughters-in-law rolling about on cabbages in their chadoors and veils should attract urchin ribaldry. But I couldn't for the life of me see why Bunter riding side-saddle on an outsize donkey should do the same.

But as the light faded we became less conspicuous and were able to lose our following. By the time we turned into Great Coram Street all that followed us was a large, stout, weary-looking, mud-stained fellow riding a bobtailed flea-bitten grey

with a head like a fiddle and ribs that would have done very well
as toast racks. Our own animals were moving so reluctantly by
then that the grey, though as weary-looking and mud-stained
as its rider, soon overtook us without quickening its pace by a
second or lengthening it by an inch.

Its rider, like all other riders that day, stared at us as he
passed, and I stared back. There was little enough of him to see
for his hat was pulled down over his brow and the rest of his face
was buried in the upturned collar of a prodigiously long and
roomy frock coat that covered him from chin to toe. But as that
hat was a widish-brimmed, lowish-crowned, solid-looking
affair attached to his buttonhole by a green cord that ended in a
fox's tooth, and as that coat was a red one with a great many
brass buttons cast in the shape of a fox's mask, and as he carried
an iron-headed hunting crop heavy enough to fell an ox and
had a hunting horn strapped to one side of his saddle-bow and a
pewter brandy flask strapped to the other, it was reasonable to
suppose he was returning home from a hunt.

My donkey was more interested in the grey than I was in its
rider. The sight of its bobtail bobbing around in front of us set
my amorous animal a-braying. Whereupon the grey whipped
around, made a rapid appreciation of the situation, and
jumped my mount, knocking me into the mud of Great Coram
Street in the process. There, for all his 'Come ups' and his 'Hold
hards', I was joined by the man in the red coat, and there we
sat, looking at one another, whilst the donkey brayed with
pleasure and the grey snorted with lust.

It slowly dawned on me that, although now fuller, and
framed in as fine a set of mutton-chop whiskers as you could
wish for, the face I was staring at had, in its whiskerless days,
been one that was familiar to me.

'It was only last week,' he said, looking with disgust at the
grey's strenuous antics, 'it was only last week that I gave
thirty-eight pun' and a nearly-new saddle for that gelding.
Double-patent-safety he said it was, and never a word about it
being a rig.'

'J.J.!' said I.

'I was done,' said he.

'J.J.!' said I, rather more loudly.

'Done to a frazzle. But never again. If you ever catch me buying a hoss from a Yorkshireman you can enter me for Bedlam.'

'J.J.!' I bellowed.

'Hey?' said he. 'And who the devil are you?'

'Bunter.'

'Who?'

'Your old school chum, Billy Bunter,' said I. And as an aid to identification I stood up, dusted myself off, removed the muffler and stovepipe hat, and put on my spectacles.

'God bless my soul!' said he. 'I do believe you're Billy Bunter. What in the Hell were you doing aboard that infernal donkey?'

That infernal donkey, having decided that there was more of promise than of performance in the grey, had just lashed out with both hind feet. Now there was a very real possibility that the grey was an even worse bargain than a week ago.

'I was,' I said, 'proposing to pay you a visit.'

'In that case,' said he, getting to his feet and putting his arm round my shoulders, 'what are we waiting for? There lies Number 19 not twenty yards away. There's a bottle of me green-seal Madeira waiting to have its cork drawn, and a fine, damp, rich plum cake waiting to be eaten whilst they brighten up the fire and set about cooking our suppers. Besides all of which there's me sister Maria. She's been there waiting for you to turn up these twelve months past.'

This last item – this notion of his sister playing at patience on a monument – seemed to fill him with a sudden anxiety, for he started to hurry me down Great Coram Street towards Number 19.

'Hold you hard,' said I, 'for I'm not on my own but have these others in tow,' and I pointed to the stationary cabbage cart and to Gurmakh Singh, the daughters-in-law and the babes. All of them were solemnly watching J.J. and myself and managing to ignore Joe Girdlestone, to whom they had left the

job of getting the frustrated grey safely away from my sadly
disappointed donkey.

J.J. looked across at Gurmakh Singh who, acting on the
belief that first impressions are all-important, sprang to
attention and gave him an arm-quivering salute of the sort
his former comrades-in-arms of the Bengal Native Infantry
reserved for a Major-General or upwards. J.J., not being a
Major-General, looked startled and turned his attention to the
daughters-in-law. He walked twice round the cabbage cart
whilst inspecting them, after which he lifted bits of the bunting
in which the babes were swaddled in order to get a better look at
them. After he had poked them in two or three different places
with his forefinger he said:

'Devilish fine infants. Dare say they'd go near a stone and a
half each if you put 'em on my bacon scales. And they're the
spitting image of you, Bunter, though a few shades darker. Are
these ladies their Mamas?'

'Yes.'

He looked at me anxiously and said: 'You ain't, I hope,
married to each of 'em.'

'I ain't,' said I, 'married to anyone.'

'That's a relief,' said he. 'Serious business, you know.
Transportable offence . . . seven years . . . King's Bench, hulks,
Botany Bay . . . Not to mention the other business. Breach of
promise . . . Doctor's Commons . . . enormous damages.'

'J. J.,' said I, 'I don't even begin to understand what you are
talking about.'

'Talking about bigamy,' said he, 'which is what it would
have been if you had married both the Mamas. Talking about
breach of promise of marriage, which is what it would have
been if you had only married one of 'em. But since there hasn't
been even one marriage there hasn't been any breach, and since
there hasn't been any breach there can't be any damages.
Consequence is, we can go ahead as planned.'

'Go ahead to what?'

'Why, you fat ass, to your matrimonials of course.'

'Matrimonials?'

'William Bunter, Gent. to Maria Huggins, née Jewkes, relict of late Lieutenant-Colonel D'Arcy Huggins formerly in the service of H.R.H. The Maharajah Runjeet Singh. And from what I can see, you dog...' here he leered at the Bunterkins and the sisters-in-law and gave me a nudge in the ribs '... you're a deal better equipped for matrimonials and the perpetuation of the species than ever my late brother-in-law Huggins was, or, for that matter, than that grey hoss of mine.'

I was about to protest that I had no desire for matrimonials, that I had never, to the best of my recollection, promised Maria anything even vaguely connected with marriage, and that I took little interest in the perpetuation of the species, even though I had so often had to contribute to it, when I suddenly remembered my position and how I was relying on finding welcome and succour at 19 Great Coram Street. And so, beckoning to the Singhs to follow J.J. and myself, I said nothing.

It ain't necessarily true that a chap has to marry or burn. If it were left to me I'd do neither. But rarely has it been left to Bunter. There has always been a masterful woman who decided the matter and saw to it that I should eventually burn. J.J., however, was neither masterful nor a woman. Why then did he have his mind so firmly fixed on matrimonials for Bunter? We had scarcely got inside Number 19 before he was, in a manner of speaking, publishing the banns, preparing the marriage settlement and planning the wedding breakfast. Nor was he alone in this. His widowed mother – John Jewkes Senior had been an inhabitant of St Botolph Churchyard for the past three years – never stopped beaming marriage beds and grandchildren at me. Benjamin, the boot, lamp and stable boy, leered at me whenever we met, and Mrs Beeton, the cook, started to prepare me for matrimony from the moment I first put my legs under J.J.'s mahogany: oysters and beefsteaks were never absent from any meal, and for the in-between-meals periods there were brandy possets, egg-nogs and wine syllabubs 'to revive them vital forces, Mr Bunter, what the suns, spices an' dancin'-gals of India can't 'ave done no good to.'

Indeed the only inhabitant of 19 Great Coram Street who wasn't determined to force-feed me, or to nudge me, leer at me, or breathe nuptials at me was Maria herself. From that moment when J.J. bustled me into the house shouting for Maria to come downstairs at once to see who had arrived and to Benjamin to come upstairs with clean glasses and a bottle of the green-seal – from that first moment she remained as cool as a cucumber, as unfanciful as roast beef and as stolid as plum duff.

She greeted me as though I had just returned from a half-hour stroll before supper instead of a perilous and year-long journey across half the globe. I ain't over-demonstrative myself, except when my safety or my belly are concerned, but I was probably as pleased to see her as I have been to see any female. She was a mite stouter now that she no longer had the fierce suns of Lahore to sweat some of the lard off her but that may have indeed been fancy – a stone more or a stone less is neither here nor there for a woman of her build. But her calm and not unpleasant face was still as round and as comforting as a harvest moon, and she still moved with the majestic waddle of a Michaelmas goose at graze on the stubbles.

It was Maria who, seeing that we all stood in need of more suitable clothing, straightway set about supplying it. There were few difficulties in my case. We could have searched the whole of London and failed to find a man as similar in build to myself as J.J. So, from what he had already discarded or now seldom wore, it was a simple business to rig me out, albeit a little shabbily, for anything from a fox hunt to a wedding.

This allowed me to pass on what had once been Captain Griffiths's best shore-going rig to Gurmakh Singh. But here some problems arose. Although plump enough for a Sikh, Gurmakh Singh was not, when it came to stoutness and size, in Bunter's league. Consequently what had been skin-tight on me sat as loosely on him as its skin sits on a rhinoceros. The trowsers were so much too long that they had to be hauled up on him until they were halted by his armpits, at which stage they did duty as a second, or under-waistcoat as well as trowsers. If he needed to use his hands he had to pull back his coat sleeves until he could discover his fingers. And the buff waistcoat which I had stretched to bursting point hung around his belly like an empty pudding bag. As his religion forbade him to get rid of either his turban or his beard he flapped around the house looking like an Old Testament prophet who had wandered into the wrong century and the wrong tailor.

The results were no happier when it came to re-clothing the daughters-in-law. The combined wardrobes of Maria, her Mama and Mrs Beeton eventually provided enough red flannel underwear, black bombazine overwear, stays, bodices, aprons, mob caps and ribbons to clothe Fyzoo and Ghulabi from head to toe. But neither one of 'em looked half as handsome or one quarter as comfortable in these English reach-me-downs as she had in her tattered and travelworn Indian dress. Those who came best out of this re-clothing business were the babes. Old Mrs Jewkes had kept the little caps and robes J.J. and Maria had worn when they were infants and our coffee-coloured Bunterkins certainly looked prettier in these than they had in their buntings.

Maria spent much time discussing the babes with their Mamas for she had acquired enough Urdu in her Lahore days to be able to chat with them quite freely. Those chats must have touched on me as well as the infants for, about a week after we had come to Great Coram Street, Maria said to me:

'Billy, we have business we must discuss.'

Thereupon she took me by the hand and led me into the back parlour that served J.J. as gun room, tack room, library and counting house all in one. The library part was represented by a few copies of the *Newgate Calendar* and Ruff's *Guide to the Turf* together with *Boxiana*, *Life in London*, and *Doctor Syntax in Search of a Wife*. The counting-house element consisted of a large iron safe and a small desk whose scarred top suggested that J. J. didn't always remember to remove his spurs when at work. Maria seated me down at the desk and took her stand on the other side.

'I must tell you, Billy, that both Fyzoo and Ghulabi describe you as being reluctant to copulate but remarkably quick and efficient at making a woman pregnant once you consent to copulation.'

'Oh, I don't know about that,' I said modestly.

'But they do, and they have the Bunterkins to prove they ain't making it up. Now my late husband was the opposite. Eager to copulate but never once able to make me pregnant. I have to say that, of the two methods, I much prefer yours.'

'You are too kind,' I murmured, wondering what she was leading up to.

'You may have noticed,' Maria continued, 'that J.J. takes it for granted that the two of us are going to get married. It is greatly to his advantage that we should. Under our late father's will and for so long as I am either a spinster or a widow, I own a half-share in this house, the grocery business, a farm in Hertfordshire and various properties in the City of London. But if I re-marry these become the sole property of my brother, and I acquire, by way of a dowry, £2500 in Consols and the rent from the Hertfordshire farm, which amounts to the sum of £118.17s.6d. per annum.'

'Ah,' said I, beginning to understand why J.J. had seemed so keen to get Maria off his hands.

'However,' she said, 'I would never agree to marry another man like D'Arcy Huggins. For my part, I have come to the firm conclusion that a woman's chief interest lies in the nursery, that her chief joy lies on the dinner table, and that the bed, with only the briefest exceptions, has to be treated as a place for sleeping and, if necessary, snoring.'

'Quite so,' said I, fearing what was to come but unable to disagree with much of what had been said so far.

'Ever since we were children, Billy, I've always thought that you and I have similar basic beliefs. And now there's the evidence of Fyzoo, Ghulabi and the Bunterkins to prove that your acts support your beliefs. You are, therefore, one of the very few men who could persuade me to re-marry. But before we pursue that matter, there is something I must show you.'

She removed the largest of the bunch of keys that hung from what, in another woman, would have been her waist, inserted it in the door of the safe and, when she had opened it, took out a large wash-leather bag which she brought over to the desk.

'There,' said she, untying the draw strings and emptying the contents of the bag on to the desk, 'there is the partnership property you entrusted to me that day in Lahore.'

I stared in amazement, for there indeed were the purse of gold coins and the gold and jewelled bracelets, anklets and nose-studs Mahtab Begum had stolen from her husband and from his other wives in order to finance my escape from Calcutta, and there, also, were the great ruby ring and fine string of pearls with which Runjeet Singh had hoped to tempt me into becoming his bum boy. To think of Maria carrying all these through goodness knows what perils and hardships to London, without selling even one item of partnership property to lessen her hardships, was truly heart-warming.

'Dammee,' said I, 'if it ain't all here down to the last rupee.'

'Not one rupee less, not one rupee more,' said Maria proudly. 'That's what partnerships mean. However, if you wish to end our partnership, I'll take my half of the loot together with £117.14s.9½d., which is exactly a half of what I had to spend getting it all back to Great Coram Street, and I've got the bills to prove it. On the other hand, Billy dear, you may wish to perpetuate the partnership, in which case we can put up the banns just as soon as you've signed this Concordat.'

'What Concordat?'

'One embodying our agreement to copulate only for so long as is necessary to make me a Mama once every twelve-month.'

I've never been slow to size up a situation. My position if I refused the partnership would be none too promising. Maria, as she had confirmed, had similar tastes to my own. In all that she had done since we'd parted in Lahore she had given proof of her courage, common sense, composure and good house-keeping. If she was masterful, she was more amiably and less demandingly so than any of the other masterful women who had from time to time made their claims on me.

Faced with all this, what could I do but set about the task of persuading the dear girl to marry me?

7   *47 Bedford Square*

The awesome responsibility I was about to take on in the shape of Maria might have lowered my spirits had I not, in those first weeks in Great Coram Street, rediscovered things I had come close to forgetting during the years of my Indian exile: namely the small, day-to-day pleasures of life in Old England. I don't speak here of important public pleasures such as a Lord Mayor's banquet or a hanging, but of quieter domestic ones such as warming your toes in front of a blazing coal fire or sitting down to an English breakfast.

It was breakfast, indeed, that did most to reconcile me to the prospect of matrimony. Where except in England (and most notably in Great Coram Street) could a man expect to start the day even half as well? Not in Scotland where they break their fast in much the same manner as their horses. Not in France where a ha'penny roll dipped into a bowl of *café au lait* may do very well for one of your Mademoiselles with her tightlacing to think about but would never do to keep an Englishman's ribs apart from dawn to dinner. And not, or so I've been told, in Muscovy where even the stoutest and most heavily bearded of them has to stay his morning belly-rumblings with nothing better than vodka and pickled herrings.

But in Great Coram Street I would come down in the morning to more solid fare, such as half a dozen fresh-fried eggs sitting on as many bacon rashers, this to be followed, perhaps, by a dish of sizzling mutton chops brought in hot-and-hot from the pan. The sideboard would hold cold things to carve at for the filling in of corners and such things as lemon pickles and mushroom ketchup for stinging a jaded palate into life.

All that anyone could want in the way of supplementaries would also be at hand. The muffins would be keeping warm over hot water inside the muffin dish. The hot rolls would be trying to do the same inside a napkin. The toasts in the rack would never be allowed to cool but would be whisked away and replaced by others fresh from the toasting fork. And in a whole cohort of dishes, pots and jugs, butter would keep company with cream, milk with sugar, and potted meats with conserves. Even more importantly the coffee-pot, whilst full-bellied enough to hold all I cared to drink, was also tall enough to support any newspaper I cared to prop against it.

This propping up of newspapers makes the English breakfast an intellectual as much as a carnal pleasure. Bacon and eggs with the latest court news, whether it be from St James's or Bow Street, braised kidneys with crim. con. in Mayfair, politicians blackguarding one another in and out of Westminster whilst you butter and munch your toast – where else in this world can a chap, with his mind recently refreshed by sleep, and in a silence broken only by chumpings and slurpings, absorb so much spiritual and bodily nourishment at one and the same time?

J.J. was not a reading man. He was, however, a most enterprising grocer, cheesemonger and wholesale tea-merchant. As such he advertised his goods in every London newspaper that sold more than 3000 copies, not counting the complimentaries, and because he did, those same complimentaries always arrived at Great Coram Street in good time for breakfast. I hadn't put many of those breakfasts inside me before the morning came when each of the papers reported a recent happening at Windsor which gave me considerable cause for alarm.

The nature of the happening was not in dispute although the reporting of it tended to be coloured by current political allegiance. Thus the *Morning Post*, which had recently turned High Tory, put in a good deal about the laxity of our laws which allowed 'impudent foreigners' to roam about at will and even 'threaten our venerable and beloved monarch's privacy'. *The Globe*, on the other hand, which tended to be as radical as was profitable, had never forgiven the King for his apostasy in '09 when, as Regent, he had dished the Whigs and put Spencer Perceval in it. So it kept referring to 'the superannuated voluptuary who had shut himself up in Windsor to escape the opprobrium of his subjects' and had a good deal that was laudatory to say about 'the sturdy republicanism of our undeferential American cousins who would never accept to live in such a Bourbon-like police state as Britain has become in recent years.'

All this arose from the simple fact that a person had arrived in a hackney carriage at the gate to the Lower Ward in Windsor and demanded that the sentry should take him immediately to the King. His name, he declared, was Griffiths. He was a citizen of the great state of Georgia. He had recently been engaged on secret matters of some importance to both the royal family and the nation. When the sentry pointed out that even the Prime Minister had some difficulty getting audience of the King, let alone a citizen of the great state of Georgia, the Georgian person said that he would, in that case, be prepared to see the Duke of York instead. When he was told that the Duke had been dead a year or more past, the person became violently argumentative, at which stage the sentry turned out the guard.

The outcome of this was that the person was removed to the Windsor Bridewell, where he would stay until he could be brought before the magistrates. The *Morning Post*, however, had an idea that it would not be a matter for the magistrates. The American wretch was either a Jacobin and would-be regicide, in which case it was a matter for the King's Bench and a hanging, or else he was a lunatic, in which case it was a matter for the doctors and the new Bedlam in St George's Fields.

The Globe on the other hand was principally interested in the secret matters of great importance to the royal family the American had referred to. 'It is to be hoped,' wrote the editor, 'that the fact that they are *Windsor* magistrates does not lead to any hushing up of things if, as seems probable, those things reflect adversely on the inhabitant of *Windsor Castle*. There is a deal too much hushing up in Britain today, and a deal too little notice taken of the public's right to know everything about everyone – including the hermit of Windsor.'

It was quite clear from these reports that my old shipmate Gaylord Griffiths was still determined to claim his peerage and Garter even though there was no Bunter to vouch for him. This single-mindedness I found alarming. There was every chance that, whilst the magistrates were examining him, the name of Bunter would be mentioned with the consequence that the authorities, as well as Griffiths, would set about hunting me down, for it is probably a misprision of treason to put it about that you are on a royal errand when you ain't. And even if that wasn't a misprision of anything, Griffiths was single-minded enough to hunt me down on his own.

My peace of mind was restored by the next reports of this matter which attracted no editorial comment and so were much the same in every newspaper irrespective of its politics. And what they all had to say was that no sooner had Griffiths been brought before the magistrates than a member of the public had stood up and asked to be heard. After he had added that he was Second Secretary at the American Legation permission to give evidence was granted.

The person gave his name as Mr Washington Irving. When he was asked by the Chairman of the Bench whether he was the celebrated American author he agreed that he was but insisted that he was appearing in his diplomatic or consular role rather than in his literary one. The prisoner, who stood accused of a breach of the peace but with suggestions of a more serious charge to follow was, the witness said, well known to him as a respectable sea captain. As an American, the prisoner was, of course, a republican, but he entertained what was almost an excessive respect for royalty, that respect being based on his belief that he was himself of royal descent. It was wrong, therefore, to suggest that he wished in any way to disturb the King and ludicrous to hint that he was a Jacobin or a would-be regicide. There were many in America who were neither.

The prisoner had, however, been the victim of a confidence trick. He had come to Windsor expecting to be welcomed by the monarch and thanked for what he had been led to believe had been a service to the Crown. Now that he had found that this was not the case he would gladly undertake to quit Windsor at once and the country within forty-eight hours.

The magistrates, after conferring, required Mr Irving to enter into recognisances to the sum of £500 before releasing the prisoner into his charge, that sum to be forfeit if the prisoner had not left the country within the time specified. The Chairman also required Mr Irving to sign the Chairman's copy of Mr Irving's *Sketch Book*. This having been done Griffiths was discharged.

As rather more than forty-eight hours had elapsed between the hearing of the Griffiths case and reports of that case being read at the breakfast table in Great Coram Street, I could congratulate myself on getting out of another potentially ugly scrape. Maria, who was the only member of the household taking breakfast with me, may have been surprised when I raised my coffee cup and said: 'Thank God, my dear, for Mr Washington Irving, whoever he may be. And I swear to you that when we have sold the loot and I have some money to spare, I shall buy every book he ever wrote.'

'I'm sure you will,' said Maria, 'and you've no need to read even one of 'em.'

The sale of the Indian loot I entrusted, on J.J.'s advice, to a respectable City goldsmith by the name of Pixley. He gave me full value or as near to it as could be expected for the anklets and bracelets and mohurs, and rather more than I had expected for the ruby ring. It was Runjeet Singh's pearl necklace, however, which really brought in the money. This was because the pearls were so large, and there were so many of 'em, that the trinket would have looked vulgar on anyone except a queen or a grand horizontal, they being bred, as it were, for the displaying of such things. Vulgar or not, the pearls looked opulent enough to attract the attention of the two leading money men in the City, namely Alexander Baring, head of the great house of Baring Brothers, and Nathan Rothschild. Each of these gentlemen had a mistress to support and so each bid against t'other until the necklace finally went to the Rothschild for twice what it was worth and three times what I had hoped to get for it. All of which supports the theory that market forces are ineluctably benign and there ain't anything – so long as you are the seller – that will so contribute to your well-being as a bit of enthusiastic competition.

The beauty of it all, however, according to Mr Pixley, was that the two men weren't aware that they were currently sharing the same grand horizontal and so were, properly speaking, engaged in a common enterprise. She received Mr Rothschild Tuesday to Thursday and Mr Baring during the rest of the week, and she kept the one period as distinct from the other as the two gentlemen kept their respective Sabbaths.

All of which shows how little bankers and suchlike know about political economy. If only they had studied Saint-Simon or Fourier or even our own Mr Owen, they would have realised that this was pre-eminently a situation for co-operation rather than competition. But then if they had been socialistically inclined they would not have been bankers, and I must thank God that they were the latter, for what I eventually received from Mr Pixley amounted to no less than £4385.7s.9d. This, when added to what I got from the sale of Maria's Consols, produced a very tidy sum indeed, one so much larger than any I had hitherto handled that it went quite to my head.

If it was my second task to marry Maria, my first one was to set up the home to which I would take her. The only thing that could ever go to my equable Maria's head was the prospect of motherhood. In everything else she was common sense personified. So she was all for prudent expenditures whilst I was all for dash. But as I had the handling of the money it was

I took the decisions, and the first one I took was to buy the lease of 47 Bedford Square.

Bedford Square is part of the comparatively new neighbourhood of Bloomsbury, which is a deal more fashionable than Great Coram Street. Number 47 was, like all the other houses in the square, a largish house built in the gimcrack modern style, made popular by John Nash, which depends so much on Vitruvius and stucco. However, I have nothing against modernism and speculative builders, the neighbourhood was one in which I could cut a dash and the house was large enough for my current requirements. That is to say there was room for the nursery wing Maria wanted to establish and fill. And, without taking very much away from the staff quarters, there was space in the attics for the daughters-in-law and half a dozen Bunterkins if need be.

Nurseries I left to Maria and the daughters-in-law. Everything else I saw to myself, and I doubt whether anyone could have seen to it more lavishly. I had my furniture from Willan & Hart of Regent Street, my bedding and bric-à-brac from Tratt & Atfield of Lower Brook Street, and my soft furnishing from Graham's of Holborn. My pictures I got at Christie's sales where, in my then opulent mood, I behaved like a schoolboy let loose in a pastrycook's. I had to bid high at Tattersall's before I could acquire the nearly-new chariot and spanking pair of bays sent there by Tommy Onslow himself. I bought prints from Ackermann, had Berry Brothers stock my cellar and Hatchard furnish my library with several yards of leather-bound classics.

I engaged a coachman, boot boy, two housemaids and a Mrs Rump who came to me with the reputation of being the best of plain cooks. I furnished one half of the kitchen with all that she could want: the other half I gave over to the daughters-in-law with permission to do what they could in the way of charcoal braziers, clay ovens, hand mills and so on in order to equip it as a kitchen in their native village would have been equipped. And, having attended to my own wardrobe, I had the same tailor make a livery for Gurmakh Singh which, with its black, silver-buttoned, cutaway coat, white stock and buff waistcoat, managed to suggest the English butler whilst still, with its scarlet turban, kummerbund and pajama trowsers, remembering the *khansamah*.

These things done, I married Maria and was, for a while, as content as any husband can be who still remembers what it was like to be a bachelor.

We most of us, I believe, enjoyed life at 47 Bedford Square. I can always enjoy being a gentleman of means and leisure and it wasn't very long before I had even more leisure to enjoy. For after a matter of weeks Maria was able to tell me that the first occupant of the new nursery was on its way and that I could, as a consequence, sleep tranquil of nights. Maria, in her own calm, undemonstrative way, enjoyed approaching motherhood. Mrs Rump enjoyed my enjoyment of her plain cooking to which had to be added her own enjoyment, in a plain and missionary sort of way, of Gurmakh Singh. And Gurmakh Singh thoroughly enjoyed his new and very full experience of social life in London.

That experience began in the taproom of the Running Footman, which was the public house closest to Bedford Square. Its proprietor, an old soldier, had first gone out to India with the 52nd of Foot. He had then transferred, as a drill sergeant, to the 17th Bengal Native Infantry, in which regiment Gurmakh Singh had served his time as a humble sepoy. They did not at first recognise each other. More than twenty years had passed since the one-time Sergeant Pike had bellowed and, along with his fellow sepoys, the one-time Sepoy Gurmakh Singh had stamped and quivered, had turned and about-turned, had shouldered his musket, grounded his musket, fixed and unfixed his bayonet all to the sound of that bellow. But there is something about an old soldier an old soldier will always, in the end, recognise. So, after an exploratory booze-up or two, they decided that they were indeed old comrades, whereafter they spent many an evening drinking rum and telling each other lies about their army days.

There was a deal more drinking of rum and telling of lies once his former drill sergeant had introduced Gurmakh Singh to other old India hands. Whether these were native-born in the shape of Britons who had soldiered in India or immigrants in the shape of Indian retainers who had followed their sahibs back to Bilatee, they quickly admitted Gurmakh Singh to their various circles for they could seldom have met a more engaging old rogue. As each circle was centred on some public house there were many London taprooms and snugs that, once the drinks started to circulate, began to look and sound like a barrackroom in any Indian cantonment or a durbar in any Indian village.

Such a full social life, however, needed a good deal of financing and so Gurmakh Singh was forever coming to me for money. If I showed any sign of reluctance he would talk of Sumroo and remind me of how much I owed him in the way of cash and gratitude. As this could not be denied, I grumbled and paid and thought myself lucky that the daughters-in-law were not also clamouring for money on account of their having invested all their jewellery in my escape from India.

For by then I had got to a situation where the proceeds from the Indian loot and Maria's Consols had mostly been spent, and unopened bills lay in heaps on top of the fine escritoire I had had from Willan & Hart, whose unpaid accounts formed one of the larger heaps. In short, we were surviving on a rapidly dwindling amount of cash and a great deal of credit. Since credit is a commodity that won't last for ever, and as I hadn't yet thought of a wheeze to restore a flow of cash, even I was starting to worry.

Which was why, if the daughters-in-law had required me to replace the jewellery I owed them, I would have had to add yet one more to the disappointments they were suffering from as the least satisfied inhabitants of 47 Bedford Square. They were not, of course, typical Bloomsburyites but two sturdy and straightforward young women brought up to the unremitting but companionable toil of life in a Punjaubi village. But now they could find neither toil nor companionship.

There was no jungle in Bloomsbury for communal fuel-gathering excursions, no river shallows to squat over and launder in, no well to socialise by and no bazaar to provide such agreeable opportunities for haggle and gossip. They had, instead, only the Bunterkins to look after, and as they were close to weaning, looking after them could not be made to fill the whole of a day. Worst of all was the fact that they had only themselves to cook for, Gurmakh Singh having succumbed to Mrs Rump's plain cooking. That perhaps was why, in cooking increasingly elaborate meals for each other, they found an outlet for their frustrations. As they knew nothing of English methods and materials they were fortunate that Gurmakh Singh had, through his contacts with the old India hands, found where in London he could buy the different rices, spices, ghees, pulses, pickles and dried vegetables and fruits needed for the increasingly elaborate dishes they experimented with as cures for their discontent.

Because they spoke no English, not even that of the Gurmakh Singh variety, they were timid about venturing abroad. As they were seldom abroad they seldom met men. And as they seldom met men they had little or no opportunity to get themselves into a similar condition to Maria's, although they increasingly envied her. They could not even do as well for themselves as Mrs Rump who did not bother to conceal a smirk of satisfaction every time her eye fell on Gurmakh Singh.

In short, the daughters-in-law had come close to feeling that they were living in vain, and they soon started grumbling about this to Gurmakh Singh. He, feeling that these were women's troubles, eventually carried their complaints to Maria. And she, in her own calm but commanding way, read me a bedroom lecture on the subject.

'For,' said she, 'I cannot believe that Ghulabi and Fyzoo are any different from myself in this respect. Nor can I think that your obligation to them is so much less than your obligation to me. It is entirely because you brought them here to Bedford Square, where it is most unlikely they will meet anyone more suitable, that you are duty bound to behave to them just as you have behaved to me.'

If I was duty bound to anything, it was to listen, for I had not yet been allowed to snuff the candle, pull my nightcap over my ears and settle to sleep.

'What behaviour do you refer to, my dear?' asked I.

'Why,' said she, 'the behaviour that put this bun in my oven of course.'

And that was why, when J.J. asked me one night over the dinner table, what life was now like at 47 Bedford Square, I replied rather snappishly that it was much like life at a Newmarket stud with Bunter playing the part, *nolens volens*, of the Godolphin Arab.

But it was a mistake to let my extra-marital problems divert me into a discussion of studs and stallions, for what I really wanted to talk about was the grocery trade. Luckily, J.J. hadn't taken much notice of my complaints. He was too busy considering the port which he was rolling around his tongue in a way which impeded conversation. It needed a deal of rolling, for I had given him a thick, heavy, dark sort of port, the kind I knew he liked best.

'Not half bad,' he said eventually. 'It's a sound, gob-stopping sort of wine. What did it cost you a dozen?'

'I'm glad it pleases you,' said I, and indeed I was. Every item of the unusually long and elaborate dinner we had just eaten had been chosen with the sole purpose of pleasing him, since I hoped I was dining, not just a brother-in-law, but a future partner.

8   *Fit for Nobs and Nabobs*

Now that I had more than exhausted both my capital and my credit, and could begin to smell bum bailiffs and the Marshalsea Prison just around the corner, I had been forced to accept that, for the time being at least, I couldn't continue to live as a gentleman of leisure. Money would have to start flowing into 47 Bedford Square besides flowing out of it, and the only way I could think of ensuring this was by persuading J.J. to make me a partner in his prosperous grocering business.

Persuading people ain't always easy and it generally pays the persuader to do a bit of self-persuading first since it will certainly add to the sincerity of his approach. It was fortunate that, being a logical sort of chap, I had no difficulty persuading myself that J.J. did indeed owe me a partnership as it was obvious that, if I hadn't taken Maria off his hands, he would still have been paying her half the profits of his grocering without getting even a day's work out of her in return. I on the other hand was fully prepared to do a certain amount of advisory or supervisory work for something rather less than fifty per cent.

School friendships, they say, are the purest and least venal of friendships, but what I remembered of J.J. when we were both at Christ's Hospital was that, if ever I wanted to persuade him into anything, I only succeeded if I offered him unrestricted access to the best of my grub. But what would J.J. accept now as the best of my grub? He was unlikely these days to be influenced by pork pies and jam tarts. Nor would Mrs Rump's plain English cooking, excellent though it was, settle the matter. A man who ate his way through so many aldermanic banquets, City swarrys and Hunt Suppers when he fed abroad, and who had Mrs Beeton to cook for him when he dined at home, would need a dinner that was extraordinarily different as well as extraordinarily good before he would be persuaded.

I always take food seriously, which was why it took me some time to settle the strategy for J.J.'s dinner. But once it had been settled, I went into action with all the vision, vigour and tactical flexibility of Napoleon in his prime. I told Mrs Rump to take a week's holiday which she could spend with her aged parents in Edmonton, I paying for her transport. As soon as she had departed in a fly and a flurry of gratitude I sent Maria round to 19 Great Coram Street with an invitation to her brother to take dinner with us at Bedford Square at three in the afternoon on the Friday three days away.

Next I had Gurmakh Singh and the daughters-in-law on parade in the kitchen which would, I told them, be in their sole charge until Mrs Rump had returned. There over the next three days they would plan and prepare a dinner for a special occasion, one that would be dedicated to the persuading of Jewkes Sahib. Since it was such a special occasion something extra special in the way of Indian dinners would be needed. What I had in mind was one that would, in so far as it was possible within the confines of a single meal, introduce Jewkes Sahib to all that was best in the many different culinary traditions of the Indian sub-continent.

'In Delhi in the kitchens of the Grand Moghul,' I told them, walking up and down as Napoleon might have done whilst giving his Marshals their orders for the coming campaign, 'you will find cooks at work who have been recruited from every corner of Hind. So different are their culinary traditions, so diverse their skills that they have never yet failed to serve a meal that surprises the Grand Moghul as much as it delights him. It will be your task to do to Jewkes Sahib what they do to the Grand Moghul. Never forget that it is as important to your well-being as it is to mine that he should finish his dinner so finely poised between surprise and delight as to be incapable of saying "No".'

'Bedford Square,' said Fyzoo, who was ever the more argumentative of the two, 'is not Delhi and Jewkes Sahib is not the Grand Moghul. But even if he were, what you ask of us is impossible.'

'Why impossible?' said I, ceasing to be Napoleon, ceasing to walk up and down, and reverting to Bunter. 'All I ask of you is that you exercise your skills as cooks.'

'And what skills, Bunterjee, are those? The skills of simple village women who know only what their mothers taught them and nothing of how they cook in Delhi or Jodhpur or Seringapatam? We know what we are capable of. Good plain Punjaubi cooking, yes! . . . Fussy, fanciful, foreign dishes, no!'

'Yet Gurmakh Singh has told me that in your idle hours, when you have neither Bunter nor the Bunterkins to occupy you, you spend your time cooking each other dishes of a richness and complexity seldom seen in the villages of the Punjaub.'

'Would you,' asked Ghulabi, ever the sharper-tongued of the two, 'have us die of boredom because you brought us here to Bilatee and Bedford Square? We still have minds and hands that need exercise. What then if we have exercised them on town cooking and have experimented with such dishes as you might find in the houses of the great ones in Umritsar or Lahore? Those towns are still Punjaubi towns and those dishes Punjaubi dishes such as our mothers sometimes talked about. How they cook in other parts of Hindoostan was something they never discussed with us.'

Gurmakh Singh, who had been listening in a calm and dignified silence, now intervened. 'It is,' said he, 'acknowledged in this Bloomsbury quarter, as in certain other quarters of this city, that Bunter Sahib's butlah-wallah is a person of considerably more distinction than other butlah-wallahs. That is why, at the Running Footman and other public meeting places, men seek him out and invite his friendship. Amongst those who have done this are several Indians, not all of whom are Sikhs and not all of whom know nothing of cooking. It could be that from among these I can find men able to tell the daughters-in-law how they cook in the palaces of Delhi and Seringapatam and in the houses of the rich merchants of Goa.'

When Gurmakh Singh asked me the next morning to consult with the daughters-in-law I found the kitchen crowded. It held, in addition to the Singhs, the dozen or so members of an assembly that was too sophisticated and cosmopolitan to be thought of as a mere village *panchayat* but was neither large enough nor grand enough to be described as an All-India durbar. Nevertheless it was an impressive collection of Gurmakh Singh's friends that had gathered around the kitchen table and a bowl of rack punch to debate the problems of an all-India dinner.

There was a fat white-bearded Madrassi with dozens of receipts for the curries of his region, some of them hot enough to melt a man's teeth, others as deceptively mild as a maiden's kiss. A solemn, dark-skinned Tamil kept moving from kitchen to scullery trying to work out where to construct a clay oven for the cooking of tandooris. A coal-black Portuguese gentleman from Goa kept babbling about vindaloos and a Gujerati Jain kept finding more and more complicated ways of cooking the simplest vegetables. An austere Kashmiri, who looked as if he lived on nothing more substantial than locusts and wild honey, knew so many different puddings, desserts and sweetmeats, each of them rich enough to induce a jaundice, that it took half an hour for the assembly to decide which half-dozen of them would do least harm. Finally, there was a very stately not to say self-important one-time *bawarchee* from Delhi who actually had, in his days as a cook, worked for the Grand Moghul before taking service with the Angrezi who were so much less difficult to please and far, far easier to cheat. After a lecture in general terms on Moghul and Persian styles of cookery – the two are much the same – he produced detailed receipts for a good many different pullaos and methods of dealing with game including instructions for cooking quails with almonds and raisins which had been a great favourite of the Grand Moghul's.

When each man there had made his contribution to the theory of an all-India dinner and we had, on a show of hands, decided on the actual menu, I made what I thought was a neat little speech thanking them for their help. I expected no more of them, but the friends of Bunter Sahib's butler-wallah clearly thought there was more they could do. The following morning they scattered to scour London for the scores of exotic ingredients the dishes they had agreed on demanded. And the morning after that, which was the fateful Friday, every man jack of them was back in the kitchen at 47 Bedford Square. There wasn't one of them who was prepared to trust the actual cooking of what he had contributed to the menu to anyone other than himself. The consequence was that there were a dozen or more cooks at work and the daughters-in-law weren't left to cook even a Punjaubi dish but were reduced to running around as mere scullions.

With so many different dishes and so many different cooks to cook them it was nearer four o'clock than three before Maria, J.J. and I could sit down to dinner. By five o'clock I was almost sure that the dinner was going to be a success. J.J. by then had sampled every one of the curries that had been set out at his end of the table and was steaming slightly as a consequence. After he loosened his neckcloth and mopped his face on his napkin he turned his attention to the dishes that made up the rest of that setting. By half after six, when he dealt with the removes, he had undone his waistcoat and the top two buttons of his trowsers. But there was still a healthy glow to him as he gobbled his way through the puddings and dessert in a style that commanded my admiration. I couldn't have done better myself if I had been free to make a meal of it. But I had to keep a cool head and so had eaten only one dish to his three and drunk one bottle to his every two.

When, in the end, we had finished eating; when Maria had left us and Gurmakh Singh, having put out the decanters, had also departed; when we had both used the silver pot I had bought from Pixley in the first flush of my affluence; when we had smoked our cheroots and finished whatever we had to say about studs, stallions, and gob-stopping port; when I had finally decided what my opening gambit should be and J.J. was beaming repletion and benevolence at me – why then, if ever, was the time to persuade him into a partnership.

It may have been that I expected too much of the dinner or that the dinner had been too much for J.J. and he was feeling the first stirrings of dyspepsia. But whatever his reasons for turning me down he did the actual turning down quite amiably.

'I didn't,' said he, 'get rid of Maria as a sleeping partner in order to take you on, Bunter-me-boy, as an active one. Don't want a partner of any sort. Nothing personal about it, so I hope you ain't offended.'

'Not at all offended,' I mumbled, wondering where I'd gone

wrong and feeling a sudden giddiness as though the dining-room floor was sliding away from me.

'That's a good thing then. Never have liked turning a chap down, especially an old school chum and present brother-in-law. But whatever gave you the idea in the first place? You're no more cut out for grocering than you are for stag-hunting.'

'It wasn't the grocering,' I said, 'but the money that would come out of it.'

'That's just what I thought. Your trouble is you're strapped.'

'Strapped?'

'On the rocks . . . up the spout . . . in Queer Street.'

'What makes you think that?'

'Got a nose for such things. Always known when to give credit and when to refuse it. Wouldn't have been in business long if I didn't know that much. Besides which, never forget that I know to within a shilling what you had in the way of income and capital when you first set up here and I can guess to within a fiver or two what you spent and are still spending on all o' this . . .' He swept his arm around in a gesture that took in the whole of 47 Bedford Square and its contents down to the silver pot under the sideboard and, for all I knew, the inordinate amount of expensive food and drink he had just put inside himself.

Suggesting to your brother-in-law that he owes you a partnership don't, to my mind, give him a licence to intrude into your private affairs. That, none the less, was what J. J. was doing and I resented it. But I was experiencing more than disappointment over the partnership and resentment at the intrusion. I have always believed that it is best to ignore the more unpleasant facts of life, having found that, if one does, they will generally either go away or cure themselves. Yet here was J.J. exposing with quite brutal glee all the facts of my condition I most wished to ignore. I found this frightening. I tried, nevertheless, to maintain a dignified independence and embarked on a speech that would, I hoped, put things in perspective.

'There may,' said I, 'be some trifling and purely temporary

imbalance between my income and my expenditures at this
particular moment, but . . .'

I got no further.

'Temporary!' said J.J. 'Temporary my arse!' He had picked
up a good many vulgar habits of speech from his low friends in
the shooting and hunting fields. 'There ain't ever anything
temporary about Queer Street. Them as gets into it dies in it.'

This was the most frightening thought of all, but I was still
determined to preserve my dignity. So I said, in the coldest of
tones, that I was sure I was not even close to Queer Street.

'Thereabouts, if not already there according to my calculations.'

'What calculations?'

He looked at me as though I were a village idiot, and then
chanted, rather than said: 'Original capital five and a half thou.
Outlay on lease, fittings and etceteras – including silver
chamber pot – seven thou. at the least. Income £118.17s.6d.,
paid at Michaelmas if the farmer hasn't had a bad harvest.
Annual expenditure, £1500 if it's a penny. Consequence,
me-boy . . . Queer Street.'

Listening to him I began to wonder for the first time in my life
whether Bunter really was equipped to be a survivor. What use
was it to have outwitted the Begum of Sumroo and the
Kurachee Chief of Police and Captain Griffiths if I was to end
up in Queer Street, that bourne from which, according to J.J.,
no spendthrift ever returned? I frightened myself so much with
these new-found doubts that I started to blub.

Anyone with even half an ounce of sense could see that I
wasn't, this time, blubbing for effect. Mine were the sincerest
sort of tears and in between the sobs I howled: 'I ain't in Queer
Street! I ain't! I ain't! I ain't!' The sincerity did it. J.J. started
to behave more like a friend and a brother-in-law and less like
an Examiner in Bankruptcy. He gave me his own pocket
handkerchief, poured me out a glass of brandy and made me
drink it, and then said that he hadn't meant to pitch into me
quite so hard and I musn't feel too cut up because it was his
opinion that he might still be able to think of a way of keeping

me out of Queer Street. There were, he added, more ways than one of skinning a cat.

This all sounded slightly more hopeful, so I dried my eyes, tossed off the brandy and asked him what his last remark signified.

'It signifies,' said he, 'that you don't necessarily have to turn grocer in order stay out of Queer Street.'

'Then what should I turn?' said I, and got no answer.

As between J.J. and myself it has always been easy to see which is the quicker witted. Ideas that flash into my mind seem to crawl into his. But that don't mean his ideas ain't worth waiting for, which is why, when he failed to answer my question, I settled down to wait. I could see, from the way his gaze had become fixed on some distant horizon, that he was either going to be sick or his ideas had started to crawl. So I wasn't surprised that, when he eventually spoke, what he said had something oracular about it. That is to say it was nothing to the point but contained suggestions of ultimate relevancy.

'That,' he said, 'was a damned good dinner you gave me. No! It was more than that. It was damned unusual as well. I'd call it a dinner well worth eating. A man could spend a week's income in one of those Frenchified eating-houses they call restorongs which have become so fashionable these days and not eat half so well.'

He said no more for a while but stared into the distance. A man could no more have guessed what was gestating in his mind than proud Tarquin could have guessed what was contained in the books the Cumaean Sibyl destroyed.

'If that dinner was anything to go by,' he said eventually, 'your heathen Hindoos can turn out a better dinner than your Monsewer Carême himself. And yet, as you know, you have to have a French cook these days if you are to be in fashion, and it ain't a proper dinner if it doesn't have its pottages and its consumays, its rotees and its rag outs, its à la thises and à la thats.'

There followed another silence whilst whatever ideas had crawled into his mind began to settle down there.

'Getting very popular, these days, India is. More and more Englishmen going out there and, which is more important, quite a few of them survive to come back, and each of 'em that does brings a powerful taste for Indian food back with him. It could soon be worth my while to cater for them by setting up an Indian grocery department.'

This was a deal more to the point.

'I suppose,' said I, 'that because of my Indian experience you want me to take charge of that department.'

'You suppose wrong. It won't be a large enough department to support a Bunter. Besides, what I'm thinking about at this moment isn't Indian groceries but Indian dinners. Have you realised that unless these returning Nabobs have brought their Indian cooks back with them they have little or no chance of enjoying an Indian meal?'

'I haven't thought about it.'

'Then you should. It's one way you could restore your fortunes without turning to grocering.'

'I don't quite follow you.'

'Open an Indian restorong, man. Give 'em meals such as you've just given me and you'll soon make it the most fashionable eating-house in town.'

Although it had taken some time to arrive, it certainly wasn't the worst of J.J.'s ideas. None the less I could already see faults in it he hadn't as yet got round to.

'There ain't enough Nabobs in London to keep such a place going.'

'Then you will have to attract the Nobs who have never been to India as well as the Nabobs who have.'

'And how can I do that?'

'People who come up from the country don't stay at inns any longer. They stay at places called hotels, which are much the same thing Frenchified. You must open an Indian hotel alongside your Indian restorong. Most people like to dine where they sleep, so you'll soon train a whole new generation of country landowners and squires to go for Indian rather than for French grub.'

My mind was already racing around and adding to the idea J.J. had arrived at so ponderously.

'It would only work,' said I, 'if it was done in absolutely tip-top style. It would have to be a better hotel and a better restaurant than any other in London. It would need to be somewhere near St James's for the clubmen and to Westminster for the politicians, yet not so far from Bond Street and Piccadilly as to be inconvenient for the shops. We would, of course, call it Bunter's Indian Serai . . .'

'Serai?'

'Indian for hotel.'

'I like the sound of it,' said J.J.

'There is, however, one major difficulty,' said I.

'What's that?'

'It will cost thousands and thousands to set up.'

J.J. buttoned up his waistcoat, tried to do the same to his trowsers and failed, whistled to himself for a moment or two and then said: 'Just because I wouldn't take you on as a working partner don't mean you shouldn't take me on as a sleeping one. You work out what it will cost, find one half of it in one way or another, and I'll be good for the other half.'

'And how do you think I'll find my half? I couldn't find half the cost of a sentry box at this moment, let alone half the cost of a hotel.'

'You'll have to talk someone out of it. That's something you've always managed, one way or another. And now I'm sure Maria's waiting for us in the drawing room with the tea tray, and as I supply her with her tea, I know it will be my best Bohea from Fukien.'

He stood up, obviously determined not to let me ask him to stump up both halves of the investment he'd suggested. I was equally determined to persuade him otherwise. But then the door opened, Gurmakh Singh came in and said:

'There is a Captain Sahib wishing to see you.'

If it hadn't been for all I'd eaten and drunk I'm sure I would have turned pale.

'You don't mean Captain Griffiths?'

'Not Captain Griffiths, Sahib. He is speaking Angrezi and not Americano, and is telling me that he is being old friend of yours and his name is Captain Manning.'

It ain't my practice to remember and cherish every attachment I've ever formed. To do so could become burdensome. If I have a rule in the matter, it is that those friendships that have been, and still could be, useful have to be kept in good repair. As for the others – there can be no harm in forgetting 'em. But I couldn't for the life of me remember whether Captain Manning was one of those I ought to have forgotten or not.

He had been master of the *Thomas Grenville*, the East Indiaman in which Bishop Heber and I had first gone out to India. Manning and I had been good enough friends then but I couldn't imagine how he could be of any use to me now. Indeed it was possible that he could be the opposite and had tracked me down to Bedford Square out of enmity rather than amity. For in Calcutta in '27, I may well, as they say, have dropped him in the shit.

That was when, having left Bishop Heber's service and gone into the commodity business, I consigned a cargo of indigo for China to the *Thomas Grenville*. I did so, however, without telling Captain Manning that there was enough of the best Patna opium concealed in some of the indigo barrels to make me half a dozen fortunes once Mr Jardine, my Canton agent, had disposed of it to the various mandarins and taipans who were his clients.

That the opium never reached Canton was entirely due to the fact that someone in Calcutta laid an information against me, as a consequence of which the ship was boarded by Customs officers who broke open every one of some twelve hundred barrels of indigo, so depriving me of several fortunes and a good many Chinese of one of their more innocent pleasures.

I had got wind of what was about to happen, and so had left Calcutta the day before. This meant that I never found out what Captain Manning thought of it all, for I hadn't seen him since. I was pretty sure he'd been able to establish his own innocence for he was a man of the most transparent honesty. But since John Company treated any attempt to breach their monopoly of the opium trade as a crime infinitely more serious than embezzlement and only slightly less dangerous than mutiny, no doubt he had a deal of explaining to do first, not one bit of which would he have thanked me for.

That was why, as Gurmakh Singh showed him in, I couldn't decide whether to be warm, cold, or devilish cautious with him. Manning, however, had no such doubts. As he advanced towards me with outstretched arms, he had on his face one of the widest, happiest, and altogether most agreeable smiles I have ever seen. That face, by-the-by, was quite unsuitable for an old sea-dog, being round, soft and rosy-cheeked and quite unmarked by all the hurricanes, calms, blizzards, scurvies and shipwrecks it must have seen in more than forty years' seagoing. Indeed the whole man was so small, round, and stuffed with benevolence that it could have been a stick-at-home country parson advancing on me and not the most experienced sea captain on the India run.

He embraced as much of me as his short arms could encompass, said, 'My dear, dear Mr Bunter, how delightful it is to have found you at last,' and then proceeded to waltz me round and round the room until the two of us were quite out of breath. It was only then that I was able to sit him down, pour him a glass of port, and say:

'And how, Captain Manning, *did* you find me?'

'It was,' said he, 'a deal easier than I had expected. The *Thomas Grenville* has never yet dropped anchor in the Pool of London without a certain bumboat woman rowing out . . .'

'Buttercup!' said I.

'The same,' said he. 'It was she who told me how she'd had her man pilot you to some moorings in Great Coram Street. I straightway laid a course to the same moorings where I found a boy . . .'

'Benjamin!' said J.J.

'The same,' said he. 'I don't believe, Mr Bunter, that I've had the honour of being introduced to your friend.'

'I beg your pardon. My brother-in-law Mr John Jewkes.'

'Delighted, my dear Sir, to make your acquaintance,' said Manning, getting up, shaking J.J.'s hand, sitting down again and tossing off the glass of port in what seemed little more than a single movement. 'Brother-in-law, heh? Mr Bunter, I do believe you've been and got yourself married. No, no, not a word. Excellent thing to do. I approve of matrimony, Sir, even though there is not and never has been a Mrs Manning. Of all the good things in life, Mr Bunter, a well-found wife must rank only slightly below a well-found ship. I look forward with impatience to making Mrs Bunter's acquaintance.'

At that stage he made to get up in order, I suppose, to satisfy his impatience. By that time, however, he was not the only one feeling impatient. I pushed him back in his chair and said:

'But the boy, Captain Manning. The boy Benjamin . . .'

'The boy? Ah yes, the boy to be sure. Well, Sir, once he'd told me where your present berth was I reckoned that it wasn't so far away that I couldn't get there by dead reckoning. And so here I am, my dear Mr Bunter, berthed alongside as you might say and perfectly ready to open hatches and start unloading cargo.'

'Cargo, Captain Manning? What cargo can you have for me?'

'Your indigo, of course – or rather what that Mr Jardine of yours in Canton turned it into. A shrewd man, your Mr Jardine, and one who will go far so long as the whisky don't cut him off short. It's an awesome thing, Mr Bunter, to watch a Scotsman's passion for his bottle quarrel with his passion for the bawbees. Not that I've anything against the Scots, mind you, apart from their eagerness to take everything over.' Here he turned to J.J. in a companionable attempt to include him in the conversation and said: 'Have you noticed, Sir, how they are presently running the government, the Services, the banks, John Company, India, the colonies and far too large a part of our merchant fleet?'

J.J., normally a garrulous man, merely goggled at him. It was obvious that he had never before met anyone so discursively garrulous as this rosy-cheeked stranger who was about to become, if I'd understood him aright, my oldest, dearest, and certainly most valuable friend.

'Captain Manning,' said I, 'a glass of port with you. And tell me some more about the indigo. Didn't the Customs men confiscate it when they discovered the opium?'

'Well now, that opium . . . There could have been difficulties if it had been consigned by anyone but yourself. But knowing you as I do, Mr Bunter, I also knew that you could have known nothing whatsoever of this cunning plot to hide opium in the cargo, and I told the Customs men as much.'

'And they took your word for it?'

He sat up in his chair and looked as dignified as any round-faced, rosy-cheeked, roly-poly little man can.

'I have,' said he, 'spent forty years sailing backwards and forwards in John Company's service. In that time I have brought out, as pale-faced boys not long left school, most of those who now sit on the Council in Calcutta. What's more, I've carried back, as gouty, sallow-faced Nabobs, a good many of those who now sit in the Court of Directors in London. They know me well and I know them even better, as a consequence of which I'm *persona grata* with the powers that be no matter which end of the voyage you're looking at. So it would be a brave Customs officer in Calcutta, Mr Bunter, who took it on himself to doubt Captain Manning's word.'

'So what did they do?'

'They confiscated the opium of course, but they reloaded the indigo on to the *Thomas Grenville*, every barrel of which I handed over to your Mr Jardine when I got to Canton. And less than twelve months later, when I sailed once more to Canton, he had sold every scrap of indigo. I don't know what he deducted by way of commission, but he brought on board for delivery to you, Sir, forty-eight chests each holding one thousand tael.'

'And what,' said I, swallowing hard, 'is a tael worth in real money?'

'A tael, Mr Bunter, is a silver coin or token weighing exactly one ounce. So you can see you will need more than a handcart when you come to collect your cargo.'

'I shall be at the docks with my coach tomorrow,' I said, 'and two stout men to do the carrying, for if I've worked it out right there will be better than a ton of silver to lift. I don't suppose, Captain Manning, you know what silver's worth an ounce at the moment?'

'Something over five shillings,' said J.J., who had taken a keen interest in our conversation and was now looking worried.

I made another calculation, barely refrained from whistling at the answer I came up with, and, fighting for calm, said: 'My dear Captain Manning, I am vastly obliged to you for the way in which you have looked after my interests. I will admit to you that I never expected to get such a fair price for my indigo.'

'Never expected to get anything at all,' muttered J.J. who had made the same calculation and was, as a consequence, looking even more worried. I ignored him.

'Captain Manning,' said I, 'my dear wife Maria is waiting for us. You will, I hope, take tea with us.'

'It's the best Bohea,' said J.J., 'and as you're just back from Canton you'll know what that means.'

'Indeed I do, Sir. There are eight hundred chests of various teas in the holds of the *Thomas Grenville* at this very moment, and I have no doubt that, by the time the merchants have had their way with them, they will all end up as the best Bohea.'

That, for the moment, silenced J.J. who hung back as Manning eagerly made for the door. Before I could follow him out J.J. grasped me by the elbow and said:

'You won't, of course, hold me to my undertaking to match you pound for pound and tael for tael in this matter of an Indian hotel.'

It's amazing how quickly a chap's confidence can come flooding back. I gave J.J. a friendly enough smile, patted his shoulder and said: 'Don't fret, my dear fellow. I dare say I'll be able to cut you in for a small share in Bunter's Indian Serai.'

PART THREE

APPOINTMENTS AND DISAPPOINTMENTS

9 *83 Jermyn Street*

For what I had in mind, Jermyn Street seemed right both in its geography and its character. It lay between the Palaces of St James's and Westminster, was as convenient for the Horse Guards and the Foreign Office as it was for Covent Garden and Drury Lane, and was no more than a five-minute stroll from the Park. These topographical advantages are reflected in its character, for it is a street wholly given over to the unostentatious gratification of the rich.

Number 83 had shown how sedately and genteelly this gratifying could be done. It had, up to her death the previous year, housed Mother Comfort's discreet establishment. There her young ladies had, in their various ways, seen to the needs of politicians proceeding northwards from Westminster, clubmen popping around the corner from St James's, and City magnates dropping off on their way home to Bayswater. But the Great Reaper had, with one swing of his scythe, put an end to Mother Comfort's services to mankind and dispersed her young ladies.

Since then the building, which was too large for private use, had stayed empty and was starting to dilapidate, so the lease, which belonged to the Bishops of London, was to be had cheap once the Chancellor of the Diocese had been satisfied that Bunter, like Mother Comfort, was a respectable member of the Church and vouched for by bankers.

I entrusted the rebuilding and refurbishing to Mr Tom Cubitt, a speculative and jobbing builder who was beginning to make something of a name for himself, especially when it came to Eastern architecture, for he had done much of the work on the Regent's pavilion at Brighton. He was quick, therefore, to see what I had in mind, which was to bring the flavour of

Indian architecture as much as the flavour of Indian cooking to the citizens of London.

The building, which was a large, plain, four-square brick affair, had a mansard roof. This, fortunately for us, was low and well set back, which made it possible for Cubitt to cover it with what was, in effect, a wooden lid. Most of that lid was built in the shape of a great dome but there was also, sprouting from each of its four corners, something that can best be described as a mini-minaret. When the whole of this lid had been covered in stucco and painted a dazzling white; when the low parapet had been replaced by one with Moorish machicolations; when the plain lead gutter-heads had all been cloaked with plasterwork elephants waving their trunks to the skies – then even the workmen who had never seen any other than London roofs admitted that the skyline had an Indian look to it.

It was more difficult to Indianise the frontages. These, which faced Duke Street as well as Jermyn Street, Number 83 being built on a corner, were also covered with stucco which was then painted to resemble marble at street level and given broad horizontal bands of red and yellow higher up. And by the time the entrance had been given a Moorish arch and the ground-floor windows had been given elaborately fretted wooden jalousies such as are used in India to screen the zenana, even the façades looked un-English and spoke more of the Great Maidan in Calcutta than they did of Jermyn Street.

The interior had, of course, to be rearranged as well as Indianised. A large Indian kitchen was installed in the basement. The ground floor, which had once contained a series of salons in which Mother Comfort and her young ladies had received their guests and conducted their preliminary business and preliminary entertaining, was gutted to provide space for a large hotel lobby and an even larger restaurant. The restaurant had a marble fountain in the middle and a sort of cloister of Moorish arches resting on barley-sugar pillars occupying most of the rest of the room. Wooden screens of the same sort of latticework as the jalousies divided this cloister into a series of alcoves or booths each of which was furnished on three sides with a divan little more than a foot off the ground. It was proposed that our Indianising clients should either recline or sit cross-legged on these, so placing themselves not very many inches above the large brass tray on which their meal would be served. On Tom Cubitt's advice, however, half a dozen of these booths were provided with quite ordinary tables and chairs, these being for those of our future clients who found either lolling or crouching over their food played the Devil with their digestions.

A hotel lobby ain't the easiest of places to Indianise. However we did our best with another, though similar fountain, Indian rugs on the floor, paintings from Mr Zoffany's Indian period on the wall, two parrots (which actually came from the Brazils) in a cage over the head porter's desk, and a liberal scattering of Benares brassware.

When it came to the two upper floors we were obliged to compromise a little. The thirty-odd workrooms once used by Mother Comfort's young ladies may have provided a cosy enough setting for those who would occupy them for an hour or two or, at their most enthusiastic, for the whole of a night. But they were too claustrophobic for even a single person needing longer-term accommodation. So we knocked every two of 'em into one and ended up with around a baker's dozen of reasonably sized and quite civilised bedrooms.

It was in the Indianising of these that we had to make our compromises on account of the difference in climates. No matter how much other Indian furniture and bric-à-brac we might use we still had to have four-posters instead of charpoys, fireplaces instead of punkahs, and good thick curtains instead of tatties of fragrant kuskus grass.

It was with my all-India staffing rather than with my architecture and interior decorating that I came closest to bringing India to Jermyn Street. The Singhs, of course, had to be given at least nominal positions of power, I owed them as much. So the daughters-in-law who were, by-the-by, already demonstrating that the demands they had made on me had not been made in vain, were placed in overall charge of the kitchens. Gurmakh Singh was given a roving commission, which put him in charge of everything else. He was made titular major-domo, maître d'hôtel, head porter and groom of the bedchambers all rolled into one and he walked around, as a consequence, with rather more pomp and circumstance than anyone had displayed in London since the last Lord Mayor's Show.

But if the Singhs had monopolised what might be described as all the dignified functions, others had to be found to do the down-to-earth, day-to-day work of Bunter's Indian Serai. And since it *was* an Indian serai it was necessary that they should be Indians. So I turned, in the first instance, to those who had planned and cooked J.J.'s all-India dinner. I offered each of them half as much again in the way of wages as their Sahibs were currently paying them and almost limitless opportunities for vails. In addition I told such of them as had sons, younger brothers or men from their native village who were willing to work as waiters, porters, boot boys or grooms that there would be posts for them as well.

The consequence was that there were not a few angry Sahibs around and I had engaged a larger staff than I needed some time before the Serai could actually open. I was sharp enough to realise that this excess of servants would be no bad thing. Every Indian establishment of any importance had a superfluity of servants, many of whom did nothing but squat around. If they performed no other service, they at least served to advertise their master's importance, wealth and liberality.

In the course of my career I have learnt never to under-estimate the importance of advertising. It doesn't matter whether you're a shopkeeper, a politician, an author, an opera singer or a world-conquering hero, the right sort of advertising is always at least a third of the game. And when I say the right sort of advertising I don't mean a column inch in *The Times* in which Figg, the grocer in High Holborn, informs his customers that he has just received a fresh consignment of fine plump raisins from Smyrna. I mean something that will force all who chance across it to take notice.

Supernumerary staff, I thought, might just do that. They would, in the first instance, be Indians, and Indians are still a rarity in Jermyn Street. They would, in the second instance, be wearing the livery I had designed for them, which was one of fairly startling Oriental splendour. And lastly they would be visible for most hours of the day since, having nothing else to do, they would either be squatting at the entrance to the Serai or else leaning against its walls. And if that made passers-by take notice – which it would – it was worth thousands of column inches in *The Times*, and ten times whatever I would have to pay them in wages.

As it was, passers-by were beginning to notice the Serai, even though Mr Cubitt had not yet finished refurbishing the interior and even though the supernumeraries had not yet begun to squat. The dome and the minarets and the colours and the jalousies were having their effect. I tested this one day by standing on the opposite side of Jermyn Street and counting the number of people who stopped to stare if they were on foot or rode with their heads over their shoulder if they were on horseback.

Eventually one of the pedestrian starers, seeing what I was at and so assuming that I must have some connection with what he had been staring at, tapped me on the shoulder with his cane and said, 'Perhaps you can tell me, Sir, whether it's going to be a Turkish hammam, a Cairo bordello or a Bosnian mosque.'

He was a tall, portly, handsome old party, carelessly but richly dressed, and if his expression hadn't been one of easy good humour, I would have taken more exception to his question than I did. Instead I said:

'That building, Sir, is none of those things, as anyone who has any knowledge of the Orient would tell you.'

He looked at me a bit more carefully and then said in his drawling, lazy voice: 'I accept the reproof, Sir, although I have done some travelling in my time. I meant no more than to jest, but I confess that I would like to know why the East has come in such a conspicuous fashion to Jermyn Street.'

The apology was handsome enough and so I said, very

civilly, that the building would shortly open as Bunter's Indian Serai.

He gave me a long look and said: 'You've got, if I may so put it, a certain well-fed and proprietorial look to you. Would I be wrong, Sir, if I guessed that you were the Bunter part of Bunter's whatever-it-is?'

'William Bunter, Sir,' said I somewhat curtly. 'And a serai is an Indian inn or hotel.'

'Bunter ain't a common name. Only Bunter I ever knew was the head pastry cook at Bellamy's. Made the best pies in the whole of Christendom. I ought to know. Eaten hundreds of 'em. The House of Commons has never been the same since he got himself killed in Waterloo year. Relation of yours?'

'Grandfather,' said I, and bowed.

'Well,' said he, 'I'm a William also. And as an old House of Commons man and one who's never eaten Indian but has always said that the stomach is the seat of health, strength, thought and life, even though Lord John Russell is always telling me that I eat too much . . .' here he seemed to lose the train of what he was saying and fell silent for a while.

'There's a fine old cod for you,' I said to myself, and indeed, with his vast expanse of white waistcoat he looked something like a great cod stood on its head. He looked at me again and suddenly said:

'You don't look a scrap like your grandfather. He had a skeleton look to him always. But you remind me of someone . . .'

He stood there, looking puzzled until he suddenly remembered something: 'Damme, you must be Dorothea FitzThistlethwaite's boy. Knew her when she was Dorothea Bunter.'

'She still is,' said I.

'Still is what?'

'Dorothea Bunter – and Mrs Lutz as well, of course.'

'I suffer from the gout these days and live far too chaste. But she was a confoundedly handsome gal in those days and I hadn't the gout. Might have taken more than an interest in her myself if it hadn't been for Freddy York . . .' Here he smote himself on the forehead and exclaimed:

'That's it. That's who you remind me of. He looked a deal like you when he was your age, did you know that?'

'I never,' said I in dignified tones, 'had an opportunity of knowing the late Duke of York at any age.'

'None the worse for that,' said he. 'York never had the feelings of a gentleman. He may have known what they were, but he never possessed 'em. I hope I haven't offended you.'

'My mother, Sir, would have agreed with you, and so must I.'

He was looking at me by now with a deal more friendliness. 'You will, of course,' said he, 'open this establishment of yours with some sort of banquet.'

'Of course,' said I, not having even considered that possibility.

'Then,' said he, 'you must send me a card for it. As one William to another.'

'Certainly,' said I.

He lifted his hat which was an old-fashioned one with a curly brim to it, twirled his cane at me and set off in the direction of Westminster.

'Hold hard,' cried I. 'William who?'

'It would have been William Lamb last year. Now it will have to be Viscount Melbourne.'

10   *The Clubbability Factor*

Whilst Cubitt's men were putting the finishing touches to the Serai I spent much of my time trying to determine why some of the hotels and restaurants now replacing the inns and taverns of our ancestors are more successful than others. I soon became convinced that it wasn't solely a matter of grub, service and ambiance. Nor was it just one of fashion, even though anything Frenchified is bound to be fashionable in these post-war days. There was clearly some additional factor involved, and when I finally discovered what it was I called it 'the clubbability factor'.

What I had discovered was this. The most successful establishments were those that came nearest to acting as supplements to, or even substitutes for, the clubs in which men of similar tastes and trades foregather. And the more one of these establishments attracted one particular type of client, the more it prospered. One had only to look at the way in which Ibbetson's attracted parsons, Stephen's military men, Fladong's naval officers, and Limmer's the sporting fraternity, to see what an essential part clubbability played in profitability.

I now began, therefore, to ask myself what sort of client I wanted the Serai to attract. And I didn't need to be a Ricardo or a McCulloch to come up with the answer, which was – to put it in a nutshell – none but the rich.

That may sound materialistic. I know that people sometimes think of me as an earthbound creature, one seldom capable of rising above such base things as grub, money, and being well-hung. But this, I swear, wasn't just one more question of Bunter being greedy. It was a question of his being practical. For a man with one glass eye and a squint couldn't fail to see that there must be more profit and less work involved in serving a single undeniable plutocrat than there would be in serving any three of the only-moderately-rich. Indeed, there was so much logic, so much poetic truth in that proposition that I found myself murmuring, along with Dryden:

> None but the rich,
> None but the rich,
> None but the rich deserve the Serai.

Poetic truths, however, butter no parsnips. I had to translate 'em into commercial realities. The rich would never be attracted to the Serai merely because it was Indian, or as near

Indian as anything could be in Jermyn Street. Nor would they be attracted just because Dryden and I wanted them to be. They would be attracted only if the Serai seemed clublike and they themselves were clubbable.

Which set me off on a study of the rich, about whom I really knew very little. It didn't take me long, however, to establish that any of 'em who were clubbable weren't clubbable because they were rich. Quite the contrary. The rich, it seemed to me, didn't want to be birds of a feather who would flock to Bunter's purely for the joy of one another's company as the parsons flocked to Ibbetson's and the sailors to Fladong's. This was partly because being rich ain't a trade or a matter of taste, and partly because, although the rich are very different from us, they are also very different from one another. Your Lancashire cotton king is no more like your Indian nabob than a retired Liverpool slaver is like Dick Gurney, the Quaker banker.

Indeed the rich, for all I knew, might actually prefer not to be in one another's company. If that were the case, and if I couldn't think of something that would do for the rich what the clubbability factor did for parsons and sailors, then a large part of my Indianising of 83 Jermyn Street would have been wasted. That, then, was my problem and, as I was determined to start as I meant to go on, it was an increasingly urgent problem, thanks to Lord Melbourne. For he, by foisting a grand inaugural banquet on me, had turned a long-term dilemma into an impending crisis.

Defining a problem ain't by any means the same thing as solving it. Sweat away at it as I might, I couldn't think of anything to make the rich as eager to come to a banquet at Bunter's as parsons would have been to flock to one at Ibbetson's. Nor was it any good turning to J. J. for advice. His concept of the rich never rose above the followers of the Surrey Staghounds and the honourable members of the Grocers' Company, and they, for my purposes, ranked as the not-even-moderately-rich.

It was at this point that my thoughts turned to my chance encounter with Lord Melbourne. He had, I told myself, been amiability itself. He'd been interested in the Serai and had suggested that he might become a client. He had been an admirer of my grandfather's and my mother's and had shown considerable respect for the name of Bunter. He might not, himself, be wealthy enough to satisfy my definition of rich, but he certainly knew more of those who would be than anyone else I could think of. And since it was he, I said to myself, who told me to have an inaugural banquet, let him now tell me who to invite to it and how to persuade 'em to accept.

It was with that last thought hot in my mind that I hurried round to his Lordship's house in South Street and told the butler to inform his master that Mr William Bunter had done himself the honour of calling. He soon came back to say that his master was in his dressing gown and dressing room, and would receive me there. When I looked surprised at this, since it was halfway through the morning, he said:

'I see, Sir, you are not accustomed to his Lordship's ways. He makes up for being a late riser by receiving visitors the moment he gets out of bed, whether he's in his nightgown, his dressing gown or his bath.'

With that he took me upstairs to the dressing room where I was somewhat surprised to find Lord Melbourne shaving himself. It was only later that he told me that, ever since Castlereagh had cut his throat with a penknife, he would never allow anyone to come near him with an open blade of any description. 'For,' said he, 'I'm sure I'll never cut my throat myself, and I'll make damned certain no one else gets the chance.'

That, however, by the way. When I entered the dressing room he had already finished scraping the left half of his face and was wiping his razor on a twist of paper. He looked at me through the lather and said:

'I thought so. It's the Mr Bunter of the Indian what's-its-name, is it not? Have you brought me my card to your opening? I take it kindly of you to do so in person.'

'No, my Lord,' said I. 'It ain't the time yet for cards. I come for advice.'

If a man can look amiable, mildly interested, and faintly surprised all at the one time and with half his face still covered in lather, then that was how Lord Melbourne looked now.

'I . . . don't . . . know,' said he, spacing out his words because he'd got to the difficult part of shaving where the lower lip runs into the chin, 'that . . . I . . . can . . . give . . . useful advice on Indian what's-its-names,' – he had turned the corner and was on the comparatively safe plateau of the right cheek.

'It's not the what's-its-name, my Lord. It's the banquet.'

'Ah yes, the banquet. Well, I've eaten my way through a good many of those and my best advice is to see to it that the plates are hot and the champagne cold.'

'It's not *what* to give at the banquet that worries me. It's *whom* to give it to.'

'Fiddlesticks. You must know better than anyone else whom you want as your guests.'

'I know who I want,' said I, 'but I'm damned if I know how to get 'em.'

'You'd best explain yourself,' said he.

Which I did. My attempts to measure the clubbability of the rich so interested him – for he was, in spite of his indolence, of a naturally enquiring and philosophical turn of mind – that long before I'd finished he had put down his razor with half a cheek and all of the upper lip untouched and the lather rapidly drying on him. When I finished he said:

'I must tell you, Mr Bunter, that if you had come here to ask me for introductions to rich men of my acquaintance as a matter of business I'd have had you kicked downstairs for your impudence. But this question of clubbability is a philosophical one, since it touches on the nature of, and reason for, groupings of any sort, whether they be social, economic, intellectual, criminal or political. I'd never before considered clubbability to be a factor, and so I must thank you for mentioning it. The philosophy of groupings is naturally of interest to me seeing that I've had to belong to more of 'em than most. I speak of political groupings, of course.'

'Of course, my Lord.'

'My social grouping was determined three generations ago by old Penistone Lamb. He may have been no more than a Nottingham attorney, but it was he who set the Lambs on their upward path. Since then there have been three or four great heiresses, any number of Members of Parliament, a baronetcy and two peerages in the family. We have now more or less reached our ceiling, which is why, Mr Bunter, my social grouping is fixed even though my political one is not. When it comes to politics I'm a man of principle.'

'I'm sure you are, my Lord. And the very best principles, I'll be bound.'

'Principle, Mr Bunter, in the singular. I've never found the need for more than one.'

'One sound principle is enough for any man and too much for some. May one enquire which principle you chose?'

'I'm of a liberal frame of mind, Mr Bunter, which means I'm generally in danger of being too open-handed in my dealings. But that will never do in politics. So it's my principle to concede as little as possible as slowly as possible and yet contrive to concede just enough quickly enough to discourage our native sans-culottes from setting up their guillotines in St James's Square.'

'What principle, my Lord, could be sounder than that?'

'Yet it has made for what some would say was a peripatetic political career.'

'You are a great walker?'

'I spoke metaphorically. It's only a few feet from the Opposition benches to the Government ones, and I walked them often enough when I was in the Commons. I've been, Mr Bunter, a Radical Whig with Fox, a Whig of All Talents with Grenville, a Tory sort of Whig with Canning and a Whiggish sort of Tory with Wellington. And I don't doubt that, with the mob howling as it does for Reform and if the Whigs like to come back and cede it to 'em, I'll need to turn Whig again if only to stop Lord Grey conceding a deal too much Reform too soon. So you will see why I take such a philosophical interest in any grouping, even one of such little importance as the group of moneybags you want for your Indian what's-its-name.'

'But is it a group? The moneybags you refer to ain't, so far as I can see, inclined to be clubbable.'

'That, as Quintilianus would have had it, is your *vis argumenti*. But as I have it, they may be clubbable, since they have at least one thing in common.'

'And what is that?'

'Discontent.'

'We are talking, my Lord, about the rich. How can they be discontented who have so much?'

'Oh, they're contented enough with what they have. It's what they haven't that makes 'em discontented.'

'And what is it that they haven't?'

'What I have.'

I stared at him in frustration, and he grinned happily back, enjoying what he clearly believed to be a Socratic dialogue, one in which he, of course, played Socrates. I hadn't the slightest desire to play Agathon or Alkibiades or any other ghastly old Greek, but I had to humour the man.

'Then what is it, my Lord, that you have, they haven't, and are discontented for not having?'

'Position, Mr Bunter. I've a tolerably good position in the political parties and a tolerably good position in society, and your first generation moneybag fellows have neither. So what follows?'

'I'm sure I don't know.'

'Tuft hunting follows, Mr Bunter. Sycophancy and grovelling and toadying follow, Mr Bunter. And as a consequence, your first generation moneybag, who wouldn't give sixpence to rub shoulders with others like himself, will give almost anything to rub shoulders with those like myself who are a few generations on.'

'You will forgive me, my Lord, if I say I'm damned if I can see what that's got to do with who comes to the banquet.'

'It's got this to do with it. There ain't a moneybag in the kingdom who won't feel clubbable and who won't go on his

knees for an invitation to that banquet once he knows that half
the Cabinet and half a dozen out-and-out social swells will also
be there. Doesn't that settle your problem?'

'Not entirely, my Lord.'

He had picked up his razor and was about to tackle his upper
lip, but this made him put it down again and ask what the Devil
I meant.

'I mean that I've no way of getting half the Cabinet to the
banquet, nor even a quarter. And if I had, I'd still have no way
of letting the moneybags of this kingdom know they were
coming.'

'You may have no way, but I have. And what's more, I'll lay
you two to one in hundreds that I'll succeed.'

'Pounds or guineas?'

'Betting in pounds is vulgar. Done, then?'

'Done, my Lord. And since I won't mind losing the bet,
perhaps you will tell me how you propose winning it.'

He thought for a while and then said: 'It will need two quite
different arguments depending on which Cabinet is involved.
My future colleagues in the Cabinet I am bound to enter
shortly will contain several old Whigs like myself who, having
started under Charley Fox, will have been trained to show a
proper appreciation of food. I shall talk to them about your
grandfather.'

'My grandfather, my Lord? Why my grandfather?'

'To remind them of his veal pies, which were certainly the
finest in Europe. And to remind them also of how he did so
much, upstairs in Bellamy's, to make such time as we had to
spend downstairs in the Commons Chamber tolerable. After
which, if I tell 'em that they owe it to his memory to come now
to the aid of his grandson, they are bound to agree.'

'And your former colleagues in the government you have just
left, my Lord, what of them?'

'Well now, Mr Bunter, you're talking about the Ultras, the
stern-voice-of-duty men like Wellington who would think it
frivolous to owe anything to the memory of a mere veal pie. But
they are, every man jack of 'em, the most inveterate and

absolute royalists, so I'll just tell 'em that they owe it to the immortal memory of the Grand Old Duke of York to come to the support of his bastard.'

I didn't mind being reminded that I was Bunter of Bellamy's grandson. No one with any store of sensibility minds having a great artist as his ancestor so long as that ancestor is no longer tantruming around but is safely tucked away in the churchyard. Being called a bastard when it's not in the way of business is, however, a different matter, and I told Lord Melbourne so pretty sharply. He had just started again on his upper right cheek and before I had finished he was laughing so much that he nicked himself and had to use a towel to staunch the blood. It was only when the laughter and bleeding had stopped that he wagged the towel in front of me and said:

'Do you see that blood? There are two reasons why I would hesitate to call it the blood of a Lamb. The first is that some might think it slightly sacrilegious. The second is that it's more likely to be the blood of a Wyndham . . . '

'You mean you also . . . '

'I mean, Mr Bunter, that my mother had four sons and a great many admirers and although it would be vulgar to be precise when it comes to attributing which to whom, it would be disgustingly middle class to ignore the institution of bastardy. That's the trouble with the middle classes. The higher and lower ones now – there's some good in 'em, and they'd just as soon be bastards as not. But your middle classes, Mr Bunter, they're all affectation and conceit and pretence and concealment and as the grandson of a great artist and the son of a Royal Duke you ought to have nothing to do with 'em.'

'I don't, my Lord, I assure you.'

'I'm delighted to hear it for I've just realised that you and I ain't far off from being related.'

'Does that mean, my Lord, that I have a Lamb ancestor or that you have a Bunter one?'

'It means neither. If we *are* related it's through bastardy and the Royal Princes who must, in the course of their randy careers, have done much to make one half of this kingdom kin to the other half.'

'Which Royal Prince did the trick in this case?'

'None other than our present sovereign. When he was still Wales, and a deal less obese and doddery than he is now, he was one of those admirers I mentioned. That's why my youngest brother George is so Guelphlike and why the first Lord Melbourne was made the first Viscount Melbourne and a Lord of the Bedchamber. So it's fair to assume that brother George and you are cousins by bastardy, though what that makes the two of us I haven't worked out. Nevertheless, I think I shall call you William and not Mr Bunter in future.'

'And what shall I call you?'

He grinned wickedly and said: 'It's perfectly true that one of my mother's earlier admirers was Lord Coleraine. It may be true that Lord Egremont bought the reversion off him for £13,000, which is why this ain't the blood of a Lamb and why I possess a good deal more sensibility than any Lamb or Milbanke I've ever heard of. Lord Egremont was known to possess so much sensibility that the fading of a rose was sufficient to throw him into a prolonged melancholy. But, be that as it may, I *am* the second Viscount Melbourne and you ain't the Duke of York. So though I may "William" you, you, Mr Bunter, must keep "my-Lording" me.'

His cynicism so shocked me that I might just as well have been tainted with the middle-class morality he'd been speaking about. But he was, *au fond*, a kindly man. So, seeing that he may have shocked me a little, he went on:

'Perhaps you would care to consider which of my future Cabinet colleagues you would like for your banquet, Mr Bunter. It will be a reforming government so they are bound, on the whole, to be a blackguardly lot. But what would you say if I enlisted the two who'll make the most noise in the world? Palmerston's a bullying sort of fellow, but he'll be made Foreign Secretary, and Brougham went to a Scottish university, which always makes a man vain, important and pedantic. He's a drunken ruffian as well and greatly addicted to laudanum, but he's bound to become Lord Chancellor and he hopes to step into Grey's shoes after that. So what would you say to those two?'

'I'd say that I'm grateful but still puzzled.'

'Dammit, man! What have you now got to be puzzled about?'

'How you are going to win the other part of your bet.'

'Heh! Heh! What other part?'

'The part about letting the moneybags know that all these great politicoes will be guests at the banquet that marks the opening of Bunter's Indian Serai.'

'Poh! Nothing could be simpler. Didn't I tell you I'm known to be a man of principle?'

'You did, and I agreed with you.'

'And so does every London paper, each of which knows that I'm bound, sooner or later, to end up in a government it supports. That means there ain't an editor who'll refuse me a favour. If I ask any of 'em, from Barnes of *The Times* to Black of the *Morning Chronicle*, to put in a puff for your Indian what's-its-name along with a mention of who will be your guests at that banquet, they'll rush to oblige.'

He had dealt with everything in such an easy and open way that I couldn't for the life of me decide whether he was a great humbug or a great realist. Then I decided he must be the latter as I couldn't think of a single reason why he should waste his humbug on Bunter. So I bowed, backed towards the door, said I was his Lordship's most obleeged, most humble etcetera, and left his Lordship to his razor.

The banquet, to judge by the numbers who angled for invitations, by the amount that was eaten and drunk, and the spirit in which they departed swearing that Bunter was the finest chap in London and his Serai ten times better than any club – to judge by these, then, the banquet was a success. Not even the fact that Brougham got so bosky that he ended up in the fountain, from which he had to be rescued before he drowned himself, subtracted by one jot from anyone else's enjoyment.

Melbourne, who wasn't entirely unbosky, was almost the last to leave. 'I hope,' said he, 'that I've solved that clubbability problem for you.'

It was a moment for parting with money with as good a grace as I could muster: 'Your hundred guineas, my Lord,' said I, 'will be brought to you in the morning. And as long as Bunter's Indian Serai exists, there will be an alcove and a table kept for your sole use.'

'I ain't exactly a moneybags,' said he, 'so I'll ration my acceptances to what I can afford.'

'There will,' said I, good grace getting the better of me, 'never be a bill so far as Lord Melbourne is concerned.'

'Thankee,' he said, 'and that reminds me that I've one more thing to warn you about.'

'What is that, my Lord?'

'Never give any of the moneybags credit. The richer they are, the less they enjoy paying a bill.'

11   *The Zenana Room*

The Bengalees have a saying to the effect that great mango trees from quite small mango stones do grow. My Serai had grown, in the material sense, just as quickly as stucco, paint and plaster elephants could be put together. But it was in the immaterial sense, that is to say in its reputation, that it made its most rapid growth. Even I, in whose mind a scheme can sprout and burgeon ten times more quickly than cress on wet flannel – even I was amazed by the speed with which Bunter's Indian Serai became not merely fashionable but *de rigueur*.

So many wished to patronise it that I was soon obliged to change my policy of catering for none but the rich to one of

catering for none but the *very* rich. And to ascertain who these
were I consulted Sir Coutts Trotter, the senior partner in
Coutts and Co. whom I had made my bankers. I put the names
he gave me on a list, added the names of those few Melbourne
had told me were truly important in politics and society, and
gave the final tally to Gurmakh Singh.

'These,' I told him, 'will from now on be known as the listed.
Get their names by heart and learn, as the opportunity arises,
to recognise the faces that go with them. For, whomever else
you turn away from the Serai, you must be sure that it is never
one of the listed.'

'On my head be it,' said he, after which I told him to make
the prices even more exorbitant and to instruct the waiters to
treat any of the unlisted who'd been admitted with the coolness
they deserved. But I added that they weren't to be over-cool
with those who might be reasonably expected, in due course, to
become postulants for listing.

It didn't work as well as it should have done. My prices
didn't seem to deter a sufficient number of the unlisted. This
puzzled me until I realised that such people are always inclined
to believe they ain't getting value for money unless they are
being over-charged. And as such people never expected an
Indian to be anything less than awe-struck when dealing with a
Sahib, even an unlisted one, they saw nothing in my waiters'
attitude towards them but the awe natural to any member of
the Indian race when confronted by any member of the British
one.

As for myself, I saw no more need to spend all my time in the
Serai than a general needs to spend on the barrack square.
Nevertheless I did, like any general, make frequent tours of
inspection. As I passed through the always-crowded restaurant
I would stop to pay my humble respects to any of those who'd
been put up for Bunter's by Lord Melbourne himself. I would
be rather less humble and rather more affable with those who'd
been put up by Sir Coutts Trotter. But with those who'd never
been put up by anyone – viz: the unlisted – I made sure I was
neither. Instead I did my best to ignore them, never speaking to

them if I could avoid it and making sure to be rude to them if I couldn't.

But even this failed to deter more than half of the merely-rich and less-than-rich. The other half kept coming to the Serai however roughly we treated them. In the end I realised that your true social climber, like your true mountain climber, will fail to enjoy himself unless the going *is* rough. What is more our climbers seemed to believe that Bunter had a positive duty to be rude. Some of these lickspittle wretches, I discovered, would go around actually boasting of the number of times I had insulted them.

Yet despite the unlisted the Serai soon began to leave its mark on social life in London. For one thing, people talked about Bunter almost as often as they talked about Wellington, or Tom Cribb, or Harriette Wilson, or any of our national heroes and heroines. The newspapers, originally alerted to my existence by Melbourne, had little paragraphs about me whenever they were short of something better in the way of gossip. Sometimes I would be 'The Nabob of Jermyn Street', and sometimes the mysterious Mr W.....m B....r. Sometimes they would wonder how I had amassed the money with which to start the Serai and sometimes they would hint at a criminal past in India. One paper referred to a rumour of my being closely connected to a late R. . .l P......ge and thought it shabby treatment that I had to earn a living as a restaurateur, but it was a sheet well known for its republican views.

And then it could be said that I started a general argument about which nation had the best cuisine. It had been accepted, even in quite middle-class homes, that this honour belonged to the French. But now, because of what was served at the Serai, it became fashionable to argue that the Indians could rise to heights of refinement and subtlety in their cooking, which the French could never match, however much they might accuse themselves of being the only truly civilised people in the world. Society physicians, who always latch on to whatever is currently à la mode, began to warn their patients against French cooking and to advise them, for reasons of health as much as of taste, to eat Indian whenever they could. They had, they said, discovered that most French dishes were inflammatory, costive and fattening, whereas most Indian ones were reductive, lenitive and diuretic.

Many who had hitherto praised the skills of their French chefs (most of whom, by-the-by, were really Swiss or Italian) now thought better of it. So out on the streets and back to their homelands went Monsieur Ragoût and Signor Risotto, and in came their Indian replacements. The trouble here, however, was that few worthwhile Indian chefs ever came on to the London labour market. All that could be counted on was a supply of Indian sea-cooks who had, before they jumped ship, fed the lascar seamen on the East Indiamen. As all that can reasonably be expected of Indian sea-cooks is Indian sea curries, this left it to the Serai to show what, in so far as Indian grub was concerned, could really be achieved in the way of refinements and subtleties.

All of these considerations brought an ever-increasing number of would-be patrons to the Serai and caused an ever-increasing number of 'em to be turned away for lack of room. This turning-away ceremony was conducted by Gurmakh Singh with all the awesome dignity and sorrowful solemnity of a judge putting on his black cap to pronounce the death sentence. It was a ceremony so regularly performed and so impressive in its performing that people came to watch Gurmakh Singh do his turning away in much the same way as they would come to watch Jack Ketch do his turning off. A very young penny-a-liner from the *Morning Chronicle* who signed himself Boz actually wrote an article about it under the heading of 'Blackballed for Bunter's'. He was so young and so green that I doubt he intended the pun.

This glut of would-be patrons gave rise to what soon came to be accepted as a long-established and self-evident truth: namely that it was quite as difficult – and therefore quite as desirable – to get oneself listed at Bunter's as it was to get oneself elected to the Jockey Club or Almack's. This truth seemed to become even more self-evident after I reached my agreement with the Lady Patronesses of Almack's, which agreement had its origins in a conversation I had with Lord Palmerston.

Lord Melbourne and Lord Palmerston were not exactly two of a kind. They differed somewhat in character and temperament. Nevertheless they had a good deal in common, including Lady Cowper, who was Melbourne's favourite sister and Palmerston's favourite mistress. It was an arrangement that strengthened the regard each man had for the other and did not even greatly upset Lord Cowper.

The two of them were as comfortable in one another's company as any two politicians ever could be, for they had been either political opponents or political colleagues for better than twenty-five years. As hedonists they very openly enjoyed the world's pleasures and guttled and guzzled and womanised as they wished. When it came to the womanising Palmerston did a deal more wishing than Melbourne, and was said to go at his women like a bull fresh turned out to the cows. Melbourne's weakness was for prolonged sentimental attachment to other men's wives, which was something strange considering what he himself had suffered as Caroline Lamb's husband. That it was a weakness was proven every time one of the husbands, thinking there may have been more of adultery than of sentimentality in the attachment, threatened action for crim. con.

But at this period it was for political as much as for belly reasons that the two of them dined together so frequently at the Serai. Palmerston was, like Melbourne, a man of principle. This meant that though the two of them had resigned from his government, they still agreed with Wellington in being opposed to Reform. They believed, as he did, that it was not within the wit of man to improve on our ancient institutions, and that only a lunatic or a Jacobin or an out-and-out Reformer (who would have the qualities of both) would want the Commons made a whit more democratical than it was.

But, the temper of the times being what it was, these were not sentiments two future ministers in a future and reforming Whig government would want to publish to the world. When the time came the Radicals would have to be dished and they would help with the dishing. Meanwhile they needed a quiet meeting place away from the hurly-burly of Westminster and the chitter-chatter of the clubs where they could plan how to do it. Being the men they were, they planned best where they dined best which, unfortunately, meant the Serai where the alcove I had so altruistically placed at Lord Melbourne's disposal suited their requirements to a T.

I say unfortunately because, by my original outburst of altruism, I had debarred myself from ever presenting Lord Melbourne with a bill for his dinner. And as Lord Palmerston (who generally had to be put in court before he'd pay a bill) always insisted that he dined as Lord Melbourne's guest, he was never paid for either. I could have afforded the two of them eating hearty and drinking deep at my expense whenever they wanted had it not been that I had to worry about the example they set. They were far from being the only politicoes to use the Serai and, human nature being what it is, many of those others must have wondered why they had to pay so extravagantly for their dinners when Melbourne and Palmerston paid nothing at all.

It took that uncouth, half-crazed, drunken windbag Brougham to put their feelings into words. 'Bunter,' said he, 'if Melbourne and Pam have found free quarters here, then why haven't I, who am a greater man than either of 'em? Never you doubt but I'll be kissing hands as First Lord of the Treasury when each of 'em will still be wondering whether what I'll offer him will be the Board of Control or Woods and Forests. So if it's the future you're looking to with your free dinners, Bunter-me-boy, Henry Brougham's your man.' Then, fortunately, he slumped back in his chair and fell asleep. But I had no doubt that there were a good many others, from Peel to Huskisson who, if they had had only half Brougham's impudence, would have said something similar.

All of which has taken me away from the Lady Patronesses and the moment when I paused during my inspection of the restaurant to pay my respects to Lord Melbourne and Lord

Palmerston. They had finished eating, were about to start on the last of many bottles, and being slightly bosky were inclined to hold me in conversation.

'That,' said Melbourne, 'was what I would call a good meal, Mr Bunter.'

'It was what I would call a damned good meal,' said Palmerston, who was the boskier of the two.

'I'm glad of it,' said I.

'Confound it, man,' said Palmerston, 'don't stand there looking like an overweight Archangel about to blow the Last Trump. Sit down and take a glass with us, for I've something to discuss with you.'

Since I was paying for this bottle, as I had for all previous ones, I saw no reason to refuse.

'I was,' said Palmerston, 'talking about this place of yours to Emily . . . '

'He means Lady Cowper,' said Melbourne.

'Lady Cowper, by all means,' said Palmerston. 'And she said that they had been talking about it at Almack's, and that all the Lady Patronesses had deplored the fact that they were unable to enjoy this new Indian experience everyone is talking about.'

'I would be delighted,' said I, 'to have the Lady Patronesses dine here.'

'Don't be such an ass,' said Melbourne. 'They are all respectable females with reputations to consider.'

'So they are,' said Palmerston who, if rumour was correct, had tupped at least five of 'em, sparing only the Countess of Sefton who was virtuous and Lady Willoughby who had long been a grandmother.

'I don't suppose,' said Melbourne, 'they would care to disguise themselves as men – just once, and for the experience.'

'Their interest,' said Palmerston, 'lies in something more long term and something that could be made available not just to themselves, but to all female members of Almack's. Have you any notion, Bunter, of how this could be arranged?'

I thought for a while before answering.

'If we were in India,' I said at last, 'there would be a zenana . . .'

'That's it, by God,' said Palmerston. And that is how the notion of a Zenana Room for Bunter's Indian Serai was born.

It was built as an annexe with its own entrance from Duke Street and, except for a corridor to the kitchens, no access to the main body of the Serai. It was, from the start, extremely popular with the ladies of Almack's who were now able, singly, in pairs, or in groups, to enjoy the 'Indian experience' that had been available to my male customers for the past twelvemonth. I could not, since it *was* a zenana, allow them to have male guests, not even if they were married to them, but I gathered that this was, if anything, one of its greatest attractions.

I have never believed that females belong to a different race, or, indeed, that the differences between male and female are a scrap greater than what is essential for the perpetuation of the species. Nothing has so confirmed me in this belief as the way in which my zenana customers began to behave once they realised there would be no male audience apart from the Indian waiters. They were, if anything, slightly less ladylike, which is to say slightly more uninhibited than most of my male customers.

They never shrank over what has to be done over curries, which is sweat. Far from toying with their meal they drank as deep and ate as hearty as any man, and if they had to have their stays loosened in order to do so, they would perform this task for one another as automatically as one loosens the girth on a horse. They guzzled and gobbled and belched and quarrelled and swore. They talked bawdy about their own and other women's husbands and lovers. They bullied the waiters although some of the younger ones might also get ogled. They sometimes left without paying their bills, and when they did settle, they would often quarrel with Gurmakh Singh, whom I'd put in charge, over the amounts. In short, they acted natural, enjoyed themselves, and departed swearing that the Zenana Room at Bunter's was the only public place in which a woman of breeding and reputation could feed well, behave as she pleased, and still afford to be seen.

For a time I was delighted with this increase in my trade. But that time passed when I was obliged to realise this had been one of my more unfortunate ventures. There were several reasons. One was that the Lady Patronesses insisted on treating the zenana as an extension of Almack's. That is to say they reserved the right to decide who should and who should not be admitted. And in doing so they refused to work along my own lines of the listed and the unlisted, but followed instead their Almack's rules of the socially acceptable and the socially unacceptable. The two methods couldn't cog. For whilst, in the male side of the Serai, I was very content to admit the very rich, the Lady Patronesses, on the female side, were equally content to exclude their wives as socially unacceptable.

I didn't realise what they were doing or what effect it would have on my trade until I received a note from Sir Coutts Trotter requesting me to call on him at the bank. This did not surprise me as I knew my account was not as healthy as it had been. It cost more than I anticipated to build the Zenana Room and several of my listed customers were insisting on signing their bills without being over-eager to pay up when their accounts were sent to them at the end of the month.

Trotter didn't get up to greet me, nor did he offer me the customary glass of Madeira and slice of seed cake. Instead he looked at me sourly and plunged straight into it:

'Mr Bunter,' said he, 'I'll not deny that I've always enjoyed dining at your Serai, but you mustn't expect to see me there in the future.'

'Are you leaving the country, Sir?'

'I am not, Sir.'

'Then why?'

'My wife, Sir, Lady Trotter, Sir, Lady *Coutts* Trotter, Sir, has been refused admission to your Zenana Room. She was born an O'Hagan, Mr Bunter, youngest daughter of The O'Hagan, and she ain't accustomed to being refused admission to anywhere. When she lived in Dublin she was frequently

invited, I'll have you know, to soirées at the Castle. Now, Sir . . .'
here he took up a sheet of paper ' . . . your account with us is in
debit to the tune of £1287.8s.6d. We must ask you to make that
good, after which, Sir, we must ask you to take your account
elsewhere.'

If this hadn't been serious I would have burst out laughing,
for I've never seen a little cock-sparrow of a man try so hard to
puff himself up to look like an indignant turkey-cock. But I
knew that, as a cock-sparrow, he was sorely henpecked, so I
said nothing and left.

Losing Trotter was bad enough. But when I lost six or seven
more of the listed, and for the same reason, I began to worry.
Very few of my very rich had wives the Lady Patronesses would
have thought acceptable, and I would probably have lost the
lot of 'em if they had all had wives curious to investigate 'the
Indian experience'.

Then I started to lose the custom of some of the politicoes
and other important people recommended to me by Lord
Melbourne. They left because, however much freedom they
permitted their wives, that freedom didn't extend to their
playing Potiphar's wife to my Joseph. This Potiphar's wife
business had its origins in a certain amount of quite innocent
horseplay in the Zenana Room. Certain of the more tomboyish
ladies who had dined rather better than usual, started to pinch
the bottoms of the younger Indian waiters. Women run most
things in India, but they don't run the bottom pinching. That
has to be started by the man. My younger waiters, therefore,
were considerably distressed and they complained to Gurmakh
Singh who, without consulting me, complained straightway to
the Lady Patronesses.

'Is no good,' he told them, 'Memsahibs pinching bottoms of
young Indian mans. Indian mans is always expecting to pinch,
never expecting to be pinched, and always he is pinching brown
bottoms. He would not be liking white bottoms too much. But if
it is the well-hanging the Memsahibs are looking for, then I am
telling you Bunter Sahib was being most well-hanging man in
whole of India. If ladies are not believing, please to be referring

to Begum of Sumroo who is tip-top expert and is knowing all about Bunter Sahib's hangings.'

That, of course, did it. Horseplay turned into something more serious. From then on I had quite a number of defensive battles on my hands, some of 'em running ones. I'd never for a moment imagined there could be so many Potiphar's wives amongst the members of Almack's.

And here I must say something about those who have criticised me for referring to the indisputable fact that I'm remarkably well hung. Even to mention such a thing, they say, is to talk dirty. I think I know where the dirtiness lies, and I have to tell those gentlemen that we are what Nature makes us. A chap can no more avoid the consequences of being well hung than he can avoid the consequences of possessing a pretty face or the physique of Hercules. I think of my own particular endowment as more of a misfortune than anything else. But as it is a misfortune that has helped shape my life, it would be an odd sort of modesty that stopped me referring to it when it starts doing another bit of shaping. No, gentlemen! It would be as futile trying to follow the fortunes of Bunter without ever referring to his being well hung as it would be to follow the fortunes of Lord Nelson without referring to the sea.

But then when I mention, in my plain, blunt, unvarnished way, some of the unfortunate consequences of being well hung, these same gentlemen accuse me of empty boasts that besmirch the fair name of womanhood. Now women, as I've already said, differ from men only in certain bare essentials, and randiness ain't one of 'em. So to those who deny that a woman is ever influenced by the fact that a chap's well hung I would say this. Whenever you see, as you so frequently will, a tolerably handsome woman hanging on the arm of some long-nosed, spindle-shanked, squint-eyed paragon of ugliness, don't ask 'What the Devil does she see in him?' Look, instead, at the paragon's wallet. And if that ain't bulging look next at his codpiece, which I'll guarantee is.

With the hope that I have now given my critics reason to hold their tongues I return to the subject of the Serai where I was losing listed customers I could ill afford to lose. But I've made it a rule never to start worrying about money until I have spent a good deal more of it than I've got, and I wasn't at that stage yet. For I still owned what was certainly the most unusual and possibly the most talked-about hotel and restaurant in the whole of London, if not in the whole of Great Britain, and if I was losing a certain amount of custom from the top end of the market, customers from lower down were still queuing to get in.

Meanwhile, even though I was currently losing money over the Serai, all I needed was enough cash to settle with Coutts & Co. and to keep my next bankers happy until the Serai came into profit once again. It was, in short, a question of arranging some re-financing, and if I couldn't arrange that, my name wasn't William Frederick Augustus Bunter.

What I had in mind to do was to form a small private joint-stock venture – a friendly little consortium in which two or three people I knew well would invest, not just for a per centum return on their money, but also out of friendship for me and for what they hoped they could make for themselves on the side. I calculated that the Serai needed another £5000 of working capital and Bunter £1000 of spending money, and that this would be met by selling three one-tenth shares in the company at £2000 a time.

The investors I had in mind were J.J. (who hadn't yet been allowed to subscribe a penny), Captain Manning (whose ship had recently docked) and Buttercup (who was certainly the shrewdest and probably the wealthiest of the three). The side benefits I thought to offer them were these. J.J. would be given the sole right to supply the Serai with all its Indian groceries from his new Indian grocery department. Captain Manning would have an opportunity to ship on his own account and without necessarily informing his owners all the Indian commodities needed for J.J.'s grocery and my Serai, including, if necessary, a fresh supply of Indian cooks and waiters. Buttercup would be offered a profitable outlet for all her market garden and other produce, including her doctored liquors.

I mentioned none of these things until after they had looked over the Serai and dined, and I took care to wine them and dine them in such a manner that Indian good living seemed likely to run out of their ears. Then I gave them as a toast 'The Jermyn Street National and Imperial Investment Company', which came off the tongue so well that it was drunk with a three times three, after which I outlined my proposal. Manning was the only one to agree immediately and without conditions. Buttercup, who had been much taken with the bedrooms, wanted the use of one of 'em, complete with Bunter, whenever she was in this part of London, as an extra inducement. J.J. said that he wanted to look at the books.

This rather set me aback, as the only book-keeping done was done somewhat imaginatively by Maria. It was because of this, perhaps, that J.J. finally declared that the £6000 the three of 'em were being asked to invest might not be enough to support the company until the Serai came into profit.

'What you must do, Billy,' said he, 'is sell two more tenths, thus providing fluidity and assuring us that our one-tenths will be safe.'

'But then,' said I, 'Bunter's Indian Serai will no longer be controlled by a Bunter.'

And there, after a deal of arguing, we had to leave it, for J.J. had infected the other two with caution and they wouldn't agree to the Jermyn Street National and Imperial Investment Company until I could assure them that I had sold two more one-tenths.

This left me in a state of considerable agitation. Of all the enterprises I had undertaken, the Serai that bore my name seemed likely to be the only permanent monument to my entrepreneurial skills. I wanted to be able to say on my deathbed, as Christoper Wren may or may not have said on his '*Si monumentum requiris*, 83 Jermyn Street *circumspice*'. So I kept saying to myself, 'Bunter's Serai must stay Bunter's Serai', until I suddenly realised that there was at least one other Bunter in the world who might help it stay so.

Ever since she became a disciple of Mary Wollstonecraft and

a firm believer in the rights of women my mother had insisted on remaining Dorothea Bunter, which was the name she was born with, no matter how many husbands she married. Her latest one, so far as I knew, was a Colonel Antoine Lutz who commanded the British garrison on Corfu. A colonel's lady, I said to myself, is unlikely to want for a thousand pounds or two, what with foreign allowances, what can be made out of the troops' pay and rations, and whatever pickings came out of the nearby war in Greece where every sort of bandit is raiding and looting and murdering the unfortunate Turks. So I sat down and, for the first time in ten years, wrote to my mother in distant Corfu, telling her that I was in the fortunate position of being able to put a highly favourable investment her way and that all she had to do was send her cheque for £4000 by return.

No cheque came. But about six weeks later, when I was just about to begin my inspection of the Serai, Gurmakh Singh came hobbling up to me in great distress. He had, he said, been hurt in his dignity as much as in his body. Never before had he, when engaged in the turning-away ceremony, had the person he was turning away hurl him roughly aside, go storming into the Serai, and seat himself in Lord Melbourne's alcove, where I could find the *badmash* even now.

I didn't much like the sound of this, but carried on with my inspection which soon brought me to Melbourne's alcove where, sure enough, a man I had never seen before was standing and arguing with a waiter. He was a great, tall, ugly, raw-boned, red-haired sort of chap with Sawney written all over him, and he kept saying slowly and loudly:

'I don't want to eat. All I want is Mr William Bunter.'

'Please?' said the uncomprehending waiter.

'Mr William Bunter,' repeated Sawney.

I waved a hand at the waiter, sending him on his way, and said: '*I* am William Bunter.'

He looked me up and down, seized my hand, shook it, dropped it, and said: 'Didn't know you were so fat. You ain't at all like your Mama.'

I didn't like his tone, so I said, pretty coldly: 'I may or may not be like her. But what I want to know is who the Devil are you?'

'Didn't I tell you? I'm Lord Cochrane.'

When I was a schoolboy, most of us at Christ's Hospital were agreed that Lord Cochrane was the greatest of all contemporary heroes – greater to our minds than the late Lord Nelson or the Game Chicken himself. Although Cochrane was then in disgrace and exile, we knew all about what he had done in the French Wars and could reel off the names, tonnages and values of the prizes he had taken when in command of the *Speedy* or the *Pallas* or the *Impérieuse*.

We might argue between ourselves as to whether he had been more heroic over the taking of *El Gamo* or the defending of Fort Trinidad, but we agreed on sending Admiral Lord Gambier to the Devil for what that psalm-singing, tract-pushing, Methodistical old woman had failed to do during the action at the Aix Roads. If only he had supported our hero better on that occasion, Cochrane would have won a greater victory even than Trafalgar. We deplored his frequent imprisonments and applauded his equally frequent escapes. And being normal, dirty-minded schoolboys, we invented new and nigh-impossible delights he would have enjoyed in the course of his elopement with the beautiful sixteen-year-old Kitty Barnes.

True I hadn't followed his career half as closely since then, but no one could have helped hearing his name mentioned, year after year, and for one daring exploit after another. Now here I suddenly was, face to face with the man hailed either as Liberator or terrorist in three continents and a dozen different countries; the man who had destroyed so many foreign governments and so often made long fingers at our own; the man who would have sprung Boney from St Helena to make him Emperor of all the South Americas if only Boney hadn't snuffed it beforehand.

So I invited Lord Cochrane to seat himself in Lord Melbourne's own alcove and ordered up a couple of bottles of my second-best claret.

When I had got Lord Cochrane seated, had seated myself opposite him, and had poured each of us a glass I said:

'I am delighted to make your Lordship's acquaintance.'

'I'm here,' said he, 'as a messenger from your Ma.'

'I didn't know my mother counted the hero of Rosas Bay, the Liberator of Chile and the Brazils amongst her acquaintances.'

'No more she does, Mr Bunter, no more she does. But she counts him amongst her friends – her closest, sincerest and most affectionate friends.'

I remembered where not a few such friendships had landed my mother. But as I've never allowed her lapses to concern me, I merely said: 'That must be a cause for pride as well as pleasure to her.'

'And to me, Mr Bunter, and to me,' said Cochrane who was turning out to be what I would describe as a double-barrelled sort of conversationalist. 'A free and fearless spirit, your Ma, as I recognised the moment I clapped eyes on her.'

'Where was that, my Lord?'

'In Corfu, Mr Bunter. Your Ma's soft heart led her to open her house to me just as soon as I landed there.'

My mother's heart, from all I remembered of her, would have been better described as sinewy. But she has had a strong fancy for famous men ever since her youth and her early involvements with such men as the Duke of York and Lord Byron. I felt pretty certain, therefore, that she had needed little or no coaxing to persuade her to play Lady Hamilton to Cochrane's Lord Nelson. But whether Colonel Lutz had been equally ready to play Sir William Hamilton's part of *le mari complaisant* could be another matter.

Lord Cochrane, meanwhile, had not done simpering over

my mother, and anyone who has watched a gawky, raw-boned, red-haired, poke-nosed Sawney simper will know that it ain't the pleasantest of sights.

'A ministering angel, your Ma,' he said, 'an angel when I was most in need of one. For you will never know, Mr Bunter, what three years as Admiral and Commander-in-Chief of the Free Greek Navy had reduced me to.'

'No true-born Briton,' said I, half-bowing to him across the table, 'has failed to admire the uncompromising and self-sacrificing manner in which you have spent yourself leading those valiant Greek mariners against the barbarous Turks.'

I don't know whether it was the reference to the mariners or the spending that wiped the simper off his face.

'Brave Greek mariners, my arse,' said he. 'And if I spent myself in their service, it was just about the only spending that *was* done. Have you ever had dealings with a Free Greek Government, Mr Bunter?'

'Never.'

'"*O fortunatus nimium*" as my tutor used to say. Rather a Sanhedrin of Shylocks, Mr Bunter, than a Free Greek Government. At least Shylock's word was his bond, but I'm still owed three years' back pay, not to mention the titles, estates and other rewards they promised me.'

I thought I might cap his hackneyed tag with one even more hackneyed, and so I said: '"*Timeo Danaos*", hey, my Lord?'

'Not even that,' he growled. 'The only gift involved was the gift I made 'em of my services. And a fat lot of good that did 'em, seeing what cowards their sailors are.'

'Cowards? Surely not, my Lord. Remember Salamis.'

'Salamis be buggered. All your modern Greek mariner is capable of is a great deal of arguing and a bit of petty piracy.'

'But what about Navarino? That was recent enough.'

'Recent enough to be sure, but it had nothing to do with my brave Greek sailors. By the time they had finished arguing over whether they should run away before the fighting started or do a little fighting before the running-away started, blowing the Turkish and Egyptian fleets out of the water had to be left to others. And that, Mr Bunter, is why Cochrane ain't the hero of Navarino and Codrington is.'

He actually had tears in his eyes, which made me remember that heroes need a deal more buttering up than ordinary everyday cowards like myself.

'You who have already won so much of it, my Lord, must leave a scrap or two of glory for the Sir Edward Codringtons of this world.'

'You ain't a sailor, Mr Bunter. If you were you would know that it isn't the glory that matters: it's the prize money.'

Now I'm as fond of money as the next man. But then I ain't a hero and so set no value on glory. But if ever there was a hero listed and passed as A1 at Lloyd's, it was Lord Cochrane. That was why his down-to-earth, profit-and-loss attitude to glory shocked me.

'You seem,' he said, 'surprised by my attitude. So allow me, as a dear, dear friend of your Ma's, to give you some advice.'

'Willingly, my Lord.'

'Never, never, never, Mr Bunter, become a national hero. It ain't a paying proposition. I was one for most of the French Wars, and what was the consequence? Why, Sir, I was thrown out of the Navy, out of Parliament, out of the Order of the Bath, and into chokey. And why do you think that was?'

'Wasn't it because you tried to rig the stock market with a false report of Napoleon's death?'

'Not at all. That was what my uncle and Berenger tried to do. No, Mr Bunter, I ended up in chokey for no better reason than that I'd become a national hero.'

'With all due respect, that sounds like a *non-sequitur*.'

'It ain't: it's an entirely logical *sequitur*. Look at it this way. Because I'd become a national hero I got elected to Parliament. Because I was in Parliament the public thought it should listen to what I had to say. Because what I had to say was said bluntly, as befits an honest seaman, I made enemies of the King, the Cabinet, the Lords of the Admiralty, and every naval officer senior to myself. Result – they had no other choice than to throw me into chokey. One thing followed the other as naturally as a string of sausages.'

'I see some connection, my Lord, but if your countrymen have shown you scant gratitude, think of the millions of foreigners who daily bless your name and call you Liberator.'

'And that's another losing game.'

'What is?'

'The liberating business. I have, in my time, helped to liberate the Spaniards from the French, the French from Boney, the Chileans from the Spaniards, the Brazilians from the Portuguese, and the Greeks from the Turks, and there wasn't one of 'em who ended up paying me the rate for the job. I'd have done a deal better if I'd gone privateering, or engaged in a bit of straightforward piracy.'

He was so passionately interested in money that he would, if I'd let him, have spent the rest of the day talking about liberation economics and the miserably low returns to be got from being a national hero. But I had other things to do, so I steered him back towards his starting point.

'I trust,' said I, 'you left my mother in tolerably good health.'

'In bounding good health, Mr Bunter, positively bounding.'

'And my step-father Colonel Lutz? Also in good health?'

'All I can tell you about him is that if your Ma hadn't been widowed by the time I landed in Corfu she has been by now.'

'She makes an excellent widow, my Lord. But I'm sorry about the Colonel. Was it some lingering Eastern disease?'

'Not what you'd call lingering. At the best instantaneous, at the worst a matter of a few hours.'

'You mean . . . ?'

'I mean if the court martial's verdict was confirmed, a British firing squad. But if he was handed over to the Greeks, impalement.'

'Surely no British Governor would hand a British officer over to the Greeks for impalement.'

'He commanded the Corfu garrison, you see. That's why both sides were so cross.'

'I don't follow you.'

'Being in command gave him control of all the arms depots and magazines on the island. And that allowed him, once he'd bribed a few quartermasters, to sell arms to the Free Greeks.'

'The great British public, my Lord, is strongly in favour of anything that will help the brave Greeks drive out the Turks. So I'm damned if I can see why the Governor had Colonel Lutz court martialled, let alone shot.'

'I'll give you three reasons. In the first place the great British public has never actually met a Free Greek. In the second place the Turks are still England's ally, even though Codrington misunderstood his orders and blew their fleet out of the water. And in the third place no British government, however much it wishes to foster individual enterprise, can afford to be caught countenancing the sale of so much public property for private gain.'

'That still doesn't explain why the Greeks should want to impale him. He was, after all, trying to help them.'

'That would indeed have been the case if the arms he sold them had been serviceable. But what the Greeks paid him for, Mr Bunter, was consignment that had already been condemned by the Board of Ordnance.'

'You mean he managed to sell the Greeks a pup?'

'All the cannon had worn-out barrels, all the muskets had faulty locks, and all the powder had been spoiled by damp. And yet he persuaded them to pay in gold and in advance, something I could never persuade them to do. A man, Mr Bunter, of considerable ingenuity and resource.'

'My mother would never have married him else.'

'Yet lacking in foresight. He failed to anticipate how the Greeks would react. They had never been cheated on such a scale before. Your step-father never allowed for what that would do to their national pride. It was the hurt to their pride, far more than their inability to shoot at the Turks, that led them to complain to the Governor and demand his surrender to them for impaling.'

'How dreadful! The mere thought of it makes my fundament itch.'

'I'm a blunt, plain-spoken man, Mr Bunter, but I'm sorry if I've upset you.'

'Nothing connected with my mother ever upsets me, my Lord, for it's never predictable. But I am curious to know how my mother is placed now that she's lost yet another husband.'

'From all that she's told me, she's placed pretty well. Your late step-father was a careful, not to say miserly fellow, which is one more reason why your Ma ain't exactly mourning his demise.'

'Then he left her some money?'

'Colonel Lutz, Mr Bunter, had been soldiering for nigh on forty years. That means he had forty years during which he had muster rolls, pay rolls and ration allowances to play with in addition to his own pay and whatever he made out of the Greeks. All in all he managed to leave your Ma a very tidy sum indeed.'

In that case, I said to myself, Cochrane must have brought with him the £4000 I'd asked my mother to invest in the Jermyn Street National and Imperial Investment Company, and I was as good as home. Cochrane, however, hadn't broached the matter as yet, so I poured him another glass and said:

'I suppose she is considering how best to invest her money.'

'Not any longer.'

'What?'

'She has it invested.'

'But you said you had a message for me.'

'So I have Mr Bunter, so I have. I'm to tell you that she may, in due course, return to England, but if she does, you are not to look to her for money. And as for the investing of what she has, I'm also to tell you that she places a deal more faith in Consols than in Indian Serais.'

It was my turn to have tears in my eyes, but mine were of rage.

'It's a damned shame,' I roared, 'for she's put an end to the most promising joint-stock venture of the year.'

Cochrane gave me a curious sort of a look – the sort of look Sir Coutts Trotter might give to a client, or a pork butcher to a fat pig still frolicking in its sty, but not the sort of look one would have expected of a national hero.

'In my time,' said he, 'I have invested in a good many joint-stock ventures, and could do again. I believe the sum in question is £4000?'

'It is.'

'Well then, Mr Bunter, if you can persuade me that an investment will yield what is, in my judgment, an adequate per centum of profit, I could be your man.'

'Allow me to fill your glass, my Lord.'

After that, Lord Cochrane never spent a day in London without wining and dining extravagantly well at the Serai. But he refused to pay for anything he consumed, arguing that, as a £4000 venturer, he had already paid handsomely for all that he ate and drank. When I pointed out to him that this meant that he was eating and drinking some of his own per centum return on his investment, he was willing enough to agree but still not willing enough to put his hand in his pocket.

In the end we came to a compromise. He could continue to eat and drink free so long as he never did so alone. He must always bring paying customers with him. From then on the alcove reserved for him never held fewer than half a dozen of his cronies, most of them half-pay naval officers who had been press-ganged into dining with him and most of whom grumbled at having to pay for the privilege.

Cochrane, unfortunately, spent the whole of that winter in London instead of in Florence which was nominally his home in exile. He was determined to end his exile, obtain a free pardon, get back the money he'd paid in fines, and be reinstated in the Royal Navy. But he still had enemies in high places.

One of these was the King, who wouldn't have Cochrane back in the Navy because of all the secret weapons he was always inventing. He had already perfected a scheme for gas warfare which he swore was such a deadly deterrent that war would become unthinkable. The King greatly objected to this.

He thought such methods ungentlemanly and likely to take all the interest out of naval warfare.

Then there was the Duke of Wellington, who was, at that time, Prime Minister, and who had long hated Cochrane because he had, twenty years earlier, insulted the whole of the Wellesley tribe in public. It had happened this way.

Just before Cochrane was thrown out of Parliament he had been conducting a campaign to stop corruption and improve conditions in the Services. There wasn't a Wellesley at that time who wasn't in enjoyment of the perks of some office or other and Cochrane had calculated that the sinecures amassed by that tribe brought them in £37,729 per annum. But, he told the House, when a naval lieutenant had the misfortune to have his leg shot away, all he got by way of a pension was £40 per annum. This meant, he told applauding Members of the Commons, that the Wellesleys were as valuable to the nation as 426 pairs of naval lieutenants' legs, and he wanted that interesting fact recorded in the Journal of the House. Since the Wellesleys have always been supportive of one another, the Duke of Wellington was still disinclined to help Cochrane return from exile.

Nevertheless, Cochrane had some cause to hope. It seemed unlikely that King George would survive for very long, and he would be succeeded by his brother, the Duke of Clarence, who was an old shipmate of Cochrane's and would, as a Sailor King, know what was due to a naval hero. That would dispose of one lot of opposition. When the King died, Wellington was bound to fall and, because of the clamour for Reform, he would be replaced by Cochrane's old political ally Lord Grey, and that would dispose of another lot of opposition.

Meanwhile, however, the Serai was never without Lord Cochrane and his cronies, none of whom could afford to be lavish spenders. As they took the place of some who were, we lost by their custom. It was Buttercup who first put this problem into words at our Annual Shareholders' Meeting.

'Your Lordship,' said she, 'you're a-losing us money.'

'Not any more, I'm not,' said he. 'Look at all the customers I bring in.'

'They've most of 'em got the wrong sort of bums,' said she.
'What the devil have bums got to do with it?'

'We've only got so many seats in the restorong, which means
that there are only so many bums as can sit on 'em, which
means we want as many of 'em as possible to be sat on by what
you might call free-spending bums, what the customers you
bring in ain't.'

Cochrane wouldn't have accepted such bluntness from
anyone else, but he had developed a rapport with Buttercup
whose commercial acumen he greatly respected and with
whom he yarned endlessly about Peninsula days. So, although
he went a bit red in the face, he answered her respectfully.

'But they're all friends o' mine, Ma'am, whatever their bums
are like.'

'Of course they are. That's why they're all either naval men
on half-pay or out-and-out Radicals. The first don't spend very
much and t'others tend to scare off customers who do.'

'I hadn't thought of it in that way,' said Lord Cochrane.

A few days later Lord Cochrane dined again at the Serai. This
time he had only one crony to keep him company. As I stopped
by his table to pay him my respects he said:

'Mr Bunter, allow me to introduce you to an old shipmate
of mine, Mr Clarence.'

13   *By Appointment*

Mr Clarence was a portly, red-nosed, weather-beaten old party
with a jolly, if sometimes silly, look to him and an oddly shaped
head. This last, which sat on his shoulders with almost no
evidence of any intervening neck, was remarkably full at the
jowls but tapered away from then on until it ended in
something resembling a point. This made it look much more

like a pineapple than most heads do, and just as that fruit had a few spiky leaves sticking up from its top so he had a tuft of grizzled, reddish hair. I wondered how he ever managed to keep his hats on and only discovered later that they had to be specially padded.

These things apart, the bald forehead, bulging light-blue eyes, receding chins and straining waistband had already told me who he really was. So after Cochrane had introduced me I bowed and said nothing. Mr Clarence looked at me pretty sharply, after which he got up and trotted round me two or three times for an overall view before he resumed his seat and said:

'So you're Dorothea Bunter's boy, hey?'

I bowed once more.

'D'you know who I am, hey?'

'If Lord Cochrane says that your Royal Highness is Mr Clarence then clearly Mr Clarence you must be.'

'Neatly put. He ain't entirely silly, Cochrane, is he?'

I thought he was coming it a bit seeing that he was known, even in his own family, as 'Silly Billy'. But I said nothing and let him carry on. Indeed, I couldn't have stopped him, for there never was a man so in love with the sound of his own voice.

'Did your Ma tell you that I was groomsman at her wedding?'

'She did once mention that fact, Sir.'

'Once! Why the Devil only once? It ain't often I act as groomsman. Only other time I did anything of that sort was way back in '87 at St Kitts when poor dear Nelson got married and I had to give Fanny Nisbet away. Damned if I can understand why your Ma mentioned me only once. I ain't someone to be ashamed of.'

'As I told you, Sir,' said Cochrane, 'Bunter's Ma has turned republican and feminist. She refuses to remember anyone she knew or anything she did in her Mary Anne Clarke days.'

'Can't say I blame her,' said Mr Clarence magnanimously. 'The way Fred treated her was enough to turn anyone republican: I'd have turned Jacobin myself. But Fred never did know how to handle women even though he handled a good many of 'em. I'll wager his Dorothea would never have turned republican if only he'd handled her half as gently as I handled mine.'

'Never knew you had a Dorothea as well,' said Lord Cochrane.

'Don't be a bloody fool. La Jordan was a Dorothea – Dorothea Bland to be precise. She only called herself Jordan after she'd crossed the water from Ireland. Bit of a pun, you see.'

'I see,' said Cochrane.

'I wasn't the first by any means,' said Mr Clarence, 'but there was no Mr Jordan among those who preceded me. In fact she never once got married.'

'Wouldn't have mattered to you if she had,' said Cochrane.

'No more it would. Thought of ourselves as husband and wife right from the moment when I set her up at Bushey to the moment when I had to leave her to search for a wife who might provide an heir to the throne. But do you know . . .' here he turned to me '. . . what me father said when he heard I was keeping Mrs Jordan?'

'No, Sir,' said I. Cochrane groaned to indicate that he'd heard all this before.

'That's all very well, Cochrane,' said Mr Clarence, 'but there are many who think it an excellent imitation.' Thereupon he stuck one hand behind his back, t'other into the breast of his coat, and said in a falsetto that would have made a parrot raise its eyebrows:

'Hey! Hey! What's this, what's this? You keep an actress, they say.'

'Yes, Sir,' said Mr Clarence in Mr Clarence's normal voice.

'Ah well! Ah well! How much do you give her, hey? Hey?'

'One thousand a year, Sir.'

'A thousand! A thousand! Too much! Too much! Five hundred quite enough. Quite enough.'

'And those,' said Mr Clarence, throwing the falsetto away,

'were the commands of one who was both monarch and parent. So what d'you think I did, hey?'

'Cut her down to five hundred?'

'Not on your Nelly. The Jordan was such an excellent, useful creature I couldn't bear to economise on her. She was highly domesticated for an actress: ran the house well and was a doting mother. Produced ten FitzClarences, reared eight, and still managed six or seven months on the boards between each one. Never was a woman like her for persistence and industry. So what else could I do but keep paying her in full until the money ran out?'

'And what,' I asked, 'happened when it did?'

'Why then,' said Mr Clarence, 'she paid me. Until she got too old to play romping young Misses and too fat to play Principal Boys she earned more as an actress than I did as Lord High Admiral.'

'I recall,' said Cochrane, breaking into the conversation, 'that someone – it may have been Home – wrote a squib about it.'

'Home, hey? Well he was rude enough about George and Fred so what did he write about me?'

'So far as I remember,' said Cochrane, 'it ran something like this:

'As Jordan's high and mighty squire
Her playhouse profits deigns to skim,
Some folks audaciously enquire
If *he* keeps her, or *she* keeps him.'

'Splendid! Splendid!' cried Mr Clarence, somewhat to my surprise. 'Couldn't have put it any better meself. Didn't I tell you she was an excellent, generous, hard-working creature? And didn't we just Darby and Joan it all those years! And wasn't I right to do my best by her and the children, whatever my father ordered, and however often the Commons refused to increase my allowance pay off my debts?'

'You were lucky to find her,' said Cochrane, in what I thought a grudging tone. 'She gave you a good deal more than those black whores you were so fond of when you were on the West Indies station. All they ever gave you was the pox.'

Mr Clarence ignored this and said to me: 'Ah, Bunter-me-boy, if only Fred had done as much for you and your Ma as I have done for Jordan and the children, you would not now have to be running a chop-house. None of the eight FitzClarences have to run chop-houses.'

'It ain't a chop-house,' said Cochrane, defending his investment. 'It's an Indian Serai.'

'And what could be better than that?' said Mr Clarence in the voice of a man wholly unprepared to quarrel with anyone. 'I haven't had a decent pilau or a proper curry since I was on the East India station in the old *Pegasus*, and that was nearly forty years ago. *Eheu*, Bunter, *tempus fugaces* etcetera. I was young enough and game enough then for anything *les dames de couleur* could provide.'

With which the foul-mouthed old whoremonger started on a detailed account of what *les dames de couleur* had provided that I found so lurid that I excused myself on the grounds of having to see to their dinner. As I left, Lord Cochrane gave me a triumphant wink. He knew, as I did, that he had now more than made up for all the half-pay captains and seedy Radical politicians Buttercup had grumbled about. Mr Clarence might be a hoary old sinner, but he was no more than a death rattle away from being the next King of England. As such, and as a customer of Bunter's Indian Serai, he could do more to bring the nobs and snobs flocking back to 83 Jermyn Street than anyone else in the British Isles.

I saw to it then that the two of them had the best dinner and the best wines ever served to anyone at Bunter's. Mr Clarence, according to Gurmakh Singh who waited on them, ate and drank for two and was now concentrating on the brandy. He had also sent for me. 'I am thinking,' said Gurmakh Singh, 'that he is wanting to thank Bunter Sahib for tip-top grub.' Mr Clarence was pretty well done up when I arrived, but was nevertheless bullying Lord Cochrane for not drinking level with himself.

'I see some of God Almighty's daylight in that glass,' he was saying. 'Banish it.'

He may have forgotten who I was, for he looked puzzled at first. Then he said, 'I remember you. You're Fred's bastard and look it. But I can't remember your name.'

'Bunter, William Bunter, Sir.'

'Of course it is, and Dorothea Bunter was your Ma, was she not?'

'She still is, Sir, although I haven't seen her these ten years past.'

'You don't look much like her. You ain't handsome enough for a Bunter. But you're more than ugly enough for a Guelph. Damme if you don't remind me strongly of Fred when he was your age, though he weren't as fat as you and didn't need glasses.'

The memory of Fred when he was my age so upset him that he needed a glass of brandy before he could proceed. But he was still concerned with inherited likenesses, and carefully explained to Cochrane the dominance of Guelph blood.

'No one can claim,' said he, 'that we don't stamp our progeny, legitimate or otherwise, though there ain't many of the former in this generation, only little Vicky. She's Guelph all through, however, and the spitting image of Edward, or will be if ever she goes bald.'

'I hope,' said Cochrane, 'she will be spared that.'

'At any rate,' said Mr Clarence viciously, 'she don't look much like her bitch of a mother.'

I wasn't brought up to be a courtier and was getting tired of standing there at Mr Clarence's elbow listening to his twaddle about the Guelphs, so I said: 'You sent for me, Sir?'

'Did I?' he looked puzzled for a moment, poured himself some more brandy, belched, and then said, quite unexpectedly: 'You're Fred's bastard and bear the same name as meself, so I shall call you Billy when we are in private.'

I wouldn't have said there was a good deal of privacy at that moment for all the other customers were straining to hear what was being said and Mr Clarence neither spoke nor belched *sotto voce*. But since it was all to the good that others should hear as much as they could so long as they subsequently repeated it all to their friends, I bowed and waited for him to continue. Instead of doing so he looked long and mournfully at me until, in the end, two large tears ran down his cheeks. If they had been collected and tested they would, no doubt, have proved to be ninety per cent alcohol. But what had given rise to the other ten per cent wasn't clear.

'I am,' he said at last, 'thoroughly upset.'

'Our curries,' said I, 'must have been too much for you. But we have, on the premises, a most commodious water closet of the very latest type. I shall have Gurmakh Singh show it to you . . .'

'Bugger your water closet and bugger Gurmakh Singh,' he roared. 'Your curries were very well, and have nothing to do with it. I ain't upset in me guts: I'm upset in me family feelings. I don't care to have even one of Fred's bastards running a chop-house.'

'Serai,' said Lord Cochrane.

'You hold your tongue, Cochrane,' said Mr Clarence. 'This is between me and Bunter.'

'I have to earn my living, Sir,' said I.

'No Guelph ever did that, whether he was a bastard or not. Fred really should have provided for you, even if it was only with a bishopric or a seat in Parliament. Damme if I won't do something for you meself just as soon as the time comes.'

'But I don't want to be a bishop or a . . .'

'Mark you,' said Mr Clarence, ignoring my intervention entirely, 'it won't be anything in the money line, however I'm placed. I never have money enough for the FitzClarences, let alone the Bunters. And at the present moment I can't do much in any other line. But the time will come. The time will come.'

As he thought about the time that was to come when his brother George would be in the grave and he would be on the throne Mr Clarence seemed to forget that I had upset him by keeping a chop-house. Indeed he seemed to forget who I was entirely and he nodded me my dismissal as cheerfully as though I didn't have a distinct look of the late Duke of York and as though he himself had never acted as groomsman at my mother's wedding. He had, in the inconsequential way of drunks, suddenly remembered another toast. So he told Cochrane to re-charge his glass, rose unsteadily to his feet, held his own glass dangerously aloft and said:

'I give you *les yeux qui tuent, les fesses qui remuent, et le cul qui danse, honi soit qui mal y pense.*'

He then poured the best part of a quarter of a pint of brandy down his throat. In the silence that had fallen over the crowded restaurant Mr Clarence's voice, though somewhat slurred, carried far – as far, indeed, as the Zenana Room. For it was from there that, after a few seconds, the sound of giggling could be heard followed by a clear female voice calling out 'Bravo!' Mr Clarence kissed his fingers in the direction of the voice and this seemed to remind the male diners of their duty, for they, too, joined in a chorus of Bravos. One or two of 'em – there were a good many of the unlisted that night – started to clap. One tall, thin, very tipsy stockbroker remembering, in the way that tipsy men do, Mr Clarence's naval connections, started to sing 'Hearts of Oak'.

All of this seemed to excite Mr Clarence who blew kisses all round, placed his hand on his heart, bowed and, unable to recover himself, slipped to the floor where he straightway fell asleep.

'Best thing he could do,' said Lord Cochrane. 'Otherwise he'd have begun to remember all the other smutty toasts he'd learnt in his youth in half a dozen different wardrooms and three times as many bordellos.'

'That's as may be,' said I, 'but we can't leave him there.'

'I don't suppose we can,' said Lord Cochrane.

So Gurmakh Singh and three waiters took a limb apiece and, amid respectful murmurs from the other alcoves, the four of them carried the now snoring Mr Clarence out to his carriage. That, by-the-by, was a new-fangled, two-horse, four-wheeled affair with a hood, and windows that wound up and down,

which the coachmaker who'd designed it had called a Clarence
in the old soak's honour.

One visit from Mr Clarence, once news of it had spread, would
have been quite enough to bring the nobs and snobs streaming
back to the Serai. Mr Clarence, however, was not content with
a single visit. Every now and again a message would come from
Bushey to reserve an alcove for Mr Clarence and friend or
friends. Indeed this happened often enough for him to become
what could almost be described as a regular Jermyn Street
attraction. Whenever he came and whoever he came with the
proceedings were nearly always the same. At some stage he
would send for me to discuss, more or less soberly, the things he
would do for me, other than in the money line, once he was in a
position to do anything for anyone. After that it was always
gobble, guzzle, toasts and bawdry until Mr Clarence had either
to be carried or led to his carriage.

But it was Mr Clarence, and Mr Clarence alone, who put the
Jermyn Street National and Imperial Investment Company
back into profit. The business he attracted to the Serai,
however, gave me a deal more work than I had time or stomach
for. So I began to think of engaging someone who would, by
acting as secretary, personal assistant and general factotum,
take some of the burden off me.

I hadn't long been thinking along these lines when, of all
people, who should pop up in Bedford Square but one of my old
sparring partners who should still have been in India! I was at
breakfast when Gurmakh Singh showed him in, and he was so
changed that I couldn't, at first, work out who he was. For the
school bully who had persecuted me at Christ's Hospital had been
a handsome, smart, brash young cockerel; the young subaltern
who had travelled out to India on the same ship as myself had
been even brasher, smarter and handsomer; but the seedy hang-
dog-looking fellow with frayed cuffs and cracked shoes who stood
timidly in the doorway was none of these things. Indeed, it wasn't
until I noticed his lop ear that I recognised a bit of Bunter's
handiwork and remembered Horace Augustus Coker.

I also remembered, with a growing funk, that I was responsible for some at least of his battered appearance. Not only had I damaged his ear in some crossing-the-Line horse-play. His sidling gait and lop-arse were due to the large slice I had cut out of one of his buttocks when we had all – incorrectly – thought he was suffering from a cobra bite. And if he was still missing the tip of his pecker, it was because I had shot it off in a duel he had forced on me, a duel in which he couldn't see straight, being drugged, and I couldn't see at all because I had my eyes shut.

He'd always been vain and he'd always disliked me, so it wasn't strange when these alterations I'd made to his looks, gait and performance turned that dislike into hatred. Indeed, he had chased me clean across India, a year or two earlier, howling for my blood. My first thought, therefore, was that he must still be howling for it.

I had a knife and fork in my hands, a white napkin around my neck and a great steaming dish of sausages, bacon and buttered eggs in front of me. When I at last realised who he was, I jumped to my feet wondering whether I should dive for the window or go for the poker when he rushed me. But he didn't seem to be in a rushing mood. He stood there in the doorway with his eyes glaring, not at Bunter, but the sausages. His nostrils twitched as the smell of the bacon got to him and, all in all, he had the look of a man who hadn't had his breakfast, or, for that matter, his dinner and supper, for a few days at least. So I sat down again and said:

'Care for some breakfast, Coker?'

'Do you mean that?' said he.

I speared a sausage and looked at it. 'There are more of these than I can manage. Pull up a chair and I'll ring for another plate.'

'I say, Bunter, that's most awfully decent of you,' he said, and then started to blub.

I took the napkin from my neck, tossed it to him, and said: 'Mop yourself and don't let the sausages get cold.'

He sat down, still blubbering, and said between sobs: 'Such

kindness . . . quite undeserved . . . must forget old scores . . . only one to whom I could turn . . . God bless you my old . . .' and then, unable to contain himself, he reached for a sausage.

And that was how I turned an old enemy fallen upon hard times into the most supportive, willing and industrious personal assistant any busy man of affairs could wish to have.

As the spring of 1830 passed into early summer, rumours of a worsening in the King's health multiplied. He was, they said, so bloated with the dropsy that he had to be tapped as regularly as a beer barrel, but not even tapping, brandy and laudanum could keep him going for very much longer. Everyone (except the Tories) looked forward, therefore, to celebrating, first a royal funeral and then a coronation. When Lord Melbourne and Mr Clarence dined together at the Serai one day towards the end of June it seemed to me that Mr Clarence must be the only man in London who wasn't wondering when the old voluptuary at Windsor would call it a day.

The two had reached that stage of the dinner where general, even serious conversation had not yet given way to toasts and talking dirty. They were, Heaven knows why, discussing authors.

'Authors,' said Mr Clarence, 'are greatly over-rated creatures, which is why they give themselves such insufferably high-and-mighty airs.'

'There I agree with you, Sir,' said Lord Melbourne, and I, hovering nearby, wondered whether he was thinking of Lord Byron.

Mr Clarence considered this question of authors whilst he chewed on another mouthful of roast spiced peacock. 'I know no person,' he finally said, 'so perfectly disagreeable and even dangerous as an author.'

'It is an excellent thing, Sir, when these authors die.'

'Of course it is. It means one scribbler the less.'

'Unfortunately not. They breed like flies. But once they're dead someone will bring out their Collected Works which you put on a top shelf and then you've done with 'em.'

At this moment Mr Clarence's coachman, who was also something of a crony of his, came into the restaurant and rushing up to his master whispered something in his ear.

'Bunter,' said Mr Clarence, grinning all over his face, 'will you fetch me my hat?'

'There are curries and other dishes to come, Sir . . .'

'My hat.'

So I went and got his white beaver. He fished in his coat pocket, brought out a length of wide black ribbon, fastened this round the hat leaving the two ends to act as streamers, got to his feet, and for the first time in all his visits to Bunter's, walked out sober to his carriage.

As he reached it he turned to me and said: 'Shan't be able to come here any more, Billy, but mark my words, I'll not forget you.'

'I trust, Sir,' said I, 'that nothing in Bunter's Indian Serai has suddenly displeased you.'

'Nothing in the least displeasing, I assure you. That spiced peacock, quite excellent. But I've just heard that Georgey has snuffed it, so I'm off to Windsor. And d'you know, Billy' – here he gave me a kindly pat on the shoulder – 'the only sad thing about today is that it will be difficult for me to be Mr Clarence again. And that means, my boy, it will be difficult for me to go into an eating-house again . . .' he thought for a moment and added '. . . or, for that matter, a whorehouse. And yet the happiest moments of my life have been spent in the one or the other. But no matter, no matter: one must be philosophical and remember that it ain't every day that a chap learns he's become King.'

With that he got into his Clarence and went off to Windsor smiling fit to bust.

Mr Clarence was as good as his word. Immediately after his coronation there was published in the Gazette a preliminary list of those tradesmen who were immediately entitled as warrant holders to put on their signs the royal coat of arms and the inscription 'By Appointment to His Majesty King William the Fourth'. Bunter's Indian Serai came first on that list and, so far as I know, was the only restaurant, Indian or otherwise, ever to be so honoured.

14 *Disappointment*

I now found that one or two of the problems of success were no easier to solve than the problems of failure. The Serai flourished and, because it did, I began to have staff troubles. Since there now wasn't an alcove in the restaurant, a table in the Zenana Room, or a bed in the hotel that was ever unoccupied, my staff was increasingly overworked. I couldn't relieve them by immediately hiring extra cooks and waiters as I had already hired every suitable Indian in London who was hireable. I did toy with the idea of hiring Italians or, at a pinch, Englishmen, putting them into Indian clothes and applying brown boot polish, but I soon realised that this could destroy the unique character of the Serai.

I knew, in the long term, that the problem was soluble. Gurmakh Singh had an abundance of relatives back in Sumroo and he had assured me that they, like almost every other Sikh in the Punjaub, would jump at any chance of emigrating to Bilatee. I consequently decided to consult Captain Manning when he next docked in London about the cost of shipping me further supplies of Singhs. But meanwhile, and in the short term, we were badly understaffed, which meant that such staff as I did have were dissatisfied and grumbling. This was particularly the case with Gurmakh Singh himself whom I had been obliged to demote from his largely ceremonial and dignified duties and set to work on more menial ones in the Zenana Room, where he was now the only waiter.

This was because ever since the bottom-pinching incident no waiter in the least pinchable would agree to serve there. Only Gurmakh Singh looked old enough and fierce enough to be pinchproof. And so, willy-nilly, he was set to waiting on the Memsahibs. But there were now so many of these Memsahibs, all of 'em members of Almack's and so eligible for Bunter's, that I soon had to admit to Gurmakh Singh that he would have to be given assistants. So, feeling as Ney must have done when he threw in the Old Guard at Waterloo, I moved the daughters-in-law from their near-nominal duties in the kitchen to far more than nominal duties in the Zenana Room.

Unfortunately they had been so long away from Sumroo as to have lost the habit of hard work, and this meant that they found all the trotting backwards and forwards with heavy trays extremely exhausting. It also meant that, sturdy though they were, they were too weary by the time they got back to Bedford Square to do anything but fall into bed and sleep. They didn't even have the energy to play for a few minutes with the little Bunterkins who were now in their second editions. Far less did they have the energy to press me into collaborating with them in the production of third editions, but for that I was thankful.

They, however, were not in the least thankful. What they resented even more than the hard and exhausting work was that, whilst they sweated in Jermyn Street, Maria remained a lady of leisure in Bedford Square. Their resentment seemed to increase proportionately to the increase in Maria's girth. For she, having exacted from me my annual tribute, was now well on the way towards producing her own second edition of Bunter.

How deeply they felt about this was brought into the open one fine summer evening in August when the swallows were swooping over Bedford Square and the sparrows were still squabbling with the starlings over the horse droppings. I was in my study giving Coker his orders – I had put him in charge of food purchasing – when Ghulabi and Fyzoo just back from Jermyn Street burst in on us.

'We have come to tell you, Bunter Sahib, that we are not slaves,' said Fyzoo.

'No more,' said Ghulabi, 'than Maria Begum is a slave.'

'Maria Begum,' said Fyzoo, 'does not have to go every day to Jermyn Street to wait on skinny, bad-tempered, loud-voiced Angrezi women.'

'Maria Begum,' said Ghulabi, 'has time and energy for the sweeter things of life.'

'All we have time and energy for is to trot, trot, trot with heavy trays from kitchen to Zenana Room and back,' said Fyzoo who still had energy enough to prance up and down with her arms stretched out in front of her to demonstrate to me what she meant by trot, trot, trot.

'Too much jogajog, no jigajig,' said Ghulabi, who was always the more practical of the two.

This last must have been the nub of their grievance, for they now drew breath, although they continued to look alarmingly fierce.

'You must,' I said, 'be patient. I shall soon be sending to Sumroo for further supplies of Singhs. As soon as these arrive the two of you can go back to your supervisory work in the kitchens.'

'And will we then,' demanded Fyzoo, 'be able to make more Bunterkins?'

'If that is what you want,' I said and shuddered.

'We want,' they said in unison, and went up to bed.

'Phew!' said Coker. 'Talk about fishwives.'

I said nothing, but mopped my brow. It was, as I've said, a fine, warm evening.

'I tell you what, old chap,' Coker went on, 'you oughtn't to let yourself be bullied like that. You're far too soft with 'em. It's your kind heart letting you down again.'

'Do you think so?'

'Sticks out a mile. You never did learn how to deal with Indians. Why don't you leave 'em to me? The Bengal Army taught me how to handle 'em, and that was a school you never went to.'

'They ain't sepoys, you know. You might find them more difficult to handle than you expect.'

'Not me – elementary exercise in man-management . . . and woman-management. Nothing simpler. Good discipline, clear orders clearly given, clean latrines and see the beer canteen is closed early on Saturday nights.'

'That don't sound particularly relevant to my problems.'

'Of course it ain't. Merely an example of how straightfor-wardly the military mind works. That's what those two bibis need – straightforward handling. So do the rest of 'em.'

'Well,' I said not very whole-heartedly, 'we could try it.'

'Splendid, old chap, I owe it to you to take some of the burden off your shoulders. Besides which I want to show you what an old chum can do.'

I never thought to hear Coker describe himself as a chum, but his doing so finally convinced me that a spot of the Bunter magnanimity generally pays in the end. And it was certainly a fact that, as soon as Coker took over staff management, the grumbling stopped, waiters scurried where they had formerly strolled, Gurmakh Singh sprang to attention every time I looked at him, and Ghulabi and Fyzoo trot, trot, trotted about contentedly and smiled at Coker no matter what orders he gave them.

The old King had snuffed it towards the end of June 1830 which meant that a royal funeral, a coronation, and a general election all had to follow. These kept people in London who would otherwise have been taking the waters or travelling abroad prior to travelling from country house to country house in order to shoot quite small birds and commit adultery. Now that the new King was known to be the Serai's patron, and that half the new Cabinet were among its more constant customers, it attracted as many nobs and snobs in those late summer days as it did at the height of the Season. It was truly the Serai's *annus mirabilis*.

The late King's artistic temperament had attracted him to all forms of pageantry and ceremonial. Just as he had himself invented most of his coronation ceremony so he had now left detailed instructions for his lying-in-state and funeral. In all such matters he had displayed more good taste than you could find in any three confectioners or pastry cooks taken together. The burial, therefore, was a very splendid and highly expensive affair. Some said the new King looked altogether too cheerful for the occasion and chatted away to everyone as though they had gathered for a jolly drink rather than an interment. But there weren't many in the country who had liked the old King while most of 'em were ready to like the new one.

This was partly because he had been a sailor (always a popular calling in Britain) and had announced that he would like to be popularly known as 'Our Royal Jack Tar'. But it was also because he was rumoured to be a man of liberal tendencies and had no objection to being known, alternatively, as 'The People's Willum'. What being a liberal means I have never properly discovered. Some say it means encouraging the lower classes to believe that they have unlimited rights, whereas non-liberals would encourage them to believe that they only have unlimited duties. As I'm proud to say that I know nothing about politics and haven't one drop of liberalism in my veins I can't say whether this is a sufficient definition or not. But I've not yet met a self-confessed liberal who didn't pride himself on being more moral than everyone else, or who would allow anyone the right to dispute that belief, or would ever consider that he himself had a duty occasionally to question it.

That, however, is by the way. Meanwhile 'The People's Willum' was cheered all the way back to London, and had to make the journey leaning out of the carriage window alternatively spitting, as had always been his habit, and waving to his recently acquired and loyal subjects lining the roadside. But those same subjects found less to applaud when it came to the coronation. If his predecessor had spent like a drunken sailor on that ceremony, he spent like a sober one. What had cost Georgey a cool quarter of a million cost Billy less than one-tenth of that sum. This meant that, after a shabby sort of show at the Abbey, mighty few of his subjects were given an opportunity to feast and booze at the Royal Tar's expense, and that was regretted by all ranks of society.

I don't rightly know whether the Almack's Project was conceived in order to emphasise King Billy's penny-pinching or to atone for it. The first I heard of that project was from Lord Palmerston, who came blustering into the Serai one day at the end of, I think, November, and said to me:

'Bunter, Emily . . .' by which he meant Lady Cowper . . . 'has just told me that the Lady Patronesses of Almack's have decided on a project which could be of considerable interest to you. She wants to consult you about it, so see that you're at the Russian Embassy, 36 Harley Street, at three o'clock this afternoon precisely.'

I blinked at him though my spectacles and said in tones that doubtless expressed my surprise: 'But why the Russian Embassy, my Lord?'

'The Princess Lieven, as you know, is wife of the Russian Ambassador besides being one of the Lady Patronesses. She has been asked, on both accounts, to collaborate with Emily on this project.'

If I was surprised when Princess Lieven's name was mentioned, I was positively alarmed when Lady Cowper's cropped up. Although she was Lord Cowper's wife, Lord Palmerston's *maîtresse-en-titre* and would never see forty again she was still, as I discovered after the bottom-pinching affair, remarkably flirtatious. So even though she was one of the best customers the Zenana Room had, I found it necessary to treat her with a great deal of reserve and refuse all invitations to meet her anywhere outside the Serai.

With the Princess Lieven the situation was quite otherwise. The poor lady, as a consequence of having been brought up in the semi-Oriental and entirely feudal setting of the Russian court, was an old-fashioned snob and as such quite incapable of understanding the more free-and-easy snobberies of a modern democracy. She alone, of all the Lady Patronesses, had decreed that it was decidedly *mauvais ton* for any female member of Almack's to be seen entering an eating-house even when that eating-house was the very exclusive Bunter's Indian Serai. She was, therefore, the only Lady Patroness, and very nearly the only female member of Almack's I had never met.

My alarm and surprise must have shown. But Palmerston, fortunately perhaps, got the thing arsey-tarsey and thought that it was being summoned to Princess Lieven's that alarmed me. So it was in respect of the Russian and not the English lady that he hurried to provide reassurance.

'Don't worry, Bunter,' said he. '*You* won't be in any danger from La Lieven I assure you. It ain't as if you're on a par with the others.'

'What others?'

'Grand Duke Constantine; Prinny; your . . . the late Duke of York; Metternich; Wellington; Canning; and now Grey and, if I'm not careful, meself, not to mention others of equal importance. But you ain't of equal importance, which is why you'll be safe.'

'Praise be and Amen to that,' said I. 'But what would happen to me if I were?'

'Were what?'

'Of equal importance.'

'That would depend on whether your importance was equal enough to influence our foreign policy.'

'And if it could?'

He looked me up and down, grinned, and said: 'In your case she'd probably have to think extra hard about Russia before becoming your mistress.'

'Why think about Russia at all?'

'She's a patriot. And she never commits adultery until she can be certain she's doing it for the Tsar.'

But when I presented myself at 36 Harley Street I found that I need not have worried over how either of the ladies would receive me. I found Princess Lieven amiable, Lady Cowper businesslike and not even a whiff of hauteur or randiness from either of 'em. For as it turned out, what they wished to talk to me about was nothing more surprising or alarming than banquets.

'As you know, my dear Mr Bunter,' said Lady Cowper, 'there's not been one State banquet this year even though it is coronation year.'

'Coronation!' said the Princess, looking disdainfully down her long sharp nose. '*Quelle blague!* How can one describe a ceremony so *mesquin, tellement parcimonieux*, so altogether lacking in any *grandeur*, as a coronation?'

'That is why,' said Lady Cowper, ignoring the interruption, 'we – that is to say the Lady Patronesses – have decided that we must give a small, private, and very select coronation banquet of our own.'

'But not,' said her colleague, 'at Almack's.'

'Almack's,' Lady Cowper explained, 'is very well for balls and routs and masquerades, and for late suppers and early breakfasts and suchlike, but it ain't really up to banquets.'

'*Dites-moi*, Monsieur Buntaire,' said the Princess. '*Dans les Indes*, do they have banquets?'

'They do indeed,' said I, remembering all the banqueting Bishop Heber and I had suffered from in our tour of India.

'But are they really what we in England would call banquets?' asked Lady Cowper.

I remembered the elaborate ceremonial, the seemingly interminable courses, the profusion of gold and silver, the multitude of servants, the nautch girls, acrobats, conjurors and musicians even the least important Raja or Nawab thought necessary for quite small and low-class banquets.

'I really think they are,' said I.

The three of us then got down to it. Obviously they were after the Serai for their banquet, but why they should want an Indian setting and an Indian banquet puzzled me. So, after they had told me how many ambassadors, Cabinet ministers, dukes, bishops and so on, with or without their ladies, I would have to cater for, I asked, straight out:

'But why an Indian banquet? And why Bunter's?'

They looked at one another for a while. Then Lady Cowper shrugged her shoulders and said: 'It's the Bunter part rather than the Indian part that's important.'

'May I know why?'

'To give a coronation banquet without the King would be like playing *Romeo and Juliet* without Romeo. But ours will be a private coronation banquet, and so the King, if he comes, can only come in his private capacity.'

'You mean,' said I, beginning to understand, 'as Mr Clarence?'

'Precisely,' said Lady Cowper. 'And as Mr Clarence has so frequently patronised your establishment we hope you can persuade him to patronise it once more. After all you have it above the door that you are "By Appointment".'

'And,' said Princess Lieven, with what would have been a knowing look if she'd not had such a habit of looking down her nose at everything, 'he would, in a manner of speaking, be banqueting *en famille*.'

'But why,' I asked, 'depend on me? Surely you could invite him yourselves.'

'In earlier days,' said Lady Cowper with great dignity, 'I had to push Mr Clarence off a sofa. He was, of course, only another of the fat and amorous Royal Dukes in those days.'

'And I,' said Princess Lieven, 'had to do something very similar to him in a carriage.'

'In a carriage?' cried a shocked Lady Cowper.

'He had insisted on escorting me home and put his arm around my waist to demonstrate his affection and respect for me. But he then added that, as a liberal, he could not feel the same towards the Tsar. So it was . . . Poof!' And, with a shrug of her shoulders and a wave of her arm, poor liberal Clarence was, metaphorically speaking, swept away.

'That's why,' said Lady Cowper, 'it would be unproductive if either of us approached the King. But everyone knows that you and your Serai are great favourites of his. So, if we are responsible for the banquet, will you, dear Mr Bunter, be responsible for Mr Clarence?'

At our next Company Meeting I was able to tell the shareholders that Mr Clarence had graciously consented to be the guest of honour; that the Zenana Room had been turned into an Indian pavilion with the aid of several hundred yards of muslin and dozens of Oriental rugs; that we were preparing an Indian feast of such richness and diversity as had never before been seen in London; that all the staff had been put into spanking new Indian liveries and that half a dozen of them had agreed to ask their wives if they would be willing to perform as nautch girls at the end of the proceedings. And to round it all I told them that, after some haggling, the Lady Patronesses had agreed to an all-in price of two thousand guineas.

It was that last bit that made them applaud and their applause so added to my native cockiness that I felt I must share with them a quite splendid idea that had just come into my mind.

'That the Serai should have been chosen for the only event of this coronation year worthy of being called a banquet is evidence of how successful the Serai concept has been. It has given London a taste of India that London likes. But there are more cities in this world than London, and ours is a concept that won't be held up by frontiers. Why shouldn't there be a Bunter's Indian Serai in Paris? In Rome? In Berlin? Yes, even in New York once that city has achieved the stature deserving of a Serai? Buttercup! Gentlemen! I shall soon offer you an opportunity to invest on a truly global scale. The world could be our oyster. Let us set about currying it.'

They applauded even more enthusiastically and Buttercup came across and gave me a hug a Turkish wrestler would have been proud of.

I beamed at them. Seldom have I felt cockier. Yet that cockiness should have been a warning to me.

The pavilion inside the Zenana Room was looking opulently and authentically Indian. The food was unsurpassable. The staff behaved perfectly and looked very well in their new liveries. The guests were as resplendent in their diamonds, feathers and uniforms as though the banquet were being held at Windsor rather than in Bunter's Indian Serai and, whilst they showed an increasing appreciation of each dish that had been served, they also showed an increasing curiosity about those yet to come.

Mr Clarence, not unexpectedly, did himself rather too well and we hadn't yet reached the dessert when he stood up, a little unsteadily, and gave every indication of being about to embark on one of those interminable oratorical rambles he loved so dearly. His audience resigned itself to half an hour of torpor, but he hadn't even finished his preliminaries when he first hesitated and then stopped. Lady Palmerston, who was on his left, made encouraging noises and Princess Lieven, who was on his right, poured him another glass of champagne, but neither availed. He suddenly turned extremely pale, put a hand on his waistcoat and let loose a fart that Pantagruel would have admired and Gargantua would not have despised.

But it threw Mr Clarence right out of his stride and brought his speech to an abrupt close. He looked wildly around, turned, and rushed out of the room clutching his waistcoat and calling for his carriage. A couple of minutes later he had left the Serai without so much as a fare-you-well or a thankee to anyone. This, not unnaturally, was taken as a royal signal for all to depart, which they did, and for the most part in silence.

Coker had got into the habit of calling at Bedford Square most mornings at breakfast time, and if this meant I had to share my bacon and eggs with him, it also meant that he shared the news of the day with me, for he was a great reader of the news sheets and collector of gossip. When he turned up the second morning after the banquet he was wearing a very long face indeed. He had heard a rumour that the cholera morbus was in town again and that many of those who had attended the banquet were laid low with it. The news he brought the next morning was both more definite and more disturbing. It was being said that the King could not last the week, that the Cabinet had been unable to meet, that the *corps diplomatique* was *hors de combat*, and that there wasn't one Lady Patroness still on her feet.

This threw me into something very close to a panic. When so

many I had mingled with on the night of the banquet had succumbed to it, how could I hope to escape the cholera morbus? But the next day Coker brought slightly more reassuring reports. The doctors were no longer certain that it was the cholera even though every invalid without exception was suffering from a severe and continuing flux. It wasn't until the following week that, to my great relief, they all showed signs of recovering. Indeed the King's physician let it slip in private that his patient had never suffered anything worse than a bad attack of the merry-go-whimbles.

But the merry-go-whimbles, or, to put it less whimsically, the squitters, is caused, as everyone knows, by food poisoning, and everything suddenly pointed to the food consumed at the Almack's coronation banquet. Rumours about the outlandish ingredients put into Indian food, about the habits of Indian cooks and the state of kitchens in the Serai multiplied until I began to wish that it had been the cholera morbus.

I quickly had to accept that these rumours were destroying my trade, and when I next reported to the shareholders I told them that, for weeks on end, the restaurant had never been even as much as half full, and then the customers were of a class Gurmakh Singh would in happier days have turned away at first glance. To complete our misery, Lord Cochrane produced a copy of the *Gazette* published that day. In it there was an announcement from St James's that the Royal Warrant issued to the establishment that went under the name of Bunter's Indian Serai was summarily withdrawn. In short, Mr Clarence had dis-appointed me.

It would be to understate the case to say that the shareholders were perturbed. Lord Cochrane and J.J. immediately wanted their money back. Captain Manning said it was a shame, but he was prepared to wait and see. Buttercup burst into tears. But Coker, to my surprise, stood up and spoke out boldly in defence of Bunter and Bunter's Serai, declaring he was sure the food poisoning hadn't been caused by the banquet and, if it had been, it hadn't been Mr Bunter's fault and, even if it was, this was no time to abandon ship, but we must all put our shoulders to the wheel and pull together for it was a faint heart that gave up at the first reverse whereas fortune would always favour the bold, together with a number of other similar adages and clichés.

By the time he had done I had tears in my eyes. If this was what a man who had once been Bunter's enemy now thought of Bunter, then Bunter must rise to the occasion. I felt cockiness slowly creeping back into my veins and my mind began to entertain any number of new wheezes. I told Buttercup to stop her snivelling, and read them all what was in part a lecture and in part my latest vision of the future.

'None of us,' I told them, 'can recover our money as things stand today. It is all tied up in an Indianised bit of Jermyn Street which, if we put it on the market, would find no buyers. It has now, I concede, failed us as a Serai. That don't mean, however, that we can't put it to other uses. We still have a kitchen and we still have a full staff of Indians. If the uses we put them to are no longer profitable, let us, as reasonable people, now put them to uses that are.'

'What uses would those be?' asked Cochrane belligerently.

'Until recently, my Lord, we have made a deal of money out of catering for the few. But the few, my Lord, are fickle. They flock to us when we are in the fashion and desert us when we are not. You are a sailor, my Lord. You will understand what I mean when I say it's time to change tack.'

'Change tack by all means, my bold, fat skipper. But at least let us know where your bows will then be pointing.'

'Towards the common people, my Lord, which is something you, as a Radical, will surely approve of. I've had enough of trying to please the nobs and the snobs. I propose to convert the ordinary people of this country to curry.'

Once a wheeze has got stuck in my mind I can usually persuade myself as much as others that it is the best possible solution to whatever problem is in hand. This time, however, I failed to persuade all my shareholders of the value of my scheme for taking curries to the lower and lower-middle classes. This may have had less to do with the merits of that scheme than with the windiness of my shareholders. For if the scheme lost money they would, as members of a joint-stock company, be singly and severally liable to the creditors for every penny that was owed. On the other hand if it made money they suspected that, because of my passion for expansion, it would be a long time before any of it would be left to fructify in their pockets.

So all of 'em except Buttercup decided to make their first loss their last one, and each of 'em, therefore, sold me his shares for a nominal ten guineas. Captain Manning did this regretfully, but he couldn't afford the loss, whereas J.J. and Lord Cochrane, who could, blackguarded me mercilessly as they scuttled from under. Buttercup, muttering that 'in for a penny was in for a pound, and love not cash made the world go round,' took me to bed with her.

Although the Serai only catered now for the unlisted and as a consequence was losing money, I dared not shut it down. For one thing I did not want to alarm my creditors. For another I would need it as a central production unit for my plan for feeding curries to the masses. I had to have a certain amount of new capital before that plan could be launched but, by not paying my bills, by selling off the Bedford Square plate and pictures, and by borrowing from Buttercup, I raised enough for a trial run.

Coker knew the situation and swore he'd stand by me.

Gurmakh Singh and the daughters-in-law who as yet didn't, carried on as usual. Which, as I needed them more than ever before if my scheme was to succeed, was a blessing.

That scheme was based, very largely, on my understanding of the current state of Britain. The country was in the middle of a deep economic depression. The social and political consequences of this – the rioting, rick-burning, loom-smashing and threats of revolution – were no concern of mine for if I couldn't look after myself in a republic just as well as I could under King Billy, my name wasn't William Bunter.

What did interest me greatly, however, was the effect these things had on the domestic economies of the poor. If a family was to survive in these times of low wages and dear food then, whether they lived in a farm cottage or a town slum, every member who could work had to work. This meant that no one had the time or energy left for cooking, and that, in its turn, meant that they had very largely to live on what they could buy and carry away from the baker, the cookshop and the food stall,

But these items were dear, partly because flour was dear and partly because most of the other cooked foods the poor could buy to eat at their convenience were prepared by traders who operated on the smallest scale, enjoyed none of the benefits of mass selling, and so had no savings to pass on to the consumer. In terms of what they were, the hot mutton pies, the stewed cows' cheeks, the boiled tripe and the jellied eels were priced as luxuries even though the raw materials would, if bought and prepared in bulk, represent no more than farthings per portion.

Moreover, when it came to the bulky part of a poor man's diet, rice was a more filling and much cheaper food than bread. I remembered how, at every Indian street corner, there would be an Indian squatting behind a couple of braziers and putting portions of steaming-hot rice on to banyan leaves, adding, by way of a relish, a spoonful of curry sauce and, perhaps, another of vegetable pickle. This would then be sold for a very few pice to innumerable passers-by, all of whom seemed quite content to make it their main and perhaps only meal of the day.

'Bunter,' I told myself as I thought about this, 'if you can convert the British working man to something similar and can sell it cheap enough, you'll not only make a fortune, you'll also be a national benefactor. For, although the Indian poor are much poorer than any British poor, they are also a deal less mutinous, and it could be that the blandness of their boiled rice produces an equal blandness in their natures. What wouldn't our government give to have our native Jacobins made even half as bland.'

So much for what might be called the over-all idea. But to put it into effect, it had to be broken down into a series of practical and businesslike propositions. The most important of these emerged as follows: to make the food cheap enough it would have to be purchased and prepared on factory rather than kitchen lines. But then, to make it available to the largest possible number of consumers, it had to be distributed in comparatively small quantities to the greatest possible number of outlets. Each outlet must be distinctive enough to arouse the interest of every passer-by, but over and above this local advertising at the point of sale, there must be an advertising of the whole curry concept on a national scale, and that in a manner better calculated to interest the nation than any of the current methods of advertising.

I decided that, as there was still only one Serai to act as a bulk production unit, I would have to confine the scheme initially to London. I had thirty Indians on the staff, not counting Gurmakh Singh and the daughters-in-law. Of these, ten were still needed, and would be needed in the future, to run the kitchen, even though what now had to be supplied to the restaurant was much reduced in both quantity and complexity, and even though all that would be produced in the future when the scheme was well under way and the restaurant had been closed down would be mass-produced items of the utmost simplicity.

The Zenana Room had been closed, for no lady member of Almack's would come near it. This allowed the daughters-in-law to return to supervising the kitchen and Gurmakh Singh to superintend the half-dozen waiters who were all that were now needed. That left fourteen of the younger and stronger Indians to man the Cart-A-Curry Stalls which I had designed and which Mr Cubitt had built for me.

They were constructed of the lightest materials so that they could be pulled along, like a rickshaw, at about five miles an hour if the puller trotted, and for two hours if necessary before he need feel exhausted. But besides being mobile they had to be distinctive enough to act as self-advertising distribution centres once they were on site. To this purpose I had tried to give them some of the outward appearance of the Serai, which was, in effect, their mother ship. The light wooden roof or awning had a little dome in its centre and the four posts supporting it were shaped as little minarets. The stall itself had been pierced to allow three little charcoal-burning braziers to hang down, their tops flush with the platform. Over these there stood, at each end, a cauldron large enough to hold about five gallons of boiled rice, whilst over the middle one was a little oven in which the curries and chapatees would keep hot.

The cauldrons and oven were made of gleaming copper. All the woodwork, except for the dome, was painted in bright red and yellow stripes. The dome, however, was painted white so that the inscriptions painted on it in black showed up well. These, reading from the top, ran:

BUNTER'S CARRY AWAY INDIAN CURRIES

RICE		CURRY	
Normal portion	1d	Normal portion, vegetable	$\frac{1}{2}$d
Large ditto	1$\frac{1}{2}$d	Large ditto	1d
Pickle, Small Spoon	$\frac{1}{2}$d	Normal portion, meat	2d
Ditto, Large Spoon	1d	Large ditto	3d

CHAPATEE IN WHICH TO CARRY SAME .... $\frac{1}{2}$d
ORDERS OVER VALUE OF 4d .... CHAPATEE FREE

For the Indian attendant I had developed a form of native costume which was both colourful and trouble-free. He went barefoot, irrespective of the weather, to save shoe-leather, and his pajamas came no lower than the knee so that mud splashes were not a matter for concern. The pajamas, as well as the vest worn over a white muslin shirt, were made of red flannel with a good deal of the gold embroidery added, which the Indians call *kincob*. The whole was completed by a towering snowy-white turban and a wide black kummerbund held in place by a leather belt from which a large purse swung on one side and a case containing the measuring spoons swung on the other. Taking the attendant and his Cart-A-Curry Stall as one, I felt sure nothing more distinctive could have been devised.

The prices advertised on the dome had been carefully worked out by Coker and myself as being ones that could be reasonably expected to leave profit margins of from twenty per centum on normal helpings of rice-and-vegetable-curry-without-pickles to ones of close to fifty per centum on large helpings of rice-and-meat-curry-with-double-pickles. And this last after allowing for the free chapatee.

We calculated that where the chosen site was more than five and less than ten miles distant from the Serai headquarters an averagely healthy stall attendant could reasonably be expected to transport and sell four hundred varied portions of rice-and-curry. Where the site was less than five miles distant another fifty portions became possible. Given that the average sale could be priced at threepence, this meant a gross return of £5 per Cart-A-Curry Stall per diem. Consequently, on the basis of the fourteen stalls included in the trial working every day of the year, I could expect the turnover to amount to some £25,000. If no more than one-quarter of that was profit, it still represented a much better return on my investment than the now almost defunct joint-stock company had ever got from feeding elaborate Indian meals to a small, unreliable clientele of nobs and snobs.

I realised that these figures depended for their validity on my being able to buy my raw materials at the right price, on my finding the right sites from which to sell my products, and on my engaging the right sort of advertising before I put even one stall on the road.

My first purchase, of course, was rice, and I was lucky. I found a captain of a newly docked East Indiaman prepared to sell me a ten-ton lot of the cheaper Patna rice straight off his ship and at a remarkably keen price to which nothing had to be added for handling, warehousing and all the other middlemen's profits.

For my spices I turned again to J. J. and his new Indian Spice Department. Although he had abandoned the joint-stock company, or perhaps because he had and now wanted to rejoin, he allowed me to buy at wholesale prices irrespective of quantity. But for the fresh herbs Ghulabi and Fyzoo would grind up every day with the spices, for the vegetables that would form the basis of both curries and pickles, and for the cheap meat I needed for the more expensive curry, I relied on Buttercup.

I did not now take the best she could provide as I had when the Serai was at its peak, but rather the stuff she couldn't sell in Covent Garden and Smithfield. This meant the older and staler vegetables and pulses, broken-mouthed ewes, nanny goats too old to breed or to milk, and, whenever I could smuggle one past those of my cooks who were strict Hindoos, an occasional old cow that had gone in the udder and would no longer take the bull. All in all, I dare say I managed to buy my raw materials as cheaply as anyone engaged in the mass feeding trade.

I had to do a deal of research on the ground before I could decide on the best sites for my fourteen stalls. But after I had collected a mass of data about traffic flows, purchasing powers, and eating habits as well as on population densities and class structures, I decided to site some by the entrances to the London docks, some close to the Covent Garden, Smithfield and Billingsgate markets, some opposite the coaching stations, one close to the Theatre Royal in Drury Lane and the rest in the poorer quarters of the city from Spitalfields to Seven Dials.

And then, as an essential preliminary to everything, I had to invent what amounted to an entirely new form of advertising. As quite large sections of the lower classes could now read and were rapidly acquiring the newspaper habit I concentrated mainly on newspaper advertising, although I did, for one week, have half a regiment of billboard men invade the poorer parts of the city with BUNTER in letters a foot high on their fronts and IS COMING in letters of equal size on their backs.

But it was when it came to the preliminary newspaper advertising that I displayed the greatest ingenuity and invented a new art form, the advertisement treated as literature, the production of which may, one day, develop into a new and useful profession.

Traditional newspaper advertisements, known in the trade as 'classifieds', live in column after column of undifferentiated print in which it is difficult to separate Mr Snip's Genoa Velvets and Chinese Silks from Mr Demerara's Twankays and Flowery Pekoes. Indeed, unless one is an expert, Flowery Pekoes could be a type of Chinese silk, which is why classifieds aren't much use when you're trying to interest the public in something it has never heard of before and therefore doesn't yet know it wants.

That is why instead of taking a few column inches in the classifieds I took a whole page in any London newspaper that wouldn't charge me too much for it. And then instead of covering every inch of the page in printer's ink I would, having left extravagantly wide and virginal margins, and using large and well-spaced type, publish what amounted to an elegant little essay that people would want to read, not least because it had nothing immediately obvious to do with Bunter's Carry-Away Indian Curries, although each did get round or about 'em in the end.

Although they could not know it, Montaigne, Bacon, Steele, Addison and many others all contributed to these essays, for wherever one of these fitted the subject, I pillaged him for the preliminary paragraphs. As for the subjects, they of course varied. One might be about the blessings of poverty, another about the loss of our American colonies and a third about the poetry of the late William Cowper, but whatever they were about they all eventually ended up in India.

So it didn't take me too long to discover that one of the

blessings of poverty is hunger, the sharpest sauce of all, although it is said that, where that is lacking, the sharp spicy sauce the Tamils call kari and we call curry makes an excellent substitute. It wasn't difficult to show that the loss of our North American Empire was important only because it forced us to concentrate more seriously on acquiring our much richer Indian one. Part of that richness was the food of India. How much more it had benefited us to have discovered curry than to have discovered tobacco.

As for William Cowper, I only had to get myself as far as:

> Variety's the very spice of life
> That gives it all its flavour

and I was straightaway into Indian spices and the hundred and one different varieties of curry sauce.

I won't deny that before I'd finished with these essays I'd quite begun to fancy myself as an author, and was justified in this by the stir their publication caused in literary as well as commercial circles. I suspect that it was the novel form of the advertisement rather than the essays themselves that was of interest in commercial circles, but it was certainly t'other way round in literary ones. Leigh Hunt and Southey both published articles – the first in the *Examiner* and the other in the *Quarterly Review* – attacking this debasement of the essay and the prostitution of literature to commerce. This, I thought, was partly envy, they not having thought of using their pens so profitably, and for the rest humbug. For there was no doubt that both of 'em had changed, or at least softened their politics, not, perhaps, because they'd been paid to do so, but they can't have been much surprised when they discovered that changing one's politics pays. So who, in that case, was doing the prostituting?

Charles Lamb, in one of his sober periods, actually called on me at Bedford Square to congratulate me, as one essayist to another and as one Old Bluecoat to another, on the happy marriage I had achieved between Commerce and Literature.

But the most surprising outcome was a letter from William Cobbett of *The Political Register*. It started by assuming that I knew who William Cobbett was – which of course I did – as he'd been writing before ever I'd been born and was now he assured me, undeniably the most prolific, widely-read, and influential author in Britain, if not in Europe and the United States as well. He had been interested in the advertisement he had come across recently in the 'Bloody Old *Times*' since it seemed to him I entertained notions about advertising that could be put to better use than puffing the merits of some strange Indian food.

There followed a good deal about those 'bloody ruffians, Lords Grey, Melbourne and Brougham', who would have him 'in court for seditious libel ere the year was out' before he came to the point, which was this. If he survived the libel action and was not left to rot by the vile Whigs in some loathsome dungeon, he wanted me to call on him at his office in Bolt Court, where he wished to discuss with me a matter of some mutual interest.

In short, as the rest of the very long letter revealed, he wanted to offer me the newly created post of Advertising Manager to *Cobbett's Political Register* and *Cobbett's Library*, this last being the twenty or so books he had written and published in the course of his life. I wouldn't have taken Mr Cobbett very seriously even if he hadn't ended the letter with a passage that convinced me that he was at least half-mad.

'Mark you,' he wrote, 'you will have to drop your ideas about these Curries of yours. I'll not have a man who hasn't an *Englishman's* tastes in his food and who won't accept that the bread, beef, double-brewed ale and good fat bacon that were good enough for his fathers are still good enough for him. Nor will I have anyone who is slave to the *tea-kettle* and the *coffee-pot*. I hope you weren't educated at an *establishment* vulgarly called a *boarding-school* and so think yourself a gentleman. For I'll have no one around me who isn't a Radical, a Reformer, and a hater of all pensioners and Whigs, and who isn't prepared to get ink on his hands in the print shop.'

But what effect did these advertisements have, not on literary and commercial gents, but on those they were intended for – namely the not-too-indigent poor? All I will say on that score is this. By the time my stalls had been on the streets a month Mr Cubitt had been given instructions to start preparing another small fleet of 'em. And I had told Captain Manning that on his next homeward voyage he should ship on my account twenty tons of the cheapest Patna rice he could buy and a dozen or so young and active Singhs.

And then there was Lord Melbourne. He had forgiven me, even though King Billy had not, that attack of merry-go-whimbles. He no longer, it's true, patronised the Serai (which considering the levels the restaurant had sunk to was not surprising) but he had got into the habit of occasionally calling in at Bedford Square. There he would take a glass or two of wine with me and enjoy, as he put it, 'a conversation reflecting your rascally but often refreshingly different judgment of things'.

It was on one of those occasions, and at about this stage in the history of Bunter's Take-Away Indian Curries, that he looked at me over his glass of Madeira and said:

'Men, Mr Bunter, can change the Law, depose kings, set up republics and destroy tyrants. But all that will be left of their achievements in a century or two's time will be a page or two in the history books. But you, they tell me, are likely to bring about a more fundamental and lasting sort of change.'

'Am I? In what way?'

'They say you're changing the eating habits of the people. I've never heard of any King, dictator or Parliament that did that.'

'If I'm changing 'em,' said I, 'I'm not sure it's only for the better.'

'That may or may not be so. But let me warn you that what you're achieving has not gone unnoticed.'

'What does that mean?'

'It means, William, that my colleague at the Exchequer has his eye on you and is thinking of clapping a licence fee on your curry stalls to help him with his Budget.'

I couldn't help being pleased by this. To be mentioned in the Budget as providing a new source of revenue is, indeed, to have arrived.

16   *Proper Procedures*

When the Chancellor did not, in the end, clap a tax on my Cart-A-Curry Stalls I wondered whether it was because the economy was on the mend or because there were, as yet, only fourteen of 'em. But then any Chancellor half up to snuff could have clapped the tax on the curry portions sold rather than on the stalls that sold 'em and have looked forward, in due course, to being able to do something about the National Debt.

For there wasn't one of those fourteen stalls, wherever sited, that didn't, almost from the first day, have a constant crowd of customers around it. Some of these would be waiting for their curries. Some would be packing their curries into their chapatees prior to taking them away for home consumption. And some would be eating their curries on the spot or, if they had been unable to afford the curry part, they would be eating their penn'orths of rice to the smell of other men's curries.

If I hadn't been Bunter and an optimist, I could easily have become frightened by what I had done, which was to create a demand for rice-and-curry that grew faster than it could ever be satisfied. But since I *was* Bunter, I was already looking forward to the time when I could sell Bunter's Cart-A-Curry concept to the investing public and live in idle luxury for the rest of my live.

Every evening the Indians would come racing back, even from the most distant sites, with their stalls lightened by the loss of some four hundred portions of curry and their purses made heavier by the acquisition of some five pounds' worth of coppers. And every morning a hackney cab would draw up at the Serai to carry Coker and around seventy pounds in coppers to Hammond's Bank in the Strand where, according to Coker, whom I'd put in charge of Finance as well as Staff, I now had a very handsome credit balance accumulating. Indeed, I would soon, unless I was careful, have overall solvency staring me in the face and no more excuse for not paying my creditors.

Cockiness, like love, is blind, and I, alas, am constantly subject to attacks of cockiness. The merest threat of success will send me strutting about, head in air, until I eventually trip myself up and go arse-over-tip. That was why I was so busy ordering new stalls and further supplies of Singhs, when I should have been attending to the one law of economics that concerned me most: the one Adam Smith called the Law of Elasticities. This states that, although a poor man's appetite for food will grow in direct proportion to the food supplies available, his ability to purchase it won't grow by even one farthing. Which is much the same as saying that what he spends on rice and curry he won't be able to spend on tripe and onions.

But if I took no notice of this law, there were others who did. It was late one morning at the Serai and the stalls were all long since on site. Coker had left for the bank on his paying-in and drawing-out duties and I had settled down to working out how many more stalls London could take before curry-saturation point had been reached. It wasn't a task I enjoyed for I'm a deal better at the instant wheeze than at protracted paper work. So when Gurmakh Singh showed in Ebenezer Snape, I quite welcomed the interruption until, on looking him over, it struck me that he must be a bum bailiff. Which made me wonder who, among my many creditors, had so suddenly and unnecessarily lost patience.

For Ebenezer Snape – a large, round-bellied, triple-chinned man with a spongy red nose, a fine head of well-greased black hair, and a remarkably low forehead to which three carefully arranged curls adhered – wore that look of authority combined with seediness typical of bailiffs. Moreover when he spoke he

contrived to sound both obsequious and hectoring. In addition
to which his opening remarks were those I have always
expected from a bum bailiff about to serve a writ.

'Am I,' said he, 'hadressing William Bunter?'

'You are,' said I.

'William Frederick Augustus Bunter?'

'I don't often use either the Frederick or the Augustus.'

'*The* William Frederick Augustus Bunter of Bunter's Cart-A-
Curry Stalls?'

'The same.'

'In that case, William,' said he, 'hallow me to present you
with this.' He put his hand into an inside pocket and withdrew
it holding – not a writ, but a very large and rather dog-eared
visiting card which he gave to me. It read:

MR EBENEZER SNAPE

Worshipful Master, Treasurer and Hon. Secretary

THE GRAND UNION OF LONDON PIE
SAUSAGE AND COOKED MEAT TRADERS

'Truth, Unity, Concord'

All Enquiries to be addressed
c/o The Pig & Whistle
84 Fetter Lane

I didn't rightly know what all this meant, but I was so
relieved he wasn't serving a writ that I said: 'Mr Snape, I'm
delighted to make your acquaintance.'

'You are?' he said, looking a mite surprised.

'Indeed I am, even though I must confess that I've never,
until this minute, heard of the Grand Union of . . . Pie . . .
Sausage . . . and so on . . .'

'If you find it too much of a mouthful at first you may refer to
us as GULPS. It's the habbreviation we ourselves use when the
hoccasion ain't a formal one. And at this precise moment in

time, Bunter, and as a preliminary gesture of good will but without any commitment as to the future, I propose to plump for informality.'

'Informality by all means. But that still doesn't mean that I've heard of GULFS.'

'GULPS,' said Ebenezer. 'And you may not have 'eard of us on account of we're a recent amalgamation.'

'You mean the Pies hadn't anything to do with the Sausages and both of 'em kept themselves away from the Cooked Meats?'

'In a manner of speaking.'

'Grave mistake,' I said in a judicial sort of voice. 'In unity lies strength. Now you've come together you're bound to grow.'

'Grown already. Three 'undred and seventeen members at last count, not including the Tripe Boilers what 'ave made hovertures, or the Roast Potato men who are showing signs.'

'Showing signs, hey?'

'Costermongers would join if they could, but you know what that would lead to.'

'Do I?'

'Course you do. Demarcation disputes is what it would lead to. 'Owever grand the union, you 'ave to draw the line somewhere and we draw it 'atween the cooked and the uncooked. Otherwise we'd 'ave to let people like the Catsmeat Men in. But you can take my word for it, it won't be long afore there won't be a scrap of the cooked sold in London that 'asn't been sold by one of our members.'

I thought of all the various forms of what Ebenezer called 'the cooked' that were currently being sold on the streets of London, looked once more at the visiting card, and said: 'And you run all that, Mr Snape, from the Pig and Whistle?'

He drew himself up in a dignified sort of way and said: 'We 'ave more commodious and himposing quarters in contemplation for when the Tripe Boilers and a few others 'ave entered the fold. But at this moment in time the Pig and Whistle, what is run by my sister-in-law, does very well.'

'Forgive my curiosity, Mr Snape, but which were you before the fold was created – Sausage, Pie or Cooked Meats?'

'There are,' he said rather cryptically, 'them as deal in the cooked and them as organise them who deal in the cooked. I am one of the latter.'

'Do you mean you're an organiser by profession?'

'I am, and proud of it. Where would the working man and the cooked-food trade be without a professional organiser?'

'I'm sure I don't know.'

'At the mercy of parasites such as yourself, that's where they'd be.'

I'd thought we 'd been getting on amicably until then. I am, I suppose, something of an organiser myself, which was what made Ebenezer mildly interesting. Now, however, he had, in effect, turned round and bitten me, and I didn't know why, unless it was because as a rice-and-curry man I qualified for the fold but hadn't yet entered it. If that was so, it was time for me to bite back.

'I wonder,' said I, 'whether you're not a fraud.'

'What the Hell do you mean by that?'

'I mean you may be like the man who tried the other day to get me to subscribe to an expedition that was going to descend on the North Pole from a balloon. I mean your Union of Whatsits may not actually exist.'

'Then you just wait a day or two and you'll soon discover whether GULPS exists or not. And it may ease your mind if I tell you I ain't trying to get you to subscribe to anything.'

'Oh yes you are. You're trying to get me to subscribe to your union. Well let me tell you this, Snape. Calling me a parasite won't encourage me to join GULPS or anything else.'

'GULPS wouldn't 'ave you as you now hoperate. Not at any price and whether you feel hencouraged or not.'

No one likes being blackballed for a club before he has actually put his name down for it. So I forgot, for the moment, that I had no intention of joining GULPS and said: 'GULPS, wouldn't have me! It would have to have me. I'm fully qualified. Boiled rice ain't all that different from boiled potatoes; curried meat is cooked meat. So it's not as though I'm an uncooked, like the Catsmeat Man.'

'You may qualify as cooked, I'm not denying that. But you must see you disqualify as almost everything else.'

'Nonsense,' said I.

He ticked the items of disqualification off on one stubby finger after another. 'One: your curry represents himport competition. Two: it's processed and distributed 'ere by cheap, coloured, immigrant labour. Three: every one of your stalls is in hinfringement of our Pimlico Agreement houtlawing site-poaching. Four: you don't even begin to qualify as a small or one-man business.'

'It ain't all that big a business as yet.'

He looked at me in an almost pitying way and said: 'I understand, Bunter, as 'ow you spent a lot of your working life in the East. That's why you're now so out of your depth. You've 'ad no real experience of British Unions, the British working man or the British cooked-food trade.'

'I acquired a certain amount of business experience in India, both as Bishop Heber's secretary and on my own account.'

'That's exactly what I mean. Let me put it this way so as you can understand. GULPS, like any other union since the Combination Acts was repealed, exists to promote hindividual-ism, henterprise, market forces, and whatever other freedoms and liberties the British working man may cherish from time to time.'

'Well that's easy enough to understand. I'm in favour of all of those things meself.'

''Ow can you be when you're running a mass-production henterprise in which un-unionised and unprotected wage-slaves 'ave to work along factory lines?'

'They wouldn't like to hear you call them wage-slaves. And as the most of 'em are Sikhs they are very capable of protecting themselves. What's more, I can't see what's wrong with mass-production methods and the factory system.'

'They're un-English, that's what's wrong with 'em. No free-born Englishman would ever want to work in a factory or to produce even one more item than 'e absolutely 'as to.'

'Well I suppose you could, if you stretched a point or two,

call the Serai a curry factory. But there are no free-born Englishmen working in it. They're all free-born Indians. What's more, only some of 'em work as wage-slaves inside the factory. Most of them work as wage-slaves out on the streets selling the product.'

'Hexactly. And in both cases they're snatching the bread out of my members' mouths.'

'Indians, Snape, are civilised people. They seldom snatch bread from anyone's mouth, and when they do they like it to be a chapatee.'

'I was speaking metaphorical, as well you know, but if you want it actual, I can give it to you.'

Here he took a tattered notebook out of his pocket and turned over its pages, licking his forefinger now and again, until he arrived at the right page.

'Item,' said he. 'Brother Grimshaw. Hot Pies and Pigs' Trotters. Corner of Commercial Street and Shoreditch High. Trade worse than 'alved since Cart-A-Curry Stall set up at entrance to Spitalfields Market. Item. Brother Grose. Jellied Eels, Cockles and Fresh-Boiled Shrimps. Bottom of Ludgate 'Ill. Forced to pack it in on account of Cart-A-Curry Stall corner of Fleet Street and Whitefriars. Item. Brother Brander. Tripes, Scratchings and Saveloys. Bridge Street, opposite 'Ouses of Parliament.'

'That's quite enough of that,' I said, 'and I am sorry for Brothers Grimshaw, Grose and Brander. But you have made no mention of the people who really count.'

'Ho? And 'oo might they be?'

'The public, Snape, the food-consuming public whom we exist to serve and who show by their custom whom they wish to be served by. And in this case, Snape, they have shown they wish to be served by Bunter's Cart-A-Curry Stalls.'

'I told you that you was out of your depth, but I didn't realise you was in such deep water as that. Let me try to hextract you from it.'

He seated himself uninvited, unbuttoned a coat that was stretched too tight over his belly for comfort, stuck out his legs which were encased in a well-filled pair of shepherd's-plaid trowsers, gave me an indulgent, almost avuncular look and said:

'I can't, with any conscience, let you go on in your hignorance spouting away about consumer preferences. Your British working man, Bunter, values 'is liberties as 'ighly as anyone, but there are some of 'em what 'e values more 'ighly than others. And one of them is the liberty to take no notice whatsoever of your British consumer's so-called preferences.'

'But what happens then to freedom of choice?'

'That's hexactly what I'm a-coming to. Your British consumer, Bunter, is a remarkably hamenable animal. Even when 'e's allowed 'imself to develop preferences – what don't 'appen very frequent – 'e can soon be taught not to prefer anything your British working man don't want to produce. If it ain't there, it stands to reason 'e can't prefer it. So you see what that means?'

'Dissatisfied consumers?'

'Just the opposite: it means as much freedom of choice for everyone as you can expect to find this side o' Paradise. There's your British working man free to produce what 'e likes and there's your British consumer free to like what your British working man produces. The only thing that can upset the apple cart is when someone such as you hattempts to introduce a hexotic product. It won't do, Bunter. Your curry stalls just can't be allowed to come into it.'

'But they *have* come into it. There's nothing you and GULPS can now do about it.'

'That, if I might say so, ain't communicating. It's hultimatuming and hultimatums ain't 'elpful at this stage when we're still at hinformal and consultative levels.'

'It takes at least two to get to a consultative level and I absolutely refuse to be one of 'em. It's no good, Snape, I'm sorry, but you and GULPS and jellied eels and cow-cheek pies all belong to the past. The future lies with the new technologies and Bunter's Carry-Away Indian Curries.'

''Old 'ard,' said he, a good deal less indulgently. 'That ain't the way to go into negotiations.'

'I wasn't aware that you and I were going into anything.'

'Which only shows 'ow little you know about procedures. What else do you think I'm 'ere for if it isn't procedures?'

'I don't rightly know.'

'Then let me straighten you out on procedures. First there's a statement of respective positions, each firmly 'eld of course. Then there's preliminary breakdown followed by exploratory proposal and counter-proposal. Then there's a lot of refusals and referrals followed by new proposals, maximum concessions, painful compromises, splitting the difference and a good many other customary procedures. The 'ole of this is traditionally known as the proper conduct of industrial relations. It's only when them relations 'ave really broken down that each side starts to fall back on hultimatums.'

'As I haven't much time, Snape, I suggest we fall back on them right away.'

'I wouldn't advise that, not on any account. It would amount to haggravation. Your British working man is easily haggravated.'

'Is he? Then what about me? Can't I be aggravated?'

'It's traditional for the union side to suffer the haggravation. T'other side does the provoking. And once you've got to the haggravating, provoking stage the hatmosphere is no longer conducive to reasonable negotiations and the 'ole situation deteriorates. Now we don't want that to happen, do we? So why don't we just operate procedures and move on to hexploratory proposals.'

'I have no proposals to make and nothing to explore.'

'Then I'll fire off first. 'Ow's this as a start? We recognise curry hofficially as a hindigenous food, and we allows you one – no, two – stalls, to be placed on sites determined by my Hexecutive Committee. You puts Brothers Grose and Brander in charge of them stalls and gets rid of all those Indians of yours. The way they run – actually run – when they're at work is very un-British, you know. The mere sight of them bare black legs jogging away hamounts to a serious provocation. What do you say?'

'I say you are in grave danger of provoking me.'

'That's only because you ain't yet haccustomed to procedures. If there's any provoking to be done, you do it to me and not vicey-versey. Now as a secondary proposal I'm willing, once you've got rid of your nig-nogs, to allow you hextra stalls as an' when we 'ave Brothers needing hemployment. And at that stage we'll consider hextending membership of GULPS to you.'

I've always been a man for the soft answer, for the Bunter blood don't boil easily. But it was simmering now.

'Mr Snape,' said I, 'I have listened to you with a good deal of patience and a certain amount of amazement. But I'm a busy man and I've had enough of your impudence. So get it into your head that I want nothing to do with your Union or your proper procedures, I have no intention of getting rid of my Indians, who are not, by-the-by, nig-nogs. Indeed I have sent to India for a good many more. I will not reduce the number of my stalls: in fact I propose to add to them until there's not a suitable site anywhere in the British Isles that hasn't got one of Bunter's Cart-A-Curry Stalls on it. And I don't care a fig for your Pimlico Agreement.'

'Careful, Bunter. That's close to hamounting to haggravation.'

'The door, Snape, is behind you.'

'That's done it then. Most deliberate bit of haggravating I've come across in the 'ole of my long professional career. You're a higgerant man, Bunter, and a boil – no, a scab on the fair face of British hindustrial relations, and I shall 'ave to report to that heffect to my Hexecutive. And after that, don't be surprised if you find yourself without a stall to your name.'

'The door, Snape, the door.'

He stood up and said in the patient tones of one who had had to endure such situations and advance such arguments many, many times before: 'They tell me, Bunter, that you once poisoned 'alf the nobs in London with the food you served 'em in this hestablishment.'

'They tell you a lie.'

'That's as may be. Now we in GULPS don't give a damn

what you do or don't do to the hupper classes. But we would certainly 'ate to see you poison even one member of the London working class with your filthy curries.'

'He's a hundred times more likely to be poisoned by one of your Tripe Boilers than by one of Bunter's Carry-Away Curries.'

'Ah, but if such a misfortune should befall one of me Tripe Boilers, 'e could always turn to GULPS and Ebenezer Snape for protection. Just you ask yourself, Bunter, 'oo you could turn to.'

After that he gave me a quite friendly nod and left.

As I sat there I tried to persuade myself of the utter absurdity and triviality of Ebenezer Snape. Any ordinary, rational, freedom-loving person, I told myself, would find Snape's obsession with procedures, his occupational jargon and his blinkered and reactionary attitude towards consumers and the food trade too ridiculous to be taken seriously. But I've generally been able to smell out danger long before others get even one whiff of it, and I smelt danger in Snape.

Absurd and ridiculous though he might be, he was also plausible. I know something about plausibility. But mine is, at its best, a limited sort of plausibility, a one-to-one or, at the best, a one-to-a-few glibness. Snape's, however, was different, it was the plausibility of the agitator, the rabble-rouser, the moulder and leader of mobs. I knew that if I hadn't been Bunter but had been Brother Grimshaw, Brother Grose or Brother Brander, I would have ignored Snape's seedy appearance and absurd forms of reasoning in order to listen and believe. I, too, would have accepted that curry was the cause of all, or nearly all, the nation's troubles. I, too, would have wanted to abolish Bunter's Cart-A-Curry Stalls, to send every Indian stall attendant scuttling back to India, and I, too, would have wanted to have every jot and tittle of the Pimlico Agreement religiously obeyed.

The Gulper Disturbances: Phase One

Although I was certainly the cause, the very *fons et origo* of what are now called the Gulper Disturbances, I don't propose to describe them in any detail. Whatever they may say about 'em now they were quite modest disturbances as modern disturbances go. They didn't, for instance, become as widespread as the disturbances started by poor mad Ned Ludd. Nor was there even half as much blood spilt as was spilt on St Peter's Fields in Manchester. Yet there are now historians who maintain that the Gulper Disturbances have already become part of the history of our times.

If they are right, it can only be because they were, as disturbances, so decidedly odd. But as historians seldom pay any attention to oddness, I suppose they have discovered meaningful, significant and portentous elements in 'em that have remained hidden from me. That's why I'm leaving all analytical accounts of Snape's Gulper campaign against Bunter's Cart-A-Curry Stalls to the historians. What I shall touch on here is not how the Gulper Disturbances affected the character and future of the British race, but how they affected Bunter.

Although I began to smell danger from Snape even before he got through all his ridiculous procedures, I still wanted to find out whether others would get a whiff of it. So just as soon as he got back from the bank I gave Coker a word-for-word account of all that had happened. I couldn't have found a more *agreeing* person to confide in. He agreed with me that Snape must be dangerous as well as absurd. He agreed with me that Snape must by now have decided that it was only by ridding London of Bunter's curry stalls that he could hope to set about ridding Londoners of their growing passion for curries. And he also agreed this meant Snape would have to launch his union members against my Indian stall attendants in a series of physical, and possibly armed, attacks designed to drive us from the streets of London. (Those members, incidentally, would soon be known to every Londoner as 'The Gulpers', just as my Indians would soon be known as 'The Stallers' or 'The Snowdrops': Cockneys never interest themselves in anything until they give it a nickname.)

Having shown how whole-heartedly he agreed with my appreciation of the situation, Coker set about strengthening my willingness to cope with it. 'Never you fear, Bunter-me-boy,' he said, getting quite red with excitement and starting to strut about like a turkey-cock. 'Just as long as we prepare for it we can meet 'em and beat 'em whenever they attack. I've seen Indians in action before, and I tell you they make the best troops outside the Brigade of Guards, always provided they're given British leadership. Remember Arcot, me boy! Remember Seringapatam! Remember Assaye!'

After which he gave me a second or two in which to do my remembering before he went on to say that although I must, of course, remain in overall control, I'd be well advised to put him in charge of the Defence Department as well as the Finance and Personnel Departments. I didn't need to think twice before agreeing to this. My Papa may have been a Commander-in-Chief, but that don't mean that I'm itching to lead Indians or anyone else into battle.

But although I readily agreed to Coker's new appointment, I couldn't agree to his next proposal. This dealt with the immediate arming of the Stallers. Coker argued that the better they were armed the more likely they were to deter Snape and his followers. Alternatively, if deterrence did fail, the more likely they were to lick the unarmed or more lightly armed Gulpers. He toyed with a scheme for mounting a swivel gun in the bows of every curry stall, but abandoned it in favour of arming every Staller with a brace of pistols, a blunderbuss and a rough-sharpened sabre. I turned this down, not just because of the cost, but because I wanted the law to remain firmly on our side. This meant standing unmistakably on the defensive. Pistols, blunderbusses and rough-sharpened sabres all hinted at aggression. So we compromised in the end on cudgels. The very next morning, and on every morning thereafter, Coker had the Stallers out at first light practising their cudgel drill.

But time passed and not even one of those cudgels needed to be swung in anger. This puzzled me until I received an anonymous communication which convinced me that I had misread Snape's plan of campaign. He wasn't going to open it with attacks on our stalls. He planned, instead, to start with a Petition to Parliament, and the anonymous communication I had received was a copy of the still unfinished Petition. It was complete enough, however, to reveal how thoroughly Snape was master of his trade.

Take, for example, the apparently simple matter of signatories. A less skilful tactician would have thought he'd got enough of 'em once he'd got the signatures of all the Gulpers and of such of the consuming public as still preferred cow-cheek pie to curries. Not so Snape. Once his 317 Gulpers and their 243 still-loyal customers had signed, he sent the Petition round to every known petitioner in London. This gave him close on a thousand additional signatories. Most of 'em came, as one would expect, from among the more libertarian Radicals, the more liberal Whigs, the more Whiggish Tories and the more enlightened Bishops, Deans and Canons. He also got the signatures of a good many political economists and of every well-known Jacobin, Pantisocrat, Owenite, Spencean, Abolitionist, and Emancipationist in the capital. By the time he'd finished circulating it, his Petition was supported by almost every forward-looking, liberal-minded, and Progressive person in London, and that's much the same as saying in the British Isles with the exception of Edinburgh, where they have their own indigenous breed of Progressives.

Some may wonder why all these London Progressives were so willing to support a Petition that even the most cursory study must reveal as thoroughly backward-looking and reactionary. The answer is that most of 'em have got so used to signing petitions that they seldom bother to read 'em. So long as there's a fair scattering of such talismanic words as 'Social Justice',

'Working Class', 'Brotherhood of Man', and 'Cheap Labour' they are more than consenting signatories. As Snape had seen to it that there should be a full crop rather than a mere scattering of these, not one of his signatories got round to wondering whether there might not be something almost unprogressive about denying the consumer his freedom of choice by encouraging the Gulpers to establish a closed circle around the London cooked-food trade.

Snape's Petition had a good deal to say about the damage that would be done to industrial relations, full employment, housing policies, law and order, as well as to all our traditional reasons for rioting, if Bunter's policy of using imported coloured labour were to be copied by other employers. It had even more to say about the damage that would be done to the nation's health if the curry habit were allowed to spread. Progressive physicians now recognised that curries, because of the heats and irritations they gave rise to, did a great deal more damage to the still-tender alimentary and procreative organs of the British than they ever would to similar organs situated inside an Indian, who would have been so heated and irritated from birth as to have become effectively case-hardened.

The Petition's other anti-curry arguments were no more, and no less, logical than these. I can't think that Snape intended the Parliamentarians to take them very seriously. But I do think he intended them to take the tail-end of it very seriously indeed. For that tail-end was pointed directly at Bunter, and that, after all, was the Petition's immediate and only purpose.

Snape had his signatories begin by disclaiming any desire to attack even one established British freedom. That was why they were not petitioning Parliament to make it an offence for adult Britons to eat curries in the privacy of their homes. Whatever depravities an individual may have acquired whilst serving in India were his own affair so long as he kept them to himself. It was with the prevention of a public, and not a private vice that this Petition was concerned: a public vice which, although still in its infancy, allowed evil men to plan the corruption of a nation. In short there was a plan afoot to make great fortunes out of turning the British into a race of curry addicts. The first part of this plan had already emerged in the shape of an establishment called Bunter's Indian Serai and a distributive network called Bunter's Cart-A-Curry Stalls. Preparations were now being made to extend this network so as to carry the curry habit, eventually, to every inhabited corner of the British Isles.

Parliament's duty, therefore, was plain. It had to destroy what amounted to a conspiracy against the moral and physical health of the nation. The signatories accordingly begged Parliament to make it a criminal offence for anyone to prepare, display, advertise or offer curries for sale to the public. The gravity of the offence should not depend on the amount or value of the curry offered. Whether it was a series of expensive curry dishes sold in the Serai or a penn'orth of curry sold from a Cart-A-Curry Stall, each sale must be made equally a felony, and be punished on a first conviction with a maximum of five years' penal servitude, and on any subsequent one with transportation to Botany Bay for a period of not less than ten years.

In the tail-end of this tail-end to their Petition, the signatories asked Parliament to remember that six penn'orth of prevention is better than a guinea's worth of cure. Indian curries need Indian cooks. These, given the present shortage, have to be imported. If immigration controls were made stricter at ports of entry, it could be made impossible for an Indian to enter Britain for the purpose of taking employment as a curry cook. It had been argued that it would be difficult for port officials to distinguish Indian from other coloured immigrants, and Indian curry cooks from other Indians. If that were true, it was an argument for barring all coloured immigrants rather than for barring none. That Parliament should set about doing this was the prayer of the undersigned.

There followed no fewer than 1734 signatures, almost all authentic.

I didn't rightly know what to make of this rigmarole. Nor could I understand why a copy had been sent to me well before the original was sent to Parliament. And the whole, whether in copy or not, so reeked of Snape's particular mixture of absurdity and menace that I didn't know whether to laught or to panic. Before doing either I turned, once more, to Coker. He had, by now, firmly established himself as my *fidus Achates*, and had come close to making himself indispensable. He, however, seemed even more surprised and puzzled by the Petition than I had been.

'Damned if I expected Snape to set about it in this sneaky fashion,' said he. 'It ain't worthy of him.'

That struck me as an odd sort of remark so I asked Coker what, in his opinion, would have been a more worthy fashion.

'Straightforward assault, of course. Snape ought to have had his Gulpers smash our stalls and chase our Stallers out of town.'

It was an even odder remark, coming as it did from a *fidus Achates* who had only recently been put in charge of Defence and cudgel drill.

'I thought,' said I, 'that you were going to meet 'em and beat 'em.'

He seemed surprised for a moment, but then he stuck his jaw out, looked mighty pugnacious, and said: 'And so I would have done if only the sneak had had the decency to behave in a manly and straightforward manner.'

'Well he hasn't,' said I. 'He's gone a-petitioning instead. So what do you make of that?'

'It ain't what I make of it. It's what Parliament might make of it. And as I'm not a politician but a plain honest man of action, I can't tell you what that will be.'

The plain honest man of action had been more helpful than he knew, for his answer reminded me that there *was* a politician who might be able to answer my question. So I set off, immediately, for South Street and Lord Melbourne. He didn't seem at all surprised to see me, and when I tried to give him my copy of Snape's Petition to read he waved it away and said:

'No need to read that. I've read it already.'

'With respect, my Lord, you can't have done. It hasn't been sent to Parliament yet, and I don't even know how and why this secret copy was sent to me.'

'Leaked to you,' said Lord Melbourne.

'Leaked?'

'Technical term. Whenever something that ought to have been kept secret is made known to no matter whom, we politicians say that it's been "leaked".'

'I shall remember the term.'

'You do that, for you'll often have use for it even if you stay on the very outermost fringes of politics. Leaking is an essential part of our business, the Ship of State would have foundered long ago without it.'

'That, my Lord, is a paradox.'

'I know. It ain't too bad, either, if I can produce a paradox at this time of the morning and at my age.'

He looked at me out of the corner of his eyes and gave me that sly sort of smile that told me he was once again enjoying himself at my expense. But I wasn't there merely for his enjoyment, so I said:

'I can understand why the Petition was leaked to me. Some-one – some unknown benefactor – wanted to warn me. But what I can't understand is why it was also leaked to you.'

'It wasn't.'

'Wasn't what?'

'Leaked.'

'But you've read it.'

'Of course I have, and in all its different and increasingly tedious versions. I do wish these fellows would get their Petitions right first shot.'

'I confess, my Lord, that I am even more puzzled now than when I came in.'

'In that case,' said Lord Melbourne, 'stop waving that damned bit of paper at me, sit down, hold your tongue, and I'll do what I can to unpuzzle you.'

I took a chair.

'You must have noticed,' he began, 'that I no longer dine at your Serai. That is because I couldn't survive another dose of your Serai Squitters. But I want you to understand that it is *not* because I don't still try – in moderation of course – to look after your interests. We are, after all, relations by bastardy.'

I did what I could from a seated and tongue-tied position to bow my acknowledgment of his solicitude and our relationship.

'Of course you'll know,' he continued, 'that Grey made me Home Secretary. But what you won't know is that Home Secretaries have to keep a pretty strict watch on all known conspirators, agitators, rabble-rousers, organisers, demonstrators and petitioners.'

'Such as Ebenezer Snape?' said I, quite forgetting the bit about holding my tongue.

'Such as Ebenezer Snape. He's not the best example these days, for he's getting on a bit and has come down in the world as a consequence. He's only organising piemen now, but there was a time, Bunter, when he organised much greater men. Do you know he helped Cartwright organise his Hampden Clubs, that he helped Cobbett organise all those demonstrations and petitions in support of Queen Caroline and the sanctity of marriage, and that he was lucky it couldn't be proved that he helped Thistlewood with the Cato Street Gang?'

'No.'

'Well he did. So you can see why we still keep an eye on him, however trivial his present pursuits may be.'

'How?' said I, having decided that to be monosyllabic was damned close to being tongue-tied.

'How what?' said Melbourne irritably. 'And I do wish, Bunter, that you'd stop barking at me.'

'How do you keep an eye on him?'

'In the usual way, of course. One of his piemen is also one of my men.'

'You mean he's a spy?'

'When we plant them on t'other side we call them agents. It's only when it's the other way round that we call them spies.'

'Well, this agent of yours . . . '

'Name of Oliver. Highly skilled man – trained under Sidmouth, so he's also getting on a bit now. That's why we planted him on Snape. Set an old-'un to catch an old-'un.'

'And what has he caught, my Lord?'

'Nothing of any importance except the Petition. And I

wouldn't have taken any notice of that if it hadn't been directed against you.'

'And since it was, you had Mr Oliver send me a copy?'

'I thought you ought to be warned.'

'That means you think it *is* important.'

'It could be. There are some quite impressive signatures on that Petition. All of them idiots, of course, but Progressive idiots, and we've one or two of the same sort in Cabinet who might agree with them. And since most of my Cabinet colleagues also had a dose of your Serai Squitters, I don't think they will object very much to the abolition of Bunter.'

'You alarm me, my Lord.'

'Too early to get alarmed. I can still find ways of dealing with Mr Snape and his Petition.'

'Such as?'

'Oliver tells me that there is going to be a meeting in Green Park of all the signatories. After speeches, they will march, carrying banners, placards, mottoes and so on, to Parliament Square. From there a deputation of bishops and political philosophers will present the Petition whilst the other marchers engage in a mass lobbying of Members. Now do you know what that means?'

'No.'

'It means that Mr Snape has forgotten his Tumultuous Petitioning Act.'

'What on earth is that?'

'It dates back to 1661, so Snape may be forgiven for having forgotten about it. Broadly speaking it suspends the subject's undoubted right to petition Parliament if that petitioning is done in a disorderly and tumultuous manner by factious and seditious persons.'

'Meaning the bishops and the political philosophers?'

'Meaning that Oliver will have little difficulty ensuring a certain amount of tumult and disorder. Enough, let us say, to justify my calling on the troops to disperse the petitioners before they reach Parliament Square, and by that time even the political philosophers will have qualified as factious if not actually seditious.'

He smiled at me. There was a look on his face that I thought I could recognise. It was something between the patient look an usher might wear when explaining Euclid to a particularly dull pupil and the self-satisfied smirk of the artist exhibiting yet one more example of his mastery of his art. It was, I suddenly realised, how Ebenezer Snape looked when he was exposing to my untutored gaze the intricate beauties of Procedures – the professional showing off to the amateur.

'You will not,' said Lord Melbourne when I rose to leave, 'say anything to anyone about the man Oliver.'

I bowed my agreement.

He smiled, said, '*Qui tacet consentire videtur*,' and waved me from the room.

The Dragoon Guards, when Melbourne had them turned out, used no more than the flats of their sabres on the petitioners and then not before they had left Birdcage Walk and were approaching Parliament Square. Melbourne, in this respect, was a minimalist. He would have been fully entitled, under the Tumultuous Picketing Act, to order edges. None the less a few political economists and Gulpers got their skulls cracked and a bishop or two got trampled on, and these constituted the first casualties of the Gulper Disturbances.

18   *The Gulper Disturbances: Phase Two*

The near-stalemate that followed the defeat of Snape's Petition suggested to me that the greatest weakness of the unionising classes was a certain stodgy-minded, unadventurous conservatism. Even an out-and-out professional like Snape began to look as mechanical and unimaginative as an old circus dog – the sort that has mastered all the traditional tricks and refuses to learn any new ones. For now that The Tumultuous Picketing

Act had put paid to the opening move of his anti-Bunter campaign he seemed to think the only strategy left to him was to picket me out.

Not that picketing out never works. If Snape had been organising my curry cooks and Stallers in a strike for higher wages, then a picket line to stop any of 'em strike-breaking might just have done the trick. But the half-dozen Gulpers he had walking up and down in front of the Serai and of each of my stalls weren't there to stop my Indians cooking and selling my curries. They were there to stop the British consumer buying and eating them. If Snape had only asked even the most ignorant politician he'd have been told that no policy is more certain to fail than one that attempts to deny the British consumer unrestricted access to cheap food.

But if Snape's picketing strategy revealed a failure in imagination, his picketing tactics showed a certain inventiveness. Pickets traditionally use oral persuasion to stop people crossing their picket line. They appeal to class solidarity, offer to break someone's bloody jaw, and so on. The difficulty here, however, is that their jeering and swearing and cat-calling generally drown whatever words of persuasion they accompany. That was why Snape had so trained and equipped his picketers that they were able to add certain unorthodox forms of literary persuasion to the more traditional oral ones.

In short, he turned his picketers into sandwich-board men. Their front boards all announced

'GULPS Curry-Prevention Campaign
Official Picket'.

Their back boards carried various messages. all of them in some way relevant to the joint subjects of Bunter and curry. Some would quote the opinions of the more eminent Progressive Idiots, such as:

'Curries are Ungodly: Bishop of Bath and Wells.'
'Curries are Unhealthy: Hon. Sec. Association of London Apothecaries.'
'Curries are Un-English: Daniel O'Connell.'

Others would consist of no more than collections of more or less popular slogans, such as:

> 'English Grub for English Bellies.'
> 'The Stewed Tripe of Old England.'
> 'East, West, Home's Best.'
> 'Nig-nogs Go Home.'

Then there were what might be called the Industrial Messages such as:

> 'Negotiation not Confrontation.'
> 'All Power to the People.'
> 'Bunter, the Unacceptable Face of the London Cooked-Food Trade.'

Profound though many of them were, these messages didn't stop curry customers crossing the picket line in their usual numbers, but many of them, as they crossed, paused to read each picketer, back and front. It struck me when I heard of it that this could be dangerous. Even your most hardened cheap-food consumer can, in the end, be evangelised. So I decided to meet sandwich board with sandwich board, and in no time at all I had half a dozen of my own sandwich-board men marching up and down wherever Snape's picketers were marching. Mine, however, didn't go in for abstruse or doctrinal messages. Instead,

> 'BUNTER'S INDIAN CURRIES:
> THIS WEEK'S SPECIAL OFFER'

was what was said on their fronts. And

> 'DOUBLE THE USUAL PORTION:
> HALF THE USUAL PRICE'

was what was announced on their backs.

Snape had been over-subtle. He had appealed to what are, after all, some of Man's most highly advanced and civilised instincts such as class solidarity and racial hatred. I made a simple, straightforward appeal to greed, which is his most basic one. The consequence was that the queue of would-be customers outside each curry stall grew so large that the Gulpers were overwhelmed. They could no more hope to maintain the sanctity of their picket line than an aged Pantaloon with a young and lusty wife could hope to preserve the sanctity of his marriage bed. Very soon they took off their sandwich boards and sat on them, looking frustrated and miserable.

I was now winning the game commercially as well as strategically. The double-portion-half-price offer had done the trick so well that, within a week, I was able to withdraw it along with my sandwich-board men. Even then I had to hire market carts to carry extra supplies from the Serai to the stalls, for the Stallers were now selling in two or three hours amounts of rice and curry they had formerly taken all day to sell. So whilst my trade doubled, the perplexed Gulpers sat on the side-lines and wondered what had happened to the time-hallowed and normally successful practice of picketing.

They got to looking so beaten and dejected that some of my Stallers, showing the ready sympathy of their race, started to smuggle portions of curry out to them. These, whether the picketers were Piemen, Tripe men, or merely Jellied Eel men, were greatly enjoyed. But when Coker reported this softening of attitudes to me I decided to stop it, cost what may. If my Stallers started to fraternise in any general way with the Gulpers, their soft-heartedness could eventually give Snape the victory my own stout-heartedness had denied him.

Now, if ever, was the time for stiffening the sinews and disguising fair nature with hard-favour'd rage, even if I had to inspire the Stallers to it myself by visiting the front line. As Napoleon and Wellington well knew, nothing so inspires hard-favour'd rage as the sight of the Commander-in-Chief riding calmly through shot and shell.

So Coker and I, mounted on livery-stable hacks, set out the following morning on a tour of the stalls. I don't exactly know what impression I made on the first Staller I called on, but I do know the impression I made on his picketers was the opposite of what I had hoped for. The mere sight of me seemed to re-kindle their bellicosity. They stood up, resumed their sandwich boards and, forcing their way through the lines of curry customers, did what they could to re-form their picket line. From there they shook their fists at me and followed their chanty leader in a cry of 'Bunter-Bunter-Bunter! Scab-Scab-Scab!'

I took the word 'Scab' to be a form of abuse. And when they'd finished abusing me, they turned on the Staller on whom, like as not, they'd been fawning for curry handouts only minutes before I rode up.

'Keep Britain White!' they shouted, and 'Nig-nogs Out!' And when they found this monotonous they shouted 'Black Leg! Black Leg! Black Leg!'

All of this seemed so spontaneous and natural that I felt sure Snape had rehearsed them into it. I couldn't at first understand why he'd trained them to call me 'Scab' and the Staller 'Black Leg'. But then I remembered our argument and realised that synecdoche had been at work. Snape, then, had not only had the impudence to call me 'a *scab* on the fair face of industrial relations', but had also claimed that the mere sight of bare *black legs* actually running to do Bunter's business constituted more provocation than any British working man should be asked to endure. He had clearly used the same phrases to his Gulpers, and they had now elevated them into terms of deadly abuse.

If my appearance angered the Gulpers, the Gulpers' reactions seemed likely to anger the customers, who were being held from their curries. So I hurriedly left, but what happened at that first stall was reproduced at the next and the one after that. By the time I'd got to the fourth stall I decided that Napoleon and Wellington had both got it wrong, and that the best and only sensible place for a commander-in-chief was well away from the front line. So I withdrew to Bedford Square, cursing myself for my recklessness, and hoping that the Gulpers would relapse into defeatism once I wasn't there to act as an irritant.

Speaking solely for myself, I've never known whether it was defeatism or whether the customers quietened them down.

Coker, however, had no doubts when he reported to me a couple of days later.

'I don't know how you did it, Bunter,' said he, 'but there hasn't been even one Gulper or half a sandwich board near one of our stalls for the past two days.'

'Do you really think,' said I, 'that they scarpered because of me?'

'Stands out a mile. The pickets turned up regular as clockwork every day until the day you showed yourself. And once you had shown yourself, they disappeared. I've always thought highly of you, as you know. But I must admit I never thought my old school chum could so dominate a situation by force of personality alone.'

I looked at him for a bit and then said, very quietly: 'You mustn't make too much of it, Coker. There ain't any merit in being what one is. A chap's either born with it or he's not.'

'Born with what, Bunter?'

'I suppose some people would call it leadership. I think of it as being nothing more than the ability to inspire those who follow me and to terrify those who oppose me. Boney, when he was at his best, was another who had it, and Beaky had acquired a bit of it by the time he got to Waterloo.'

'I never served under either Boney or Beaky,' said Coker. 'But I've served under a few other generals, and I've never seen one of 'em show half as much leadership as you showed the other day.'

'You mustn't exaggerate, Coker.'

'I ain't exaggerating. I know courage and genius when I see 'em.'

I waved the tribute away with a flap of my hand and said, somewhat gruffly: 'Leadership itself ain't enough. A leader's got to have men like you to lead, Coker, if he's to get anywhere.'

'It's typical of your kindness and modesty to say so.'

'Kindness and modesty have got nothing to do with it. A chap like me will always need chaps like you for exactly the same reasons as a salad dressing is nothing without a salad and a mayonnaise sauce is nothing without its cold lobster.'

'Beautifully put, Bunter,' said Coker.

Apart from a steady increase in sales, so little of note happened on the curry front over the next two or three weeks that I began to forget Snape and the Gulpers. And that was probably why I was so unprepared for a midnight intruder.

How he got into Bedford Square at that time of night I never discovered. No one could have let him in because everyone except myself was in bed, and I was dozing over my accounts in the study. It's true, as I was soon to discover, that the intruder gave the impression of being able, if need be, to ooze his way through a solid brick wall, but I'm certain that was no more than an impression. What actually happened, I suppose, was that he found an open window and climbed through it.

It was a remarkably warm night for early June: one that positively drove a chap into putting his feet up on the desk and contemplating the infinite. The infinite needs quite a deal of contemplating, which was why it took me some time to realise that there was a soft, even furtive tap-tap-tapping at the study door. I thought, for one dismaying moment, that it was one of the women of the house who was tapping. It was a night for dozing rather than sleeping: just such a night as would persuade one or other of 'em that, rather than count sheep, she might just as well exercise her conjugal rights – or her concubinal ones, as the case may be.

A little more thought, however, told me that in such cases Maria, Fyzoo and Ghulabi had never been ones to announce their intentions with a mere gentle tapping. Bursting straight in and demanding with menaces was more in their line. So feeling partly reassured, I took my feet off the desk, sat up straight in my chair, and said: 'Come in.'

Nothing happened, so I said it again, only a bit louder. All that produced was another bout of gentle tapping. A person of only average hearing would have heard my third 'Come in' as far away as the attics, and it had its effect. The study door

opened perhaps ten inches and a strangely muffled-up figure
slipped through, glided across to me, put a finger to what may
or may not have been its lips and whispered, hoarsely:

' 'Ush, Mr B. We must 'ave more 'ush or we'll be rumbled.'

I stared long and hard at the figure, not that there was all
that much to stare at. It's true that it was, in spite of what
looked like a permanent stoop, more than ordinarily tall. But it
must have been, when in the buff, more than ordinarily skinny.
Even with the clothes it had on it looked positively skeletal
when viewed sideways on. Those clothes were not entirely
suitable for indoor wear on a hot June night. It was encased
from chin to toe in one of those heavy, black, many-caped
greatcoats stage-coach drivers favour as winter wear. A
wide-brimmed, low-crowned, exceedingly hairy beaver hat
was pulled low over its brow and a thick woollen muffler filled
most of the space between greatcoat and mouth.

What with the beaver hat and the woollen muffler there
wasn't much of the face left uncovered. At first sight all that
could be seen of it was a thin, high-bridged nose that seemed to
travel a long way before it came to a point. A second look
revealed a pair of sharp little green eyes mounted close to that
nose at the top and an untidy grey moustache straggling out at
the bottom.

Anyone looking as strange and acting as mysteriously as he
did needed to be approached with caution, so I got ready to
spring out of my chair and make for the fireplace and the poker
even whilst I said, with, I fear, something of a quaver:

'Who in the Devil are you? And what are we to be rumbled
about?'

They seemed pretty sensible questions to me, but he didn't
answer them. Instead he tiptoed to the windows and looked
very carefully behind each curtain. After that he started to glide
silently round the study, pausing to look in at a closet and to
kneel in the empty grate so as to peer up the chimney. When he
eventually got to the study door he looked cautiously up and
down the corridor outside before closing it, gliding back to me
at the desk, pulling up a chair, sitting himself down, taking off

the beaver hat and mopping his shining and near-hairless pate with a dirty yellow and white bandanna. After which he said, still in his hoarse whisper:

'Name of O., Mr B. Our mutual friend will 'ave told you about me.'

Some of my alarm left me. Even if I couldn't place this mutual friend, the mere fact that he existed made it probable that O. wasn't one of those who thought being friendly with Bunter was proof of either perversity or insanity. Nevertheless, I still thought that, as a means of establishing a relationship, O.'s approach lacked precision. So I said:

'If you're convinced we have a mutual friend, then a mutual friend we must have. But I hope you won't think me stupid if I ask who he is.'

He did think me stupid. The look he gave me was the sort one normally reserves for a backward child who refuses to understand that cats sit on mats.

'Shall we,' said he, 'just call 'im M.?'

'M. by all means, but which M. is that?'

'Come now, Mr B. that won't do. It won't do at all.'

'Why not?'

'You will recolleck, of course, the matter of a certain petition.'

'Of course.'

'Then I don't see 'ow you can't also recolleck consulting this particular M., and no other, about a copy of the said petition what was leaked to you anonymous.'

'Leaked by you, God bless you,' said I, and I leant across the desk and shook him heartily by the hand. 'Why on earth didn't you mention that petition to start with and say you were the spy instead of spraying half the alphabet at me, my dear Mr Oliver.'

He withdrew his hand, looked at me coldly, and said: 'Don't you never ever, Mr B., name names in circumstances such as the present. A name named can easily be a name over'eard. And a name over'eard can mean ruin for a man in my line of business which, if you please, is agency work and not spying.'

'I do beg your pardon. I'd quite forgotten what Lord . . . what our mutual friend told me. You're only a spy when you're working for the opposition.'

'That's it in a nutshell. A great man is our mutual friend. Probably knows more about agency work than any other layman in the country with the exception of Lord Sidmouth. And Lord Sidmouth ain't active any longer, more's the pity.'

'Why do you say that?'

'Because in Lord S.'s days, S. and I 'ad much more important matters to 'andle than GULPS, or than any other trade union for that matter.'

'Surely we've now got one S. too many.'

'I ain't referring to Lord S. I refer to Petition S.'

'Do you mean that you and Ebenezer worked together in those days?'

'Not what you'd call "together". More like gamekeeper and poacher, and of course 'e's never known I'm a keeper. But in those days we 'ad giants. We 'ad the Irish rebellions and the Radical riots and the Jacobin conspiracies for 'im to organise and me to hinform on. Now there's only these unions.'

'You don't think unions are important, then?'

'Indeed I do. 'Ere to stay, unions are. Everyone ought to 'ave one.'

'Have you?'

''Ave I what?'

'A union?'

'I 'appen to be,' he said with decent pride, 'Vice-President and 'Onorary Treasurer of SAPIAS.' When he saw this left me unimpressed he added: 'Society of Agents Provocative, Intelligence Agents and Spies.'

'It almost sounds as though you cater for both sides.'

'Of course we do. Can't afford party politics or them and us when it comes to union business.'

'Well Mr O.,' said I, 'I wouldn't advise you to talk about SAPIAS to M. Many's the time he's told me that he believes all unions to be inconsistent and impossible bodies whose very existence is contrary to the laws of Nature.'

'I know. But then 'atween ourselves, good and great man

208 *Bunter by Appointment*

though 'e is, M. belongs to the past whilst unions and SAPIAS belong to the future. But we're getting away, aren't we, from why I'm 'ere.'

'Well,' said I, 'it's been interesting so far. But why *are* you here?'

'Two reasons. One . . .' here he held up a long skinny forefinger '. . . S. is planning something against you for tomorrow.'

'Oh, I don't think so. He's given up.'

'Not 'im. Too much of a professional to give up so easy. I know we've beaten 'im over the petition and the pickets, but that don't mean we've stopped 'im. *Reculer pour mieux sauter*'s always been 'is motto.'

'Well what sort of *sauter* is he planning now?'

'That's the trouble. I 'aven't been able to find out any more than it will involve all of the Gulpers, a couple of magistrates, most of the constables in the parish, and a dog catcher. But S. 'asn't let any of us know exactly what 'e's going to do with all of 'em.'

'And whatever it's going to be, it's going to happen tomorrow.'

'Only thing I can be certain about. You'll understand that's why I 'aven't communicated through the usual channels to M. Didn't 'ave the time. So 'ere I am, bringing the news direct to you.'

'Very kind of you,' said I, not knowing how seriously I should take him. 'But what about the second?'

'Second what?'

'Second reason for being here?'

He held up another long and skinny finger and said: 'You've bin penetrated.'

'Penetrated? Don't be silly.'

'Silly, is it? Then 'ow do you think S. knows just about everything you do 'ere or at your place in Jermyn Street almost as soon as you've done it?'

'He can't.'

'What you earn from your curries, 'ow much you owe, what

you've got in the bank, 'ow often you 'ave to go to bed with them
Indian women . . .'

'Impossible.'

''E even knows what you 'ad for breakfast yesterday.'

'I don't believe it.'

'Three eggs, lightly boiled, two grilled mutton chops, plate of
cold 'am, toasted muffins and marmalade, coffee.'

'Good God! How can he know all that?'

'If you're asking for my professional opinion, I'd say he's
planted one on you.'

'One what?'

''E'd call it an agent. You 'ave to call it a spy.'

'A spy, here, in this house?'

''Ere or 'ereabouts. Stands to reason 'e or she 'as to be in and
out to know what you 'ave for breakfast.'

'Do you know whether it *is* a he or a she?'

'No, but I'd put my money on its being a he.'

I looked at him miserably through my spectacles and
muttered: 'And so would I, Mr O. And so would I.'

19 *Perfidus Achates*

Mr Oliver didn't actually vanish. People don't disappear like
that outside fairy books. But it would be true to say I wasn't
aware that he'd departed until I suddenly realised I was alone.
So I went to bed.

I got no sleep in what was left of that night, but lay awake
considering the perversity of some men and the perfidy of
others. It was annoyingly perverse of Snape to be planning
fresh mischiefs against me for the morning. But that he should
be secretly helped in those mischiefs by one who described

himself as a school chum and my current *fidus Achates* was worse than perverse. It was downright wicked. For the more I thought about it the spy at my breakfast table had to be, could only be, Coker.

Looking back on it I realised that Coker had always hated me from the time we were at Christ's Hospital to the day he turned up, penniless and starving, at 47 Bedford Square. It could be argued that I had, over the years, given him reason to accumulate and treasure that hatred. But at no time had I actually intended to make him either lop-eared, lop-arsed, or half-cocked. I had always damaged him either by accident or as an act of friendship. But even if that hadn't been the case, his hating ought to have stopped the moment I saved him from beggary and became his benefactor and patron. And if it hadn't stopped, he had no right to be humbugging around as my *fidus Achates*. I could have kicked myself when I thought how I had fallen for his humbug and lapped up his flattery.

The more I considered his perfidy the angrier I became. By six o'clock I had worked up such a fury against him that I jumped out of bed three hours before my time and set off, unshaven and unbreakfasted, for Jermyn Street. It was one of Coker's duties to be at the Serai by six each morning in order to parade the Stallers for inspection before sending them about their curry vending. It was well after six by the time I got there, but Coker wasn't to be seen and the Stallers, far from having moved off to their stations, were lounging around looking lost. What with parades, inspections, cudgel training, elementary infantry tactics and all the other military flapdoodle Coker had drilled into them, they were in much the same state as army recruits fall into after their first few weeks under a drill sergeant. That is, they scarcely dared think, speak, or move except by numbers and to orders. As they were now *sans* Coker they were necessarily *sans* orders, which was why they were sitting on the stairs instead of trotting smartly off with their stalls.

I was so heated against Coker, so frantic to face him with his treachery, that not finding him added to my anger. Some of that new anger had to flow over on to my bewildered Stallers. I spent some time cursing them alternately in Hindi and Urdu, after which, much to their relief, I ordered them on to parade, which re-established routine. So they lined up for inspection outside the Serai with a good deal of alacrity, each Staller standing to his stall and each stall precisely in line with every other stall and equidistant to an inch from its neighbours. I inspected them and their stalls very carefully, which heartened them even more. Then, as it was a ceremonial occasion, I proceeded in a stately fashion to the top of the stairs which served on such occasions as the saluting base. It was from there that I would give the order 'Dismiss to your Duties' for which they all waited.

That order was never given. In the time it had taken me to move from parade ground to saluting base a large crowd had debouched from Piccadilly into Jermyn Street, had advanced smartly towards the Serai and, reaching it, had turned from column into line. It had then advanced its right and left flanks up to the walls of the building, thus preventing the Stallers from moving very far in any direction. As more members of that crowd arrived, turned, and took up position behind their fellows, Jermyn Street began to seem altogether too narrow to contain both them and the Stallers. The latter were squeezed up against the Serai, leaving their stalls to be surrounded and over-run by the surging mob.

A great, gaudily painted banner stretched between two poles, each pole being held by a sturdy fellow who was assisted in his task by two others holding steadying cords, announced that these were the Gulpers – all 317 of them by the look of things. There was in addition a sprinkling of clerical-looking persons who may or may not have been bishops and of miserable-looking ones who may or may not have been political economists.

The silences of a large crowd aren't really silences. There is always a background noise that more than anything else resembles the sound of a heavy sea breaking on a pebbly shore. It comes, I suppose, from several hundred pairs of lungs all at work breathing in and out. But now a shout of 'Make Way' could be heard. A ripple went through the tight-packed ranks as men pressed backwards to clear a narrow path, and a small group of men made their way along it. Once their leader had set foot on the stairs the crowd surged back so quickly that the group was propelled up the staircase as though from a catapult. Its leader, indeed, would have been propelled through the front door of the Serai if he hadn't been brought to a stop by colliding with Bunter. So there the two of us were, packed face-to-face and waistcoat-to-waistcoat with scarce enough room between us to breathe.

This leader was a stout, purple-faced, important-looking party wearing exceedingly tight leather breeches, a blue coat with silver buttons, and a white stovepipe hat. Behind him came a beadle, complete with laced hat, scarlet gown and staff; a rough-looking fellow in greasy moleskins and a fur bonnet; and Ebenezer Snape. Behind them again came three constables. As I had dressed very hastily, omitted to shave, and was still, although I didn't realise it, wearing a nightcap, Purple-Face must have thought I was someone else.

'Out of my way,' he said. 'I want Bunter.'

I pushed hard against his waistcoat to give myself breathing and speaking space. 'I am Bunter,' said I.

'Catchpoll,' said he to the beadle. 'You will observe that this Bunter has laid violent hands on me, the which may amount to assault and battery. It may even amount to resisting arrest.'

'Amounts to both, Your Honour,' said Catchpoll.

A constable tried to draw his truncheon but was so hemmed in by the crowd that he couldn't get his arm free. The rough-looking individual looked stonily ahead. Snape winked at me in a way that suggested he was enjoying himself. This led me to say:

'You will kindly note, Mr Snape, that I have acted solely in self-defence, this person having assaulted me by violently pushing his waistcoat into mine, no provocation having been offered.'

'I did no such thing,' said Purple-Face.

'You did so,' said I. 'And now that we're talking about arrests, I'm in half a mind to put you under a citizen's arrest here and now.'

'Don't be absurd. *You* can't arrest *me*. I'm a Common Councillor.'

'That don't mean you ain't also a citizen. And one citizen, such as myself, can always arrest another, such as you.'

'Only for good reason.'

'Reasons enough already,' said I, trying hard to think of some. 'Such as what?'

'Such as . . . Trespass? . . . Insulting behaviour? . . . Loitering with intent? Vagrancy? . . . '

'Vagrancy! Catchpoll, am I a vagrant.'

'You are not, Your Honour.'

'And why aren't I a vagrant?'

'Because Your Honour is an Alderman, a Magistrate, a Common Councillor, a Sanitary Commissioner, a member of . . .'

'That's enough, Catchpoll. Do you think Bunter here could arrest me for, say, Trespass?'

'I do not, Your Honour.'

'And why not?'

'Because Your Honour has a warrant.'

'A warrant?' said I. 'What sort of warrant?'

'A warrant to search the premises at 83 Jermyn Street known as Bunter's Indian Serai,' said Purple-Face.

'Search the Serai! Search it for what?'

'Stolen goods.'

'Then whoever issued the warrant must be mad.'

'I'll have you know, Bunter, that I issued it on the basis of evidence sworn before me as a magistrate, although I've accompanied my constables here in my capacity as a Sanitary Commissioner.'

'Evidence? What evidence, and who swore it?'

'Mr Jeremiah Witherspoon.'

'Who and what is he?'

'That's *who* he is,' said Purple-Face, pointing at the rough-looking individual in the moleskins. 'As to *what* he is, he's Head Poundkeeper and Official Dog Catcher to the City of London.'

'Worthy occupations,' said I, 'but I'll be damned if I can work out what they have to do with Bunter's Indian Serai and stolen property.'

'They are occupations that take him on to the streets late at night looking for animals to impound or put down. In recent months he has frequently observed blacks with sacks on their backs moving furtively in the shadows.'

'Did he impound them or merely put them down?'

'He followed them.'

'Why?'

'Some of these sacks *moved*.'

'What was in them?'

'That's what we're here to discover.'

'Why here?'

'Because this is where those blacks always came. Mr Witherspoon has declared on oath that he has seen three and four black men a night go into your Serai with sacks and come out without 'em.'

'So that's why you want to search the premises?'

'It is.'

I looked hard at Witherspoon. He ignored me and fixed his gaze first on the chimneypots, next on the ground, and finally on Snape.

'Tell me, Mr Witherspoon,' I said, 'how much has Snape promised you to swear to all this nonsense?'

'I resent this hinsinuation,' said Snape, 'and so does Mr Witherspoon. Don't you, Jeremiah?'

'That's right,' said Jeremiah. 'I ain't never clapped eyes on Ebenezer afore today, like 'e says, and I resents the hinsinuation. There's a law against going round saying such things.'

'So there is, Jeremiah boy,' said Snape. 'You take the fat bugger to court and make him pay.'

I gave the two of them up and turned to Purple-Face. 'Those two,' said I, 'have rogue and liar written plain on their faces.

This is a conspiracy against Bunter and against the curry-eating masses. Those two are so obviously the principal conspirators that a man would have to be mad to believe a word of what either of them swears to, even if he swears it on a stack of Bibles.'

Purple-Face didn't much like that. He turned his back on me and said to the senior constable: 'You know your duty. Get on with it.'

The constables turned into file, wheeled round Purple-Face and advanced on the Serai and myself. I was still so angry that I thought for a brief moment to resist them. I put my back against the door and stretched my arms wide, and a noble figure I must have seemed in spite of the nightcap.

The senior constable, who was leading, put a hand on my shoulder and said in a quite kindly voice: 'Now then, Sir. Be a good gentleman and don't give us any trouble. The sooner we can search your premises the sooner all this will be over and you can get back to your bed.'

As I had nothing to fear from a search it had been anger and not fear that had made me consider resistance. And with me anger will generally give way soon enough to gentle reason. So I moved away from the door, waved an arm and said:

'Search where you like, but don't linger over it. I've still got my public to consider and my Cart-A-Curry Stalls to get away.'

Whilst we were waiting for the constables to complete their business I asked Purple-Face why he allowed the Serai to be blockaded by Snape's followers.

'Those followers,' said he, 'who include certain reverend and certain learned gentlemen as well as a large number of very respectable tradesmen, asked if they could come to see that our British principles of fair play, justice for all, and support for the underdog were respected.'

'Did they, by God! And who do they think are the underdogs?'

'Mr Snape assured me that your people, who are ignorant black savages, would have no understanding of, or respect for, the law and would attack my constables with the utmost ferocity if you ordered them to. The only thing that could prevent this would be the presence of a large number of fair-minded and law-abiding people, such as his followers.'

'I have already warned you against believing Snape. My people, as you call them, are no more ignorant than yourself, there are as many of them who are brown as there are those who are black, and there's not one of them that's half as savage as any of Snape's Gulpers. And you've only to look at 'em now to see how unlikely it is that they would ever attack your constables, whether I ordered 'em to or not.'

I pointed towards the small group of Stallers who were holding hands with one another for comfort, and who neverthe-less looked so distressed and disconsolate that anyone with even a half pint of the milk of human kindness in him would have wanted to pat them on the shoulder and say: 'There, there, don't take on so.'

'I must admit,' said Purple-Face, 'that they don't look very savage to me. Mr Snape must have been mistaken.'

'He's not the only one who's been mistaken,' said I, 'as I shall tell my kinsman, the Home Secretary, when I make my complaint to him about this wanton persecution.'

'Did you say Home Secretary?'

'I did.'

'And did you mention kinsman?'

'I did.'

'My dear Mr Bunter, I hope you don't think there has been anything in the least malicious about these proceedings. I have done no more than my bounden duty, which was to act immediately on information received.'

'False information,' said I.

'As it concerns Lord Melbourne's kinsman that begins to seem, alas, all too probable.'

Purple-Face, to give him his due, seemed genuinely dis-tressed.

'You mustn't take it too much to heart,' I said. 'You've been used.'

'So I have,' said he, and his jaw began to stick out and a scowl came to his face as he turned on Witherspoon and Snape.

'Bearing false witness,' said he, 'is a mighty dangerous game, as the two of you will soon discover. Meanwhile Snape, I'll give you five minutes to disperse your followers before they become a riotous assembly.'

Snape, to my surprise, was not in the least put out.

'Don't you think, Your Honour, that it would be best to wait until the constables have finished their search?'

And at that precise moment three constables emerged, each carrying a blood-stained sack. They took these to Purple-Face and opened them, to show him what was inside. He gasped and said:

'To think that I have eaten here myself. No wonder they talk about the Serai Squitters. The villain must have come close to poisoning the half of London.'

This, however, was not sufficient for Ebenezer Snape. He stepped smartly forward, held one of the sacks up high for all to see, and then emptied its contents on to the top stair. As dead cats and dogs of all colours, breeds and sizes fell slowly out, the crowd let out a collective groan. There was another groan as the second sack was emptied. But the third produced a great roar of anger, for it contained carcasses that had been skinned and dressed, ready, apparently, for the cooking.

But Snape hadn't finished, and if ever there was a man who knew how to milk a crowd it was he. He now held up in one hand a dead spaniel and, in the other, what might well have been a skinned cat.

'What about these, then, lads?' he shouted. 'Are we going to let these Indian buggers get away with this?'

Some of the 'lads' had not only anticipated the question: they had already prepared their answers, for they had been prising up cobblestones and distributing them to their fellows. That, indeed, was the last thing I saw. One of those cobblestones took me behind the ear and laid me out, bleeding and senseless, at the top of the stairs to Bunter's Serai.

Much later I awoke in my bed in Bedford Square to a strong smell of vinegar. The surgeon called to me had applied a brown paper and vinegar compress to my cracked pate after taking three pints of blood and administering a clyster to ward off the fever. Gurmakh Singh was at my bedside, and it was from him that I learnt the sorry details of what had taken place in Jermyn Street after I was laid low.

It all seemed to happen as though to plan. My terrified Stallers were seized, beaten up, told to go back to India and then released, the majority of them determined to do what they had just been told. Their stalls were systematically smashed to splinters. The crowd, or all of it except the bishops and the political economists, then rushed the Serai, sweeping Purple-Face, Catchpoll and the constables aside, they being prepared to understand but not to countenance what was to happen. The staff inside the Serai was treated in the same way as the Stallers had been treated, only Gurmakh Singh escaping unscathed as he had hidden himself inside one of the minarets. The Serai was then looted of all that could be moved, after which anything that could be destroyed was destroyed and anything that could not had 'Nig-nogs go Home' painted on it. It was only after the mob had withdrawn that Gurmakh Singh had come down from his minaret, summoned a hackney, and brought me home.

That bit of mob violence, which historians are beginning to dignify as the Battle of the Indian Serai, was the end of the Gulper Disturbances so far as the historians are concerned. There is a bit more to add so far as Bunter is concerned, however.

A couple of days later Gurmakh Singh came into my study dragging a shrieking Fyzoo and a weeping Ghulabi with him. It took some time for the story of their betrayals to emerge, but what Gurmakh Singh had found out, and what he now made them confess to me was, to put it in a nutshell, no more and no less than this.

Both women had, of course, greatly resented being put to work in the Zenana Room, both because this left them no time for producing and playing with Bunterkins and because they had lost the habit of hard work. They complained often and loudly, but the only person to pay any attention to those complaints was Coker, in whom, as a Hindi speaker, they could confide. He, telling them that matters could not improve for them so long as the Serai remained open, gradually convinced them that it would be to Bunter's benefit as well as their own if they could, somehow or other, force it to shut.

The great Coronation Banquet to be given by the Ladies of Almack's in the Zenana Room would, he assured them, give them their best opportunity, and he, Coker, would give them the means. The means consisted of equal quantities of calomel (Hydrargyri chloridum), jalap (Exogonium purga) and Gregory's Powder (Pulvis rhei compositus) dissolved in a concentrated essence of rhubarb flavoured with ginger and cinnamon. The flavouring did something to disguise the taste and the strength of the vindaloo curry to which it was added did the rest. Here, then, was the cause of the cholera scare, the royal merry-go-whimbles, the Serai Squitters and the loss of my customers.

But the Serai did not simply close as Coker had predicted. Instead it became a factory turning out curries for my Cart-A-Curry Stalls, and the daughters-in-law were no closer to becoming ladies of leisure. It was then that Coker persuaded them that further measures were necessary and, without telling them exactly what was in them, he persuaded them, the day before the Battle of the Indian Serai, to hide the three sacks behind the carcasses of sheep and goats hanging in the meat larder.

Gurmakh Singh offered to wipe out the shame of their treachery by cutting their throats and burying them behind the stables. And now that they saw what their conspiring with Coker had brought me to, the daughters-in-law came close to advancing their throats to his knife. I could not, of course, allow any such punishment to be inflicted on the mothers of my Bunterkins so, after I had spoken very severely to them, and after several more pints of tears had been shed, they were forgiven; and I dare say, if it hadn't been for the brown paper and vinegar plaster, they'd have been at me to start making more Bunterkins, so full of contrition and affection were they.

If all this forgiving and loving had ever threatened to make me shut my eyes to the harsh realities of my situation, the package that a messenger brought to the house a short while later removed that threat. It was addressed to me in Coker's own hand, and when I opened it a bank book and a bill were revealed.

The bank book was the one that had been in Coker's keeping ever since he'd been made Director of Finance. The last entry but one showed that the Jermyn Street National and Imperial Investment Company had a credit balance of £5428.9s.4d. The last entry, which was dated a week later and written in red ink, showed that the Company was now overdrawn to the tune of £5.2s.3d.

I turned to the bill, which was also in Coker's hand.

H. A. Coker Esq. Cr. to W. F. A. Bunter Esq.

To one damaged ear	£750. 0s.0d.
To one ditto buttock	£1500. 0s.0d.
To one ditto pecker	£3000. 0s.0d.
To one passage to S. America	£183.11s.7d.
Total due	£5433.11s.7d.

The scoundrel had had the impudence to scribble at the bottom of this document:

'Settlement of this account in full is acknowledged with thanks. Signed: H. A. Coker.'

EPILOGUE – *Counting My Blessings*

I am of a euphoric rather than a melancholic disposition and so normally I count my blessings rather than curse my fate. I am glad, therefore, that my creditors had me imprisoned in Newgate, which is in every way a better place than the Fleet or the Marshalsea, where most who are in my situation end up. If a man can still pay his way though insolvent, Newgate ain't at all a bad place to be insolvent in.

That I can pay my way, and handsomely, is entirely due to Gurmakh Singh, for my creditors saw to it that I was stripped down to my bare bones before committing me to prison. But Gurmakh Singh, unknown to me, has for some time past done extraordinarily well out of lending small sums at high interest rates to other Indians, and had already acquired a tidy fortune at the time of my ruin.

That fortune hasn't gone to his head. He still thinks of me as Bunter Sahib and requires me in return to think of him as my banker as well as my *khansamah*, and to draw on him for anything and everything I may need in this place. So here I am occupying a handsome set of chambers at the top of Newgate prison, with a fine view over London from my windows and private access to the roof on whose leads I can walk if ever I need to take exercise. The Head Gaoler, whose official residence this is, has leased it to me for the modest rental of twelve guineas a week.

And here I receive and entertain such a steady flow of guests that I never, unless I feel like it, need dine alone. Nor, if I listen to Maria, Fyzoo and Ghulabi, who visit almost every day, do I ever need sleep alone, though I do so unless the pressure to be husbandly becomes excessive. Maria and the children are back in Great Coram Street, for J.J. took them in after they'd been

turned out of Bedford Square. The daughters-in-law and the
Bunterkins live with Gurmakh Singh who, to be close to me,
has taken lodgings nearby in Angel Street, at the back of St
Paul's Churchyard.

Maria, when she comes, brings the children for me to admire
and play with. She also brings me hampers of such choicer
things as the Head Gaoler's wife who cooks for me is unlikely to
provide. It's all good, plain English delicacies such as haunches
of venison, pheasants, lobsters, turbots, asparagus and straw-
berries, according to season. The daughters-in-law, not to be
outdone, bring me the Bunterkins to admire and play with
and see to my linen and laundering. They are under strict
instructions to bring me no curries.

J.J. generally dines with me once a week – fried smelts,
mutton chops, boiled potatoes and greens and a batter
pudding, all very nicely cooked and served by the Head
Gaoler's wife. He always provides the dessert and a dozen of
port, together with the half of either a Stilton or Derbyshire
cheese. The Head Gaoler supplies good ale and porter and a
drinkable claret, but his burgundies and ports are such poor,
thin stuff that J.J. refuses to tackle 'em.

Buttercup never comes to town without calling on me and
would, if I allowed it, treat Newgate as her hotel, and my
bedroom as hers. Although I prevent this nine times out of ten,
she takes no umbrage and leaves such a profusion of fat ducks,
new-laid eggs, saddles of mutton and other home produce as
she departs that the Gaoler's wife always begs me to invite extra
people to dinner for the next few days.

Cochrane seldom visits me, but Melbourne and Palmerston
are not infrequent guests. Brougham once took it upon himself
to call, wearing his Lord Chancellor's gown and wig, which
impressed the Head Gaoler mightily. My visitor was so full of
brandy, however, that it took two warders to push him up the
three flights of stairs when he arrived and four to carry him
down when he left. When he visits me in ordinary dress,
however, he is often sober. Mr Clarence, I'm sorry to say, has
seen fit to ignore my existence.

Recently more and more of my guests have been coming from literary, publishing and journalistic circles, for the impression left by my advertising 'essays' lingers. And the scribbling habit, I confess, has been growing on me, and not just because I have been occupied with this instalment of my *Memoirs*. Both William Cobbett and John Murray are frequent visitors. The first, an old Newgate hand himself, has the problem of attracting a sufficient number of Letter-Writers to fill the pages of his *Weekly Register* devoted to Correspondence. He now expects me to supply him with at least two different letters for each number. Sometimes I do and sometimes I don't, but such as he gets are always good, indignant letters written from an impeccably Radical viewpoint and signed 'Brutus' or 'Cicero' or some such stern Roman name.

John Murray knows and admires my mother because of her ghost-writing and managing of Harriette Wilson's *Memoirs*, even though my mother never gave him the publishing of it, which he wanted. So I provide him, although he pays even less than Cobbett, with good solid Tory articles of seldom less than ten thousand words under some such by-line as 'A Patriot', 'True-Blue' or 'Britannicus'. He has come close to persuading me to abandon commerce and take up the pen as my trade once I return to the world.

And return I might. For only yesterday I had a letter from my mother in Florence saying that she hoped I have now learnt not to invest in speculative ventures and wanting from me a full account of my present financial situation. I detect in that demand some intention on her part to come to my assistance to the extent of getting me out of here. But, before that happens, I will, as I said I would, present a count of my current blessings.

Item: I live as full and pleasant a life here as I did when I first married and the sale of the Indian loot had made me a gentleman of leisure. That I do this on Gurmakh Singh's money rather than my own don't detract from my enjoyment.

Item: Although still liable to be bludgeoned and bullied into bed by masterful women, I have more control over their access to my bedroom than I ever had when I was running free.

Item: I no longer have to have anything to do with Indian food and especially with curries, of which foods I have grown heartily sick.

Item: I no longer have to be either obsequious or haughty to customers, but can treat all on their merits or according to my fancy.

Item: I am at last rid of my creditors and my only indebtedness is to Gurmakh Singh who is the most accommodating banker I ever borrowed money from.

Item: I hope, if I can find an honest publisher for it, to make a good deal of money out of this plain, unvarnished account of the more recent adventures of William Frederick Augustus Bunter. I don't rule out John Murray, although I doubt I'm too serious a writer for him. But I am more than half-prepared to accept his advice and to take to the pen in one way or another once I shake the not unpleasant dust of Newgate from off my feet.